Also by Indira Ganesan

Inheritance
The Journey

As Sweet as Honey

As Sweet as Honey

A NOVEL

Indira Ganesan

 Alfred A. Knopf · NEW YORK · 2013

This Is a Borzoi Book Published by Alfred A. Knopf

www.aaknopf.com

Knopf, Borzoi Books, and the colophon are registered trademarks of Random House, Inc.

Portions of this work were previously published in the following: "Aunt Meterling"
in not enough night, Issue 1, Naropa University, Boulder (Spring 2005); "Meterling:
Chapter One" in Bombay Gin 32, Naropa University, Boulder (2006); "From
Meterling" in Square One, no. 5, University of Colorado, Boulder (Spring 2007);
"Meterling (a work in progress)" in Black Renaissance, Institute of African
American Affairs, New York University, New York (2007).

Library of Congress Cataloging-in-Publication Data
Ganesan, Indira.
As sweet as honey / by Indira Ganesan.
p. cm.
"This is a Borzoi book."
ISBN 978-0-307-96044-3
1. Island people—Fiction.   2. Families—Fiction.   3. Tall women—
Fiction.   4. Aunts—Fiction.   5. Islands of the Indian Ocean—Fiction.   I. Title.
PS3557.A495A9 2013
813'.54—dc23   2012042632

Jacket illustration by Chris Silas Neal
Jacket design by Carol Devine Carson

Manufactured in the United States of America

First Edition

For my niece
Gayatri Sinha Ganesan

Love has a thousand shapes.

—Virginia Woolf, *To the Lighthouse*

PART ONE
Marriage

So that is marriage, Lily thought, a man and a
woman looking at a girl throwing a ball.

—*To the Lighthouse*

I

Our aunt Meterling stood over six feet tall, a giantess, a tree. From her limbs came large hands, which always held a shower of snacks for us children. We could place two of our feet in one of her sandals, and her green shawl made for a roof to cover our play forts. We loved Meterling, because she was so devotedly freakish, because she rained everyone with affection, and because we felt that anyone that tall had to be supernaturally gifted. No one actually said she was a ghost, or a saint, or a witch, but we watched for signs nevertheless. She knew we suspected her of tricks, for she often smiled at us and displayed sleight of hand, pulling coins and shells out of thin air. But that, said Rasi, didn't prove anything; Rasi had read *The Puffin Book of Magic Tricks* and pretty much knew them all, and was not so easily impressed.

What was interesting, and never expected, was that Aunt Meterling married the littlest man she knew. He was four feet seven, dapper, and jolly. The grown-ups were embarrassed and affronted, for like Auntie Sita said, it was bad enough having a freakishly tall woman in the family. Yet, they were all relieved that Aunt Meterling found Uncle Archer and he, her.

The wedding was a small enough affair as weddings go, but the bridegroom did ride to town in a white baby Aston Martin decked with garlands of roses and basil. The first marriage rites took place at dawn.

Someone said how sad it was that Meterling's parents could not be at the wedding, but neither could Archer's. I wondered what Meterling's father had been like. He had named her, after all. Who had he been? A man smitten with the German language, it seemed, for her name sounded German, and smitten, too, with his family. A man who died, with his beloved wife, in a car accident, all those years ago. A man who loved his daughter enough to name her something special. A man who must be still alive in Meterling's heart, I thought.

And her mother? A small, sweet woman who must have loved her daughter, even as she might have seen something in her that marked her for a fragile future. Also absent, also loved, also missing the wedding. I could comprehend Meterling's long-ing for her family, because my own father and mother were in America, land of dreams and snow. But lose a mother and a father—no, that was impossible! I could only imagine so far.

I rubbed the sleep out of my eyes, straining to see if my aunt would change somehow after the fire ceremony, the part where she walked seven steps hand in hand with Uncle Archer, but she kept her eyes downcast, as became a modest bride, while the priests chanted all around her. She wore a reddish-pinkish gold sari from Kanchi, with twelve inches of gold *jhari* on its border and thirty-six on the paloo; she had *mendhi* on her hands and feet, aglow from a bath of turmeric and sandal. In her hair was jasmine, rose, and tulsi. She wore an engagement ring, and during the ceremony she'd get a gold ring on her third finger, left hand, and a ring on her toe. Uncle Archer would get a ring as well. He wore a white pajama suit of heavy material all the way from Bombay, a pink tie, a boutonnière, and sandals. That he was wearing a suit instead of a formal dhoti was radical enough, whispered the aunts, but to hold hands before the ceremony was too much. We knew something was afoot but were not quite sure what the problem was. He's being *intimate,* giggled Sanjay, stamping his feet while Rasi and I pretended not to know him. We just shook our heads as our aunts did—we were smart enough to know that rules were being broken left and right, and didn't need Sanjay to tell us, even if it appeared that he did know more than us. Afterwards, Auntie Pa (her real name was Auntie Parvati, but Sanjay started saying Pa when he was two and could not roll his r's, and the name stuck) said that she had had a funny feeling in her heart that something was not right, but at that moment, when they were simply standing at the ceremony and later at the reception, everything was fine and there was plenty to eat and drink and toast the couple's happiness. He was now our uncle. Auntie Pa smiled and playfully tugged Sanjay's hair.

But no one could have predicted what happened next. One minute Uncle Archer was laughing and dancing with the littlest cousins, and then he took Aunt Meterling out to the dance floor. She had gone to Western dance classes, whispered an aunt, just for this moment. No one doubted Uncle could dance; he was born to wear a suit and tails—in fact, he bore more than a striking resemblance to the Monopoly man, with a full white mustache and a round tummy. A Western waltz was struck up, and everyone left the dance floor. Some of the elders among the guests frowned and turned away, because touch dancing was severely looked down upon, even though we lived in town. As my grandmother would say, this was not Delhi, not Bombay, but Madhupur, a town on the island of Pi in the Bay of Bengal: a place as sweet as honey, where people lived decent lives. Touching was meant for *procreation*, nothing else. Once, we had looked up "procreation" in the Animal Encyclopedia, but didn't learn much except about the mating habits of the stickleback fish. But there she was, Aunt Meterling, swathed in gold tissue silk, and there was he, monocled and marvelous, and the music from the hired band began. One turn, two, three, and he was down. Uncle Archer was on the ground. A flurry of activity, then a scream, and we children were pushed aside. The youngest of us didn't understand but started to cry anyway. Rasi, Sanjay, and I didn't really understand, either. When it was all over, no one had any appetite for the plates of round halvah and sugared grapes.

We were stunned into silence. We had not been paying attention. We never would have believed it if someone told us. We grew still with shock. We were eleven, nine, and ten. Plus all of our other cousins. All of us kids. It was the worst thing we had seen, or nearly seen. He had died in an instant.

There was not even a chance to see where exactly he measured up, someone said, in a half-giggle or cry, whether to her knee ("That's silly," said Rasi), her elbow, her chin. In truth, most of the guests hardly knew him, had only seen him once or twice, and mostly from afar. And it was hard for us to see much during all of the ceremony, because Sanjay started chasing Mani, who had swiped his spin top, and Rasi joined in to help Mani, and she dragged me with her. Mary Angel from two doors down called to us to share her caramels. We forgot about Mani and Sanjay as we ate the caramels. Rasi said we had to avoid her schoolteacher. She did not look so menacing to me when I saw her, a perfectly nice woman with her husband, who smiled broadly, making me think Rasi hadn't done some schoolwork, or had skipped out on a class. All in all, we hardly saw them wed.

But their love was palpable, like a color that was visible, almost heard. Their arms reached for each other with the sweetest sigh. Fingertips touching, swish of gold, monocle flash. One step, two step, three, gone.

Meterling sobbed in a corner. She sat right down, three feet of her against the wall, another three and more stretched on the floor. Her crying was fraught and unabashed, and no one seemed to know what to do. No one had ever seen her cry, because her height made her seem protected from whatever ill might befall ordinary women. Grandmother, no slouch, sharply spoke to anyone who said "It's too bad," and gave them work to do. The other aunties crowded around; some, you know, were waiting for a moment like this, because Meterling, that awkward fish, had landed a man before they did. But others, like Nalani, just burst into tears for the loss and grief.

The marriage hall quickly cleared, and they took Uncle Archer's body away. Uncle Darshan and Uncle Thakur ushered Aunt Meterling out. I looked back at the decorated hall, the garlands of pink, white, and orange flowers trailing from the ceiling, and those crushed on the floor. A funny feeling filled my stomach as I stared at the trampled blooms. A handful of cooks and cleaners began to clear up the food and sweep up, while a priest continued to pray, and there was a loud murmur of voices all at once as we exited. Outside, the musicians bowed their hands to our grandmother, offering condolences.

We gathered on the veranda that evening, not sure what to do. In an instant, our house had gone from celebration to mourning. The family doctor had been a guest, and now she was in charge of the body. Was it a heart attack? An attack on the brain? All we heard was the muffled crying of Meterling, which made Auntie Pa want to have us stay with neighbors, but my grandmother decided we should stay home and not cause trouble.

2

Our family is medium-sized. I used to wish for sisters and brothers, but really, having Sanjay and Rasi and all our other cousins was enough. My grandmother had four daughters and one son: Rema, Parvati, Jyoti, Chandra, and Tharak. Rasi and Sanjay are my cousins closest in age. We all lived in Grandmother's house, along with Auntie Meterling and Nalani. Rasi's father, Uncle Thakur, is usually in Dubai or Singapore for business; but her mother, Auntie Pa, lives in Madhupur. Uncle Darshan, Sanjay's father, lives nearby, a few districts over, and is a college professor. His wife, Chandra, who was also the sister of my mother and Auntie Pa, died giving birth to little Appam, so Sanjay practically lives with us as well. Appam stays with Uncle Darshan's sister and her husband, who have no children and are looking after him like a mother and father would. Rasi (whose real name is Rasisvari) has two sisters who are much older than her, both already married and living in India. Nalani (who we call just Nalani, not Nalani-Acca, or Elder Sister, because she is still unmarried and young) says there are enough kids for everybody. She is the daughter of my mother's sister Rema, who died with Nalani's father, both of them on a hiking trip in Ooty, while Nalani was in school, long before Rasi, Sanjay, and I were born. Meterling is the daughter of our uncle Tharak, my mother's brother, but we still call her Aunt even though technically she is our cousin. My mother and father are Jyoti and Jai, both in America, working on their PhD's in astrophysics and organic chemistry. I'm Mina, and at the time of the wedding I was ten, Rasi was eleven, and Sanjay was nine.

We had heard snatches of their story before, of how Meterling and Archer met at a party thrown for a local nawab, minutes before Meterling was to leave to go home. A Cinderella story, only they didn't live happily ever after. And no glass slipper. Instead, Archer and Meterling spoke, captured each other's hearts without intending to, and went home determined to meet again.

"He wore funny socks," said Meterling. "Imagine wearing socks in this heat." Meterling had worn yellow and looked like a radiant flower, said Grandmother.

They met at the train station next, where they nodded hello, and Archer asked Meterling to another party. This was a more awkward situation, because Meterling was, despite her height and name, a proper girl of specific caste and region, and Archer was an unknown. Marry an unknown to a known, and who knows what the net result might be! But marriage wasn't in anyone's head, merely social edification, so Meterling was sent to the party—a reception, really, for one of our neighbors who came back from the States with a degree. The grumbling was minimal, more or less, but two chaperones were provided, just in case. Meterling was twenty-eight (too old already, according to our town's standards) and as such was ripe to marry a fat fifty-year-old from a neighboring town, Mr. Govinda, but as fate would have it, she fell in love with Uncle Archer, who was only Archer at the time, fat enough himself and close to forty.

At the second party, the hostess had decided on a theme of

jellyfish to honor the local marine biologist, and served vegetable cutlets with ketchup and multicolored badushas. Meterling stood in front of a punch bowl full of seashells, and looked
for something to drink. Archer offered her a cup of something
sea-green, tasting like a little of this, a little of that, with the
tiniest kick thrown in between.

"Vodka?" she wondered out loud, before accepting.

He shook his head, saying, "Seven-Up with food color."

Meterling had never tasted such a fizzy drink before and
immediately burped. Archer let one out too, to save her embarrassment, and that's how their fate was sealed. They decided to
go outside to see the roses. Mrs. Mohan's roses were famed all
over the district; it was rumored she ordered them direct from
England. They were large, immensely fragrant, and individually named.

Meterling smiled.

"How complicated it must be to live here as a foreigner," she
said.

"How hard do you think it is to grow roses?" he asked in
reply.

Riddles, they both thought, feeling awkward.

Then Archer looked away a bit.

Then he held her gaze.

She felt embarrassed, and wondered if anyone could see.
Who was this man anyway? A footfall prevented intimate conversation, and they went back inside.

In the American films we were not allowed to see, couples
fell in love at first sight. In fact, they did in Hindi films too. One
of my grandfather's friends fell in love when he saw a girl on
a bus, and married her within a week. My aunt did not fall in
love with Uncle Archer so quickly. She said he made her laugh,
but she could not take him seriously at first. In fact, only when

the entire family had fallen in love with him could she entertain the notion of marriage.

He was easy to love. He came to our house bearing small, funny gifts, and flirted outrageously with our grandmother and Auntie Pa. He complimented them on their saris, spoke knowledgeably about market prices for potatoes and string beans, and knew the words to old *filmi* songs. He made them smile. With Uncle Darshan, he was more reserved, but only in the beginning. He soon cheerfully played and lost game after game of Parcheesi and cards, and sometimes he and Uncle Darshan retired with glasses of gin.

He gave us a clock shaped like a cat, whose tail swung to and fro and could open and close its eyes. We were delighted. We had a grandfather clock that Grandfather had received as a gift from one of his clients, but this plastic clock seemed to represent a new age, a new era. He gave us a set of Russian nested dolls and a set of miniature sport cars. "Put a tiger in your tank!" said one, which didn't make sense, but we loved it anyway. He pulled our braids, tousled Sanjay's hair. He taught us to improve our badminton. He told us jokes that made us crack up. He reminded me of a cuddly old teddy bear, eager to please and a bit beaten up.

When he came to the house one evening to ask our grandmother if he could marry her oldest granddaughter, Grandmother did not hesitate too much. My grandfather had known his father, the Gin King, and had often played cards with him into the wee hours. When they had first met the Gin King, she thought the foreigner was a bad influence on the neighborhood, and on her husband. My grandfather said no, the man was only lonely, missing his family, who were in England. Because she remembered Grandfather's good opinion of the Gin King, she gave her approval for Meterling to wed. She worried only what people would say. Marriage across color lines, not counting religious and cultural lines, was unusual but not unheard of, even in Pi. She wanted to be sure Meterling was certain about Archer, not resigned to any marriage instead of no marriage. If he had been Indian or an islander, this question would not even have arisen. Our aunt must have reassured her, because a date was set for late September.

I was glad Uncle Archer's parents were spared his death. Grandmother herself had seen the death of three of her children as adults: Meterling's father, Nalani's mother, and Sanjay's mother. Even one was one too many, and there are people in the city who say my grandfather died of grief. I knew that the death of a child is the very worst thing that can happen to a parent. My grandmother's face was lined, soft, stoic as well. She could be cross with exasperation, and her voice could turn querulous. Maybe she knew more than we did that life wasn't to be wasted over petty things. But how does one separate petty from what is important if what is petty seems important at the time? Whenever we fought, it was always over something of importance. When we were punished for fighting—our toys being taken away, or having to write out the times table—we sometimes forgot what the fight was about.

I never saw my grandmother cry. I wondered if she cried in bed, like I did. We used to take turns sleeping with Grandmother, or we'd all tumble into bed with her. Her body was so comforting, a big mound gently breathing. She smelled good, too, not like powder or perfume, like some of the overseas aunties, but of chapati dough, wet silk saris hung out to dry, sometimes vetiver. The fan circled above, and the night's shine came in through the windows. Sanjay, Rasi, and I believed that if we slept with Grandmother, mosquitoes would not bite us at night. Look, we'd say, showing off our smooth arms and legs in the morning, no bites.

🦋

"Was Uncle Archer really a white man, Auntie?" asked Rasi one afternoon.

But Aunt Meterling didn't answer, just got that distant look in her eyes, and we threw Rasi murderous looks. What a thing to ask! She had been at the wedding like all of us. A few myopic older great-aunts had whispered "Kashmiri" as they gazed at Archer's pale face and sandy gray hair. Some thought he was Anglo-Indian, which was what Rasi was asking, but we knew better. His father, *Oscar,* was English, as was his mother; both had a fondness for Robin Hood. We knew too that Archer's father was a gin maker, although we didn't know what gin was exactly. The place he made gin was on the island somewhere. There was a card game called gin, and one called rummy, though we ourselves played "Declare" with ten cards, one sequence, no jokers. But Archer's father's gin was liquor, and *not for children,* and *no, we don't have any in the house, go run out and play.* Archer had worked for his father in *Distribution,* not *Disturbance* like some neighbor suggested, and why were we listening to all this talk anyway?— but when his father died, *yes, I am still telling you the story,* Archer decided to live on Pi instead of England, and live off the interest of his inheritance. That's why his bungalow, which we saw only once, was as sparsely furnished as an islander's, though most of the British and European homes on the island were thick with furniture and lamps and paintings, even pianos. It would have been nice, though, if he had had a piano.

. . .

Archer had invited his family to the wedding, but only his sister and a cousin attended.

Mother? Uncles? Nieces?

He had little family, most already dead. Some friends from Eton showed up.

He went to Eton?

Someplace like that, anyway.

Some friends from Eton, then, showed up, with girlfriends and wives, and kept a watch on proceedings. The family retainer attended. One of the women wore a sari, insisted on hennaed feet and hands, and spoke a good deal about a Madame Blavatsky and vegetarianism. Some of the foreign men gave Uncle Archer hearty claps on his back. An Italian couple watched the proceedings with interest while we were watching them. The woman was wearing a white silk dress, which was looked at askance by those who believed that white was for funerals. A boy with curly hair stood shyly by them, until one of the other boys befriended him. It was always like that at weddings—we kids always found our level and ignored the rest. The Italian boy grinned at me at some point, and I smiled back.

Our families will be tied together, grandmother had said to one of his friends. *Archer is top-notch,* said someone. Then, *She's very tall, isn't she, the bride?* Grandmother sighed. *Yes, we are very happy to have him here,* she said, in English. It didn't sound right. She tried again:

We are very happy he is coming to the family.

Afterwards, his friends fled back to England, after awkwardly offering condolences to everyone but the bride. The Italian family looked stricken; they went on earlier than they'd planned for a holiday in Ooty. Uncle Archer's family lawyer flew home, after speaking to our uncles. Archer had died of an aneurysm was the guess, not by poisoning, not by murder. No need for an inquest. There was a moment when the sister demanded one, convinced Archer had been murdered for his money.

My grandmother drew up to her full five-foot height and asked if the sister really believed her granddaughter was benefitting by marrying Archer. It was a painful situation, but the cousin intervened. No one knew how to approach Meterling—she was so consumed with grief.

My aunt did not go to the funeral. Uncle Archer's family, represented by the sister and the cousin, were to take the body away, to "bury on decent soil," the sister had said. It seemed like an awful lot of bother, to transport a body from one country to another. Grandmother bristled, but what could anyone do? *Antigone,* someone said, but we didn't know what that meant, and someone else said, well, it was her right, the sister's; she had refused a cremation.

"It's not right that she is not invited to the funeral," said the cousin to the sister.

"She's not really part of the family, Simon," said the sister, furious with our aunt.

"She's his wife," he said softly.

"What could he have thought, marrying without even introducing us? Who is she? *What* is she?"

"Susan . . ."

"He's my brother, Simon."

No one could get a word out of Aunt Meterling then, racked with sobs as she was.

"What of the money?" asked Aunt Pa. "What of the rights of a widow?"

But Meterling just continued to weep. If anything were to come to her, that funny-looking cousin wouldn't be telling us any time soon.

3

Rain fell intermittently each day, swelling to a steady downpour in the afternoons. I'd watch the water pour off the gutters set on the roof from the veranda, lying down on the heavy swing, sometimes resting my head in Aunt Meterling's lap. She smelled sweet, like sandal powder and jasmine. Sometimes she'd braid my hair in a five-strand braid, weaving in the flowers the kanakambaram vendor brought to the house even in the rain. I hoped my aunt was braiding away her sorrow, for I wanted to help her carry some of her pain.

Our house in Madhupur was a rambling affair built in the days when Pi was an island still under colonial rule. High-ceilinged, with an impressive swing inside the front room as well as the one outside, with windows barred, and mounted fans circling on days when the current was good, it had a kitchen in the back that held a large clay amphora for drinking water, and a storeroom that was mostly kept locked. I spent much of my time up on the roof with my cousins. There, where the mango trees weighed down with fruit made for easy treats, after the monkeys were chased off, where in the morning, crows waited, talking away until fed with offered rice, we were in paradise. We could see long drumstick beans hanging off the trees, and coconut palms with big green fruit. We had an iron spike in the yard to break open the coconuts, and a tiny steel teeth-edged wheel sunk into a slab of wood to shred the flesh. Out in the back, we had a two-and-a-half-foot mortar and pestle to grind batter out of rice or lentils. Our cook would squat and rotate the pestle with strong arms, using her hand to scoop any straying batter back into the mortar. I always feared she would crush her hand, but she never did. The doors we left open in the day, so you could run straight in and straight out, which was convenient if we were stealing snacks. At night, the heavy doors were shut, and the vertical latches were secured.

Named for the setting of *The Tempest*, the initials PI stood for Prospero's Island as well as π, that strange symbol for the eternal fraction, a moniker that appealed to the island's mathematicians, sages who could not stop the Dutch or Portuguese, the English and French as they invaded and conquered Pi, but could only scratch their heads with resigned sadness, even as the assaults became bloodier and more severe. As schoolchildren, we all knew the story of the Home Rule movement, which freed but also parted India and Pakistan—squandering Gandhi's hard-won struggle for independence with blood—and made Sri Lanka separate as well. Our island got its independence too. Pi was the tiniest crescent-shaped bindi above the eyebrows to Sri Lanka's tear, a small spit of an island floating in the Bay of Bengal, resembling Madras when Madras was Madras and not Chennai, but resembling Chennai as time went on. Looking deeper, though, it seemed a bit Greek, a bit Italian, a bit African, a portion of every world culture that claimed sea and surf.

Where we lived, Madhupur, was on the western coast, the largest city on the island. Back in 632 c.e., it was just a town built around a Pallava temple. That was when Pi was known as Manjalmallekaipoongam. As the Rajarajeshwara temple was being built in Thanjavur, gopurams on our island became larger, intri-

cate with stone sculpture. Other small towns dotted Pi, speck-
led with cave temples and some Buddhist stupas. The temple at
Srirangam in India was begun a hundred and three years before
Vasco da Gama came to the subcontinent. By the time Shakespeare wrote *The Tempest*, the East India Company was a decade
old. It was more than a hundred years later that a storm-tossed
ship landed on Pi, with a Dutch captain who named what he
thought was an uninhabited island for Prospero, a magician who
could calm sea storms. Had he been taken with *As You Like It*, he
might have selected Het Eiland van Arden; if *Romeo and Juliet*,
New Verona. White men had arrived earlier than the Dutch, but
the tribal Banacs refused to be captured, and killed these unfor-
tunate entrepreneurs who sought circus stock for their English
queen. Even today, the Banacs still lived in the hill country,
but now their men sported American T-shirts made in China
over their dhotis. Every year, poverty and disease reduced their
number, and every year, the government turned away its eyes.
That was what governments did in general, I was told, although
I wasn't quite sure what a government was. I imagined elderly
men and women playing Parcheesi, only their cowrie shells represented countries and towns.

In the north was the town of Trippi, more remote and therefore
more enticing, the hot spot for tourists looking for nirvana and
bhang and gurus. Vacationing Indians mixed with Europeans,
and the police were lenient and easily bribed. Street musicians
and magicians performed all night and day, and the bazaar had
anything you could want. It even had its own ice cream, Trippi
tutti-frutti. Surfers, though, stayed away from Trippi, happier
with seaside hideaways, where waves were seemingly endless.
This is where they came after contests in Hawaii and Australia,
where they could relax with coconut juice, and count on the

waves, beer and bonfires at night, and dawns full of promise. Villagers nearby kept a strong hand on their young women, marrying them off quickly to protect them from the charms of the bare-chested foreigners who laughed loudly and seemed to want to become friends. It wasn't only the villagers who were careful of their daughters; town and city dwellers were the same. Sex before marriage loomed large as a menace, and parents were anxious to prevent unwanted couplings between islanders and foreigners, as well as between islanders themselves. Marriage provided stability, safety, as well as status.

The seasons followed India's patterns: rainy season followed by monsoon in the winter; nearly unbearable fire heat in April and May; then a mild summer. The sea kept our moist air excessively humid in April and May, and the vegetation was lush. Flowers were in constant successive bloom. Lotus stayed constant, but different species of rose, firecracker, and bougainvillea bloomed in pattern. Mango season followed gooseberry season, then jackfruit and sapote. Sometimes it seemed as if everywhere one looked, there were flowers and birds and lizards. Drought was rare, but flood was not. Still, mostly it was temperate, even, and predictable, nearly always warm.

As far back as I could remember, evenings after dinner, just before we were summoned back from the alley where it was safe to play as the summer sun set, Aunt Meterling would teach us ten new words of English. Next morning, we'd have to recite the words to her, and write them on our slates. She used a worn paper primer with unattractive crosshatch drawings. Apple. Bird. Cat. We breezed through the first five. But then, inexplicably, came "Fig." Ph-ih-ghhh. It made no sense—not the sounds, not the spelling, not even the illustration. It looked like no fruit we knew.

"What color is it, anyway?" I asked.

"Brown," replied my aunt.

Of course. Brown, a dull color. Later I'd learn that figs could be black, or purple, or green, that they could be split open to reveal a jeweled sunburst, that a microscopic wasp was the reason it existed at all. Later, I'd love the taste, but then it was merely the ugliest fruit I had seen, with a nearly unpronounceable name. I'd start and come up with a "pa" sound, a "ba," but the "ph" sound was elusive, slippery. In Tamil, there was no such sound, although we had a near-impossible "rjzha" I can't begin to spell in English even now. That sound was found in the Tamil word for banana—a fruit, frankly, that was easy to love. And the banana, we were taught in school, was simply the queen of all trees. Its fibers could be used for rope, its leaves for baskets and hats, and the color was a lovely yellow. Who doesn't love a banana? Or a mango? No, the fig was an oddity, some dessert dish that made my lessons miserable.

"Nonsense!" chided Meterling when I disclosed my doubts about this fig. "Figs," she said, "are delicious, and in our ancient lore, quite sacred. Why, Gautama Buddha himself received enlightenment only under a fig tree!"

I remained unconvinced. There and then, I resolved that this English was not a language for me.

Mary Angel did not understand my frustration and laughed. In her house, they spoke English frequently. Mary Angel also gave me more information about this fig and its leaf.

"It's what Adam and Eve covered up with," she said.

"Covered what up with?"

"Their dishonesty. They lied to God and he tossed them out of the garden. You can see pictures in our Bible."

Later, Sanjay would tell me what exactly they covered.

I myself would have used a banana leaf.

* * *

Soon I became as fluent in English as Mary Angel. We all did, and oddly, started to like the language, even if the spelling was strange. The problem was the "gh" that could be said either "ph" or "gh." The ghost had enough of coughing. Uncle Thakur loved to quote George Bernard Shaw on language. From him we learned to play with English, just like the way he and Uncle Darshan pretended to translate Shakespeare into Tamil: *Friends, cut off your ears and give them to me. I have come to bury the scissors, not ask for the price of scissors.*

My grandmother's kitchen was built of plaster and stone, and watermarks covered its surface in many places. One day, the wind howled as if announcing a change. Although the walls were eight inches thick, it felt as if the wind had moved inside, clanging the pots eerily. My aunt Meterling and I stared at the iron skillet, thrumming now with an almost imperceptible vibration. My aunt turned her attention to the kettle, flipping her hair with a flick of her wrist. It was such a careless act, a carefree movement that belied everything up to that point. This was a woman in mourning, on an island where some women shaved their heads in grief. My aunt's hair shimmered like a lake.

"The air is warm in here," she said.

I shivered. I could still hear the wind.

"I think the kettle is burning too slowly," she said. I looked at her. What did she mean? That the water was taking too long to boil? I looked up at the ceiling, wondering if Grandmother was nearby.

Meterling ran her hands through her hair again, but more slowly this time. Then she picked up a tea bag from the box of India Golden Tips and placed it in the Jane cup. The cup had a facsimile of Jane Austen's head on it, looking oddly dour in fading gold paint. It came from a set of Famous Authors, but Keats was long gone, and Johnson had a chip.

"I should probably pour the hot water right into my mouth," she said.

I stared at her.

"I mean, we have such a conviction that tea will cure all ills, that all we ever really need is a good cup of tea," she explained.

I let out a breath. She was making a joke. I sat down on a stool. Still, nothing was certain. She could be on the verge of crack-up. That's what I was watching out for.

"Why are you staring at me?" she now asked.

"Are you feeling all right, Auntie?" I asked.

My aunt looked away. I was again conscious of the wind. I thought—but just then, Uncle Darshan came in.

"Look, that whale in London had a bad time of it and died," he said, shaking the paper. He had not noticed my aunt, and spoke directly to me. We had been following the news on the radio, about the minke whale caught in the Thames, while hundreds watched from the shore. Even the prime minister had come down for a look. Last night, a rescue boat was trying to guide it back toward the sea.

The sound of china shattering to the floor made me turn.

The teacup had slipped from my aunt's fingers.

"He should not have died," she whispered, bursting into tears. I too thought the whale shouldn't have died, but my aunt was taking it badly. The teakettle began to whistle urgently, and Uncle Darshan switched it off.

Grief was something my grandmother understood. She understood that one entire year was needed to mend the heart, to mourn and wail, to sit staring at space with no intention. One year to tie up the stomach in knots at night, and untie it every morning. She knew that grief had many names, that it came unbidden at the slightest provocation.

"Leave Meterling alone," she told us. "Soon she'll be back the same."

Maybe. But we missed her magic tricks, we missed her laughter. We even missed going to the market with her, where she never carried a list, forgot whatever really was needed for the kitchen, and could easily be persuaded to buy pistachio ices. Our tongues green, we'd run back singing at the tops of our voices until stopped short by one of the other aunts.

Love had found Meterling when she least expected it. There were no letters carefully preserved and perfumed and tied with string. There were no photographs—not even from the wedding. The photographer was near tears himself; none of the photos came out—"almost, madam," he told my grandmother, "as if the gods themselves decreed there would be no witness."

Archer and Meterling had known each other such a short while. No time for her to save movie stubs, a stolen menu; no time to press flowers into heavy dictionaries. Yet Archer must have had all the accoutrements of a suitor at some point. Surely, he must have proffered her a bloom on a walk, tucked a sprig of jasmine in her hair, and compared her to any number of objects: the sun, the moon, the stars. Was she his happy orange ("happy giraffe," said wicked Rasi), his celebrated plum? His melon full of fragrance and yielding just a tiny bit? His enchantress, his toffee, his reason for existence? My mind spins at the possibility, for Meterling won't tell.

I imagine their courtship as furtive and romantic, like
Romeo and Juliet's. Meeting in secret, at night, stealing kisses
in the dark, behind trees and bushes as they did in the films. I
have no real information to base this on; I was not privy to any
of it. I create my narrative with overheard conversation, stories
recalled and told, a bit of imagination, using what I know now,
and my eyes then as a ten-year-old.

But I was on the cusp of eleven, and after my birthday, Rasi
told me, my world would change. She sneaked Nalani's Mills
& Boon books, and read about scores of handsome, brooding
men, and heroines who never thought their looks amounted to
much, until they wore that one dress and loosened their hair.
The books, Rasi told me, all ended the same way: the hero would
crush his lips on the heroine, murmuring something like "You
little fool, I love you." I was only half interested; getting my lips
crushed did not sound inviting. But soon, I began to read them
too, secretly. Still, I couldn't help thinking Rasi would punch
any boy who called her a little fool, and I would, too.

I realized I wasn't a heroine. I actually liked the way I looked,
and practiced smiling in the mirror. I did want a cowlick when
I was seven, even though it was something little boys had in
the books. My favorite character from the Famous Five was
George, short for Georgina, and I think she might have had
a cowlick. But I had read all the Enid Blyton I could find and
so I looked at Rasi's books. No, I was not a heroine. I did not
think my hair was mousy, thinking that meant messy instead
of a kind of color. I did not wear quiet colors—but then, I did
not live in Australia or England. The men did not sound that
interesting, with their cruel mouths. Who would want to hang
out with a cruel mouth? Around me, it seemed, the boys had
soft mouths; soft, round faces. If you said boo, they'd run away.
Archer hadn't a cruel mouth. He was always smiling, it seemed,

always telling jokes and making Meterling laugh. I couldn't imagine him crushing Aunt Meterling's lips.

4

One month after the wedding, after the death, Meterling told Grandmother that she was going to have a baby. She had missed her second period, and had gone to the doctor to make sure. The baby would be born in just less than eight months. Our family again became the center of sorrow in the town.

We children didn't understand it. We were thrilled to know she was pregnant. Of course we weren't to know, but secrets are very hard to keep in our house, let alone the neighborhood. But what was wrong with our Meterling? There was a trace of something in her eyes, a whiff of guilt that colored her days. All she meant to do was love whom she loved, not bring shame to her family. The boys giggled because they had heard it was all about the scandal of it, but we girls thought that the boys were just being foolish. Anyway, maybe the baby wasn't a product of procreation (by this time, Sanjay had found out and informed us of the proper process, which we previously thought involved the doctor peeing on the mothers to produce the babies. No wonder no one wanted to go to the doctor, we thought! And now, we knew the proper process on top of everything! Who would want to get married after all that?) but an unasked-for gift from God. In the Catholic church that Mary Angel went to, babies were born all the time without fathers.

When our neighbor Shobana had a baby called a preemie

later that month, everyone made a fuss. The baby itself was pretty ugly—wrinkly and squinty, and always crying. But every once in a while, it gurgled and cooed and caught up its toes, and we children, all of us, were enchanted. We begged for turns to help Auntie Shobana—fetch her water or cane juice, or fan away the flies.

"Do you want to hold little Iskander?" she would ask finally. We children took turns, marveling at the lightness, the comfort, careful of the soft spot on his head. Before Iskander's birth, there had been all sorts of celebrations. But our house was muted, quiet with grief.

Some people wondered if the baby was really Archer's, Mary Angel told us, reporting what her parents said. If not Archer's, whose? They thought the marriage was a cover-up, that Uncle Archer knew he was going to die, that he loved Meterling so much he wanted to make sure her baby wasn't a bastard. Maybe this was why Grandmother was so angry lately with the cook, and irritated with everyone else. She had really liked Uncle Archer, and she trusted him. We weren't sure what trust had to do with it, but for a while, everyone walked around with troubled eyes.

How had he asked her to unfold, to open for him, allow him entrance to all that every South Asian girl is told to guard until marriage? *Look at Sita, unspoiled and pure even after Ravana's numerous entreaties, who would not even let the monkey god carry her to safety to avoid the destined war.* But wasn't she accused of impurity after the return to Ayodha, and Rama rejected her, and she finally returned, hurt and angry to her mother, Earth, who split open to receive her? *That was not what happened; they remained happily married. And don't ask me about Radha, you troublesome girls—some things are left best to be learned after marriage.*

Maybe it was Meterling's idea from the start. Maybe as she found that her heart was expanding to include Archer and sustain him, she thought that marriage was still remote, an impossibility, so she invited him in, despite the risks. Maybe she was being adventurous. How surprised she must have been to receive his offer of marriage, then! No, that version won't do—surely they must have agreed to marriage before untucking themselves of clothes to lie—where? Only the forest would work in our imagination—the cool earth, the soft grass, the cover of night.

In our part of the world, some brides are flogged for creeping home after being beaten by their husbands. *Not in our community,* but who could really be sure? If not physical flogging, then surely a censuring of some kind occurs. An undercurrent of disbelief, *she's lying, she deserved it, she must have been responsible* runs in some people's minds. Once when I tripped and fell and got a black eye (a shiner, because it was shiny) I remember strangers I encountered turning away, as if I were to blame somehow; even if I were a victim of home violence, it remained my fault. A girl who reports a crime can be derided in public, and if she has the misfortune of asking a corrupt policeman for help, he might rape her as well, since she is already "spoiled." We knew of such cases, where it was the police captain himself who molested the girl, causing the girl to commit suicide. Even as the parents seek justice, he will continue to work and gain promotion to commander.

And I admit, I wondered if a hooligan had made my aunt pregnant unbeknownst to anyone, and Uncle Archer, in love and in full knowledge, asked to marry her, to save her reputation (because that would be how it would be seen), to raise the bastard baby. Had Uncle Archer saved my aunt from suicide? Maybe Uncle Archer had even killed the man. And the man's family poisoned Uncle Archer in revenge. But there was no sign of anything like that occurring; they were not numb, or filled with fear, or anxious. They were at ease, happy, very much in love.

But if it was merely the two of them, in love, and eager, and ready, when had they initiated their act of love? When had they said, "Let's prepone," rush before the prayers and the sound of horns, the walk round and round seven times circling the holy fire? Had Archer known he was not long for the world? Had he a congenital disease, an inherited brain impairment? Had he failed to tell our aunt? Would she have said "No dancing, no drinking"? Would she have said "No child making"?

Grandmother did not seem to be bothered by such questions. She said little, and took care that everyone ate well, and fussed over the pregnancy. Yes, she might have been short with our cook, Shanti-Mami, a day or two, but who knew the reasons running in her head?

As for us, we began to flutter around Meterling like butterflies.

"Does it hurt, Auntie?" I asked, looking at her tummy.

"No, darling. Soon I think you can feel him kicking."

"It's a boy?"

"I think it's a boy. If it is, I'll call him Oscar."

"Oscar?"

"That's Archer's favorite name."

Here she was, with baby Oscar or Oscarina inside, and all us kids crowding around her, asking questions. Mostly she smiled, and looked past our heads, as if she could see a ship we couldn't, far away on a sea that we could not see, either.

5

After school, we threw down our schoolbags, and stretched out with her after our tiffin. I had begun reading an abridged version of *Silas Marner*, and was struck by the description of the bright coppery gold of a little girl's hair. Would Oscar have hair like that, or black like ours? Aunt Meterling did not know. She listened to our questions, answered what she could, and spoke about other things on her mind.

"Distractions," whispered Rasi.

"There are just a few requirements for good tea," Aunt Meterling said one rainy day, as if that had been our topic of conversation, when we were all sitting on the veranda. I was watching the rain pound the earth, making small puddles, beating down the plants. The rainy season was calming down. No longer did people dash by with umbrellas and overturned baskets on their heads. To me, the sound of rain was intoxicating, a conversation between earth and sky. At the beginning of the season, I knew some people held monsoon parties—"drinking as much as the rain poured," said Grandmother—and danced into the early hours. Now, the rain ceased and began again, no longer a steady presence. We were lucky to escape the flooding of the towns on lower land, the tremendous damage to crops and homes, the fierce mudslides. Madhupur seemed in a bubble, warding off ecological disaster.

"One, the tea itself must be good. Not fancy, but just strong. Then you let it sit awhile while it steeps. But when you pour it, it must be hot. And when you drink it, it must be nice and hot as well."

Here she paused to give us a look, as if imparting a secret. "But not to scorch your mouth. And a porcelain cup is good, because it will retain the heat. A little milk, a little sugar . . ." And here she sighed, relished the teacup in her hand.

"It is good around three in the afternoon, when the heat of the day is still strong. When you can feel the sun. If someone starts dinner outside a little early, then the whiff of wood smoke in the air is good. But you know, the smoke is better on a rainy day. When it is nice and summer hot, you want to smell only the sun and whatever flower the breeze carries."

Again she paused. We breathed in, seeing if there was wood smoke anywhere.

"Only the first three mouthfuls will be good. You must relish them: its heat, its flavor. After that, you will drink only the memory of that first taste, until you drain the cup."

"What about the sugar? Don't forget the sugar," said Rasi, who had heard this story before and was idly playing with a top.

"Yes, you must remember not to stir the sugar in too forcefully in the beginning. In fact, a little sugar should be left to coat the cup's bottom. Stirring too hard fans the tea and makes it cool. Now you are rewarded with a sweet ending taste."

I was still too young for tea, but my personal favorite drink was Coca-Cola, which I was also not allowed to have but had tasted once at Mary Angel's house. It was like a liquid jewel, and I planned on drinking a lot of it when I got big, and to bypass tea entirely. Grandmother's friend Dr. Kamalam, who was also our family doctor, said that tea wasn't good for children or adults, that good water, thinned buttermilk, or light juice from fresh fruit or coconut was better. But Meterling was fond of tea, and got a soft, dreamy look when she drank.

Those first three sips, said Nalani when I told her what Meterling had told us, those first three sips are so precious to her because she lost Archer. That's why she thinks the flavor can't last to the last drop. Three sips and gone.

Another day, in another distraction, Meterling told us about a poet.

"Our island has many poets, did you know that? It is always poetry we rely on, some of us, to set the tone for our days. Everyone thinks of Tagore, or Kalidas, but there are many more alive today. One of my friends is a poet, and she works, ever present, at her desk in the morning chill, moving her pen across the page. Perhaps she uses a pencil. If her window is open, you can hear the slow tap of her typewriter keys. She was my classmate at school, and she wrote poems even then."

This is what Meterling told us when we asked her if she was not sad that Archer could not see his child. We thought that sorrow would eat her up, as it had eaten others in our family, tales we heard that we never knew if they were true or not. But Meterling hugged us close, and said no, no, that was what the poet was for, what poems were for.

"She is our inspiration when we feel bad. No matter how deep our heart drops, my friend the poet will pull us up out of dangerous water, somehow, with those lines, *her* magic cards, bring us up bit by bit so we can choke out the water, pull oxygen back into our breath."

Meterling carried the poet's books about with her on occasion, but mostly they stayed in her room on a shelf, thin spines edged neatly together. There was a pile of paper bound together with a ribbon as well, blank pages for Meterling herself to fill up when the time was right. To that end, she kept some fresh pens and a few sharpened pencils in a long, narrow wooden box.

And when will the time come for Meterling to pen her own thoughts? We wondered about that mysterious force that would rise up somehow, in a cloud of ink and erasure, and take her away from us. We knew so little about writing. There was a hundred-year-old man who lived near to us, a famous author, said our grandmother. He needed very little contact with the world, it seemed, and mostly penned his famous work in foreign hotels on holiday. He asked only for quiet. Once he paid for a family of bleating goats to be removed from his neighbors' garden, supplying them with milk from his writing income to make up for their loss. He was eccentric, and just a bit scary, and the poet sounded just as bad. We certainly did not want Meterling to end up a writer!

6

There's all kinds of magic," said Rasi.

"What do you mean?"

"There's the person who just guesses really well—like the weather, or whether you'll get a boy baby or a girl. That's not magic, that's just luck."

"Uncle Thakur can predict which horse will win a race."

"That's not magic."

"Uncle Raj says it is."

"Then," continued Rasi, "there's the person who can read people's minds. That's called Especially."

"Especially?"

"Yes," said Rasi. "I read it in a book. And so, say you've got a bad thought, and that person has Especially, then you're in trouble, because that person will know what you are thinking."

"I don't believe it . . . What kind of bad thoughts?"

"Like lying or stealing or cheating. And you should believe me, because it's true."

"Amma says to look straight at her elbow if she thinks I'm lying."

"What?"

"She points her elbow at me and asks me to repeat whatever I said, except at the elbow. If I don't laugh, she knows I'm telling the truth. But I always laugh. It's her *elbow*."

"But to really be magic, it takes someone special."

"Especially?"

"*Special*," said Rasi, exasperated. "The kind of someone who can turn little boys into frogs, that sort of thing."

"A magician!"

"Yes. And on Pi, there are only eleven such magicians."

"There are?"

"Where are they?"

"Oh, they live in ordinary houses and everything, but they have great power."

"Do you think Aunt Meterling is one?"

"I don't know. I doubt it."

"She might be." Aunt Meterling did do some mysterious things.

"I saw her one day, hair not even combed, with a sword in her hand," said Sanjay.

"A sword? We don't have a sword," protested Rasi at once.

"And not only did she have the sword, which was just a plain one, not encrusted with jewels or anything—"

"Because that would make it too special!" said Rasi, rolling her eyes.

"She walked out into the garden, plunged the sword right into the ground, and walked back inside."

I didn't know whether to believe him or not. It seemed possible that maybe Archer had given her a sword, but if he had, where was it? When friends of relatives in Bengal got married, the father of the bride presented the groom with a sword, which was displayed proudly in the front room of their house. I must have been only four or so when I saw it and was very impressed. Maybe this was the sword Sanjay saw, but how did it get from Bengal to our island? It made no sense. He was making it up.

"She's a magician," said Sanjay, folding his arms against his chest.

We did know about the fakes. A practiced charlatan will pay a dishonest iron wallah or pot mender to tell him a few details about a certain family. Had there been a death recently, an old history to elicit a bit of gossip? The charlatan would not act on the information immediately. He'd wait a few months, then casually stroll into the courtyard.

"Amma, can you spare some change, and I'll tell your fortune?" he'd say.

Grandmother usually chased such cheats away, but others, like Mrs. Gupta, were not so lucky.

Mrs. Gupta lived a few houses down, with a grove of banyan trees in her backyard. Her daughter had run off at fifteen to live with an American sailor, a good-for-nothing who ditched her as soon as she got too eager, the fortune-teller said. We wondered what she was eager for. A taste for the sea itself? Who wouldn't want to set sail on salty water, look at an expansive horizon, and not know what the next port would hold? To see dolphins and jellyfish frolic on the water, to sleep soundly even though there might be a shark or two lurking nearby? In our storybooks, pirates were not always so bad, and could prove quite helpful, and we knew to eat plenty of lemons and oranges to prevent scurvy. Too bad he ditched her—we literally imagined her in a ditch, cast off, like Ariadne by Theseus. Lucky for Ariadne that Dionysus came along to rescue her. I don't know who might have rescued Mrs. Gupta's daughter. The charlatan didn't seem to think anyone did. Let's hope she became a pirate herself, wore tall boots and smoked a pipe; let's hope she learned to tie good knots, fend for her supper. Let's suppose she mended her heart, found many friends and a fulfilling life. Who doesn't have the right to a happy ending? Especially one brave enough to follow her heart.

The days right before the wedding—how spacious they seemed, filled with possibility. We followed Meterling like lambs, running after her, tumbling on the grass, pulling at her sari. "Indulge us, indulge us!" we'd cry, and she'd patiently wipe a tear, fix a hem, get the splinters out. Meterling was like a rose that kept blooming, long after everyone thought it couldn't bloom anymore. Unfurling like a flag, like a song, like joy, like love itself.

She was beautiful in her height, her face a calm, round moon. Her hair was also calm, affixed in a knot or twined around in a braid. In one photograph, she is on a scooter, her plait falling jauntily down one shoulder, sitting sidesaddle (because this was old Pi) and laughing at the camera. Before Archer, before the thought of a baby. Another was taken when she was my age. She sat wearing a pretty frock, her ankles crossed and tucked in, but her body coming a bit forward, her hands on her knees. She is almost laughing, her face full of joy, her tight braids seeming to dance for the camera. Only one photograph shows her discomfort, a school picture, where, even seated, she is a head above everyone. She slumped in her seat, and I knew she was trying to make herself disappear.

When ice cream dripped down Meterling's arm, she licked it up to savor each drop. This is why we loved Meterling so, she was our *difference* among all our tight-lipped sad women, the ones who could not take a walk in the dark, the ones who let horoscope and superstition rule all of their destiny, the ones who had no music in their feet. Tall, bold Meterling—all of us wanted to grow up and be just like her. We'd stretch our limbs, stand on tiptoe. We had to stand on each other like acrobatic clowns and still could not reach the ceiling. She couldn't touch it, either, but she was closer to it than anyone.

Most nights, Meterling went to sleep early. She drank a cup of hot milk laced with saffron threads that turned a dark orange, russet, that stained her milk with exquisite scent. With her milk, she ate a butter biscuit; she dunked her cookie in her milk, relishing the flavor, the spongy texture, the soft taste. Lately, in this her third month, she craved nursery foods, like bread thickly spread with butter, sprinkled with sugar. She wanted pale baby food. She craved rice and ghee, mushy peas and chopped-up boiled carrots.

She woke at three one morning, resolved to make her own ghee and not wait for Shanti-Mami, our cook. From the ice-box, still a luxury in the neighborhood, she removed a cold slab of butter. She placed it in a stainless vessel and lit the stove. The butter began to melt quickly, accompanied by the sound of rain, thick, splashing rain. Soon, the storm let up;

the smell of rich, buttery, nutty ghee permeated the room. She thought of how, when she was a child, her mother would let her swipe the ghee leavings on the pan with her finger, after the ghee was transferred to a clean jar. No one was to know, because there were so many pollution rules governing the kitchen, and there was no licking of pots done in the open. But it was a secret relish the two shared, licking up the ghee, sometimes surreptitiously dipping their ghee-brown fingers into a small plate of sugar.

That edge of something so unusual to be forbidden was compelling, like Colette with her burnt chocolate at school.

She savored early the idea of what could be left after the main show, what remained in the bowl.

Returning to the ghee at hand, Meterling watched as the melted butter began to clarify, the solids resting at the bottom, the clear yellow-gold liquid floating to the surface. *I am the clarification of butter,* Krishna had said to illustrate his divinity. Soon the pot was full of golden ghee.

Was this when the tremendous midnight cooking began, with that first ghee, followed by rice and sesame, then honeyed badushas, then plump eggplants filled joyously with spice, until she was banned from the kitchen for being too pregnant? Almond kheer, buttery pooris, crisp jalebis that were like slender fingers, followed by perfect coffee already waiting when we awoke? Meterling told us that a famous author named M. F. K. Fisher had once described a good cup of coffee as being "intelligently made." She loved that description, but we could think only of the name Fisher. I say it again and again: there was so much in those days that was lost on us, us children, but more that we could intuit, sense and get.

Some nights found my aunt unable to sleep despite the hot milk. Her body ached, and she woke, displaced and disgruntled.

She tried to calm her body by setting up a chair in the dark, to let the night air cool her face. It was difficult. Just as she began to fall asleep on her chair, she'd move to her bed, hoping to carry the sleepiness with her. She would lie awake. Mornings would find her having napped a bit, her left side aching, and her cheek creased by pillow folds, her nerves raw and on edge. Sleep was what she wanted—sleep and Archer.

7

Folded fortunes made of paper. Nalani was very quick in making them. She'd put down words like *happiness, wealth, joy, peace, yes,* and *no,* but Rasi never had much time for them. Too easy, paper fortunes, she said.

One of our uncles always used a coin to decide whether he was going to get another coffee, or would it be tea, the *Madhupur News* or the *Albitar Accent.* Both papers were dailies and owned by the same person. But the editors were rivals, ready to best one another. The *News* featured Moon Lieutenant, a very funny commentator who wrote piercing articles poking fun at the Madhupur City Council. At the *Accent,* it was the Silver Bullet, who systematically ridiculed the Moon's article from the day before. Uncle Raj, our neighbor, took one paper, Uncle Darshan took another, and the two compared notes over betel. Neither the Moon nor the Bullet, of course, they liked pointing out, held a candle to the late, great wit and publisher of Tamil Nadu, Kalki himself. Kalki, they said, had written it all, before it had even needed to be written.

Every evening it was the same. The uncles would settle on

the veranda with a silver box holding the paan leaf and betel nuts between them. Carefully they would attend to the matter of creating plump rolls of paan. This was done in silence. Then, chewing carefully, they would each let out their own thick red spit into the garden. Then one uncle or the other would comment on the dailies. Another stream of paan laced with tobacco followed. Then a sigh. And finally, one uncle or the other would speak of Kalki. And a third or fourth round of paan would commence.

I always watched fascinated and repulsed all at once at the thick red stream of spit.

Dreamy Nalani and her paper fortunes. There she was at the window, her hair in a loose plait down her back, and in a soft loose cotton gown we called her Juliet dress. She had a whole trunk full of such gowns, one for every day of the week, in soft purples, greens, yellows, pinks, and creams. Nalani, always sunny with her smile if you caught her by surprise. But at the window, her eyes were on her future, and she folded and unfolded the paper frogmouth she had made. *Joy, peace, love, happiness.*

Rasi said she should put in some other words, like *misfortune,* or *dire straits,* but Nalani has no use for words like that. She wanted a good life. Sometimes joy, sometimes peace. Mostly she wanted love, like Meterling had had, to share her heart with someone, romantic love, deep love, divine love.

"Shouldn't they learn French?" our aunties wondered aloud. "They are running around like wild pigs."

Their most focused talks had been about landscape. Archer had been an amateur naturalist. That was one thing his father, the Gin King, hadn't taken away. So as he traveled for his father's company, inspecting bottling facilities and such, he always took one day to appreciate the scenery.

"That must sound dull," he said, "but we so often take it for granted."

He described what he'd seen: enormous mountains stranded in mist, the vapors rising, magically, ghostlike.

He told Meterling about California, a green wonder in America, where orange groves perfumed the air, where the Pacific crashed wave after wave against the reddish-tan cliffs.

"Fat sea lions line the harbor, and pelicans roost in the rocks. Whales migrate each year—it's a sight, Meti. A sight we should see."

And so they had planned a honeymoon, a quiet trip to visit all the oceans, all the shores, all the mountains he had seen. And then a trip to all that he hadn't seen, scenery and landscape they would discover together. They'd pack a few clothes, some lotions and potions to ward off sunstroke, bug bite, and nausea. They would be easily equipped for adventure.

I wondered if Meterling had even wanted a baby. How would they have traveled? Her belly was growing. Her body began to perceptibly change, and things became heavier. She felt as if water sloshed under her skin. Everything seemed puffy. There was nausea. Some mornings, she heard birds cry out and her eyes began to fill with tears. Her arms trembled. They were the part of her body that hurt the most. Not her legs, not her back, but her arms. So much was held in, held up.

Archer had given up the gin business, but he still held the title of VP of Distribution. As heir, he could not give it up, although in reality a legion of assistant VPs and sub-VPs did most of the work. His family's company made its fortune on Black Cat O'Malley gin, named for a real cat back in 1670, when patrons at High Tom Spirits on Holburn Street in London lined up for a shot of medicinal gin. The chief attraction at the pub was a mechanical cat that held a spout from which the publican poured a shot of gin straight into the customer's mouth. The Forster family's dram shop grew to a gin palace, and the original, highly guarded recipe stayed the same until Archer's great-great-grandfather decided to open a distillery in Madhupur. He added cardamom and coriander to ten other still-secret plant oils, as well as asafetida to his gin, calling it Mulligatawny Black Cat. "Add Spice to the Kick!" was the advertising slogan, and the British colonials drank it up to ward off malaria. It was local, it was cheap, and it was British.

There was an old house on a hill station nearby to the distillery where Uncle Archer's father stayed with his family when he became president of the company. As babies, Uncle Archer and his sister had an ayah, and then they were sent to boarding school in England. Susan loved England, and begged her father to let her stay with relatives in London instead of coming back to Pi. Archer was different. On holidays, he'd return to Pi, getting tanned and following his father to the plant. He was fascinated by the way the stillman, Mr. Peaks, ran the liquor through again and again, until he deemed it perfect. In another room, the rich smell of cardamom and the other plant oils wafted to the ceiling. Archer's father hired about twenty local people in his plant, and as in the old days, the island workers were overseen by the Anglo-English, except for Mr. Prakash, who kept the books. On his holidays, Archer would often visit the Prakash family at their home, and plump Mrs. Prakash fed him sweets and savories. "Archie," she would chide, "you're much too thin. Do they not feed you at that school of yours?" In his hamper back to school, there would be lovingly made chutneys and snacks packed expertly by Mrs. Prakash.

Adolescence found him hiking in the hills, often with just a rucksack and a friend or two. After university, after a brief stretch with the idea of becoming a barrister, he settled into a job at the family business. It was an easy jump to VP—who was there to compete with him? Evenings found him and his father nursing their tonicky gins, as the shouts of night cricket were heard outside their home. Archer's father was rail thin, and liked to emphasize his points with sharp blows with a cane on any nearby object. The object had often been the back of Archer's knees for misdemeanors and backtalk. Boarding-school masters were equally fond of the cane, but Archer swore he would never use one on any child of his. What was unnerving to Archer was to imagine his father voicing those same promises when he was a young man.

His father did not die on his beloved island. He died in London, on the floor of a bank, where an epileptic seizure led to his heart stopping altogether. Susan identified the body. Somehow, she blamed the island, even though it was irrational, but when is grief rational?—and at the same time, when is grief ever irrational? Grief for her needed a focus, something to blame. She was twenty-two. When Archer reached her, she was cold, withdrawn, because she knew Archer loved the island. After the funeral, Susan poured herself into her new job in advertising. Archer poured himself a drink.

Was this why he never dated much, in love with the bottle more than with any woman? A cadre of school friends dined with him regularly until one by one, they married. Then he became a guest, the needed fourth in bridge, the possible date for Anne or Lesley. At thirty-five, he went back for Mrs. Prakash's funeral, and wondered why he ever left Pi. He moved to Madhupur permanently. His father's house was too empty, so he sold it, and took a small bungalow. Without his drinking companions, he felt less inclined to drink. Mr. Prakash, eighty, took him along to ayurvedic steams and massage, made him consider yoga. Archer thought about it, but decided he found more pleasure in rasagullas than in chaturanga dandasana, sweets winning easily over yoga postures.

8

Meterling picked up the phone. It was an old-fashioned one, black, with a heft that, if it was hurled, could hurt someone. The cradle was heavy, too. She put the receiver back. She hesitated but did not pick up the phone again. The slip of paper was in her hand with the cousin's number written in scrawled letters, haphazardly spaced, in black fountain-pen ink. She gazed out the window and saw that the goat was no longer in the garden. The sun lit up the coral jasmine tree, making the orange tongues of its flowers fire points. Momentarily dazzled by the sight, she looked away. She smoothed down her light cardigan. It was too large for her, and a thread was fraying near one of the buttons. She absently pulled at it, and then bent down her neck in an odd angle to bite it off with her teeth. She became ashamed of her own ferocity, and smoothed the sweater down again. She got up and walked to the door, but changed her mind. She began to pace. There was something on the floor. It was one of our marbles. She picked it up and held it up to the light. It had a pale green tint, with a brown cat's eye inside. Meterling wiped the marble in the paloo of her sari, and placed it in her mouth. She let it roll around against her teeth, bit down softly, and then spat it out again.

"I must be going crazy," she thought. She looked out the window once again and began to cry. She placed her hands on her ever-bigger belly and shuddered with tears.

I saw her from the doorway and ran to her to hug her. My arms couldn't reach around, but I had forgotten that. I wanted to take away her pain, moor her somehow, make it better.

Gin is made with juniper berries and a careful blend of other herbs. If Meterling was to inherit any of Archer's wealth, she hoped it would be a field of coriander, a field of cardamom, and a field of turmeric. This was all she could handle, she thought, wanting no part of the great monstrosity of a house his father owned in England, with its dark, damp walls and sweep of staircase, its foyer so crowded with photographs of unsmiling relatives and white nawabs, a house that Archer said suffered from a lack of breath. There was no money, except in gin, but Archer's family was going to see to it she got very little. Certainly there was no will; there had been no time for a will. But if there had been a will, she might have gotten three fields. That's what she had wanted, after all. For Archer did talk of his death once, a night they took a boat around the lake as the sun burnt the water with crimson. He worried aloud that he might very likely go before her, leaving her a widow. She had laughed her twinkly laugh then and told him, looking straight into his eyes, "Then leave me three fields. One of rye, two of spice."

"You are like Isak Dinesen," he said, taking her into his arms.

"Who?"

"A woman who was brave beyond her times."

And then he began to kiss her, and there really was no further talk on the subject.

Meterling found the story from Isak Dinesen that Archer had mentioned. A woman pleads for the life of her son, who is accused of arson, and the overlord asks her to plow a field of rye in one day to spare his life. She plows with the village and the overlord and his guest watching, until she finishes, her son walking beside her all along, and collapses in his arms to her death. For the freedom of one, the death of another. Sorrow-Acre. An inheritance of sorrow. A haunting tale. Isak Dinesen, who had had a philanderer for a husband, whom she still loved, some say, after their divorce. And now Archer was gone, and she had no wish for rye.

And here was his cousin, wanting her to phone, leaving a message hurriedly scribbled by Pa. She had no wish to phone. She wanted Archer.

Archer had told her about the seasons in Surrey, his old home. In March, everything became mud, as the weather shifted from ice to less ice. Then a brief, pale-lemony sun that melted the ice and softened the soil, painting the backs of rubber boots with squishy dirt.

"Once I was walking and came across violets, half-hidden in all that mud," he told her. "The trees hadn't greened yet—everything was still bare branches and gray. But the burst of violet was sudden, a gift.

"Finding you, Meterling, is like coming across those violets—a gift."

And Meterling blushed. For even though the idea of an absence of flowers was alien to her, she knew what he meant from the emotion in his voice. And again, there was nothing else to do but fall swiftly into his arms.

Later, they wondered about children.

"Yes, a good idea," she murmured, her face pressed to his neck.

"Yes," he replied, "a wonderful idea."

9

L ook at the way our neighbor conducts himself late at night," said Aunt Pa. "Who is to say he is not at war with his whole life, all of the time like that? My uncle Das was his classmate, after all," she told us, "arm in arm back in those days, one wiping his nose, the other scratching. Two peas in a pod, you know, the pair of them: and how often did my own grandmother take a broom to their shenanigans? My grandmother, who was so severe," she said—and here we looked at each other, listening to Aunt Pa's tale, astonished.

But Aunt Pa was looking off into the distance.

"You never expect your uncle to be killed so young, of course. This was your great-uncle from your grandfather's side of the family. And it was our neighbor himself who went to the stationmaster's office to demand reparation. Of course, it wasn't that poor man's fault—a train is bound to fail once or twice for all the times it runs properly. And your great-uncle, eighteen, he was fond of crossing the tracks to get home for tiffin. The train came at a quarter past, that was the schedule, and usually your uncle crossed while the roar of the departing train could still be heard and seen in the distance, receding. He liked to touch the rails, too, to feel their heat. And whose fault was it except that of the glass he struck his foot on, and later the stone he hit his head on before he passed out? No one saw him, that was the trouble, or in a wink they would have pulled him off the tracks. And that was the day the train chose to come late, too late that day.

And even though Auntie Pa was relating a story she must have related a hundred times before, and even though we had heard it before, there was something in her voice that told us that she would have given anything to have been there that day, to pull him away from the tracks, so even now her grandmother, were she too alive, could shake a broom at him still, to spare our neighbor who drinks late into the night and smashes bottles from his second-storey window onto the street below.

It wasn't only for her uncle that our neighbor got drunk, but it was the start of his downward spiral, as Aunt Pa tells it—Aunt Pa, who often rises early and carefully sweeps up the glass before most of us are up the next day.

Nalani had a funny little finger, smaller than the usual small pinkie. It was a birth defect, a stub. We loved to hold it, and compare its littleness to our own little and littler fingers. Nalani had long, thick braids, and liked to wear chiffony dupattas over her skirts. We thought her laugh was like running water, all sparkle and stream. Nalani liked to paint on glass as well as fold paper fortunes; she was the artist in our family. She painted beautiful girls from the classical period, dancing girls and musicians holding tamburas and veenas, small drums and cymbals.

She went to Madhupur Women's Art College, and took two buses to get there. There had been a row about her going, but Auntie Pa prevailed, saying that all girls should go to college; it was nonsense to think otherwise.

My own mother had gone to college, but many of my aunts had not. Nalani's mother had been in a class of four, one of the first girls to go to the local Catholic college in 1951. In those days, families who sent their girls to college were made fun of. Why do they protest, our grandfather had fumed (so we'd been told); our girls would be skilled at economy, home science, at the arts, make better wives than those without a B.Sc. Others resisted any Catholic institution, and the kneeling that went on within those walls. All this fuss over a class of four.

"What's the matter, don't you want her to get married?" persisted the neighbors, worried he had gone crazy. But my grandfather maintained that an educated woman could educate her family, and college was the natural step to take. But though the band of four was brave, there were faculty who refused to teach girls, who said "they were unteachable, that it was immoral, and even the Gita had concurred." The president of the college, versed in Sanskrit and no slouch, defended his actions, and threatened to dismiss faculty who would not cross the border. It was a bold step; in other situations, a man might say this, but in private—it would be understood that the threat would not be carried out. Clustering close and walking hand in hand in the corridors, where the men frankly stared, then hurriedly looked away, the four sought to absorb information quickly and become good scholars.

The following year, the enrollment for girls at the college dipped to two and the coed program was done away with. Then, in 1954, a new women's college was built, and the compulsory Catholic prayer with kneeling was made optional, and families sent their girls in droves, or at least dozens. My mother attended RKV Subalakshmi College and, together with her two best friends, Anu and Miriam, studied physics and chemistry. When Miriam told the girls she was going to become a nun, my mother and the other friend cried. "But, Miriam, what about your hair?!" was all they could think of to say, so shocked and hurt were they; but Miriam hugged her friends and said no shaving was involved, only a crop—"Think of Joan of Arc!"—which made the girls cry even more, followed by Miriam herself.

Everyone was full of stories about our grandfather. He had been posted to Malaysia, on assignment for the civil engineering project he was engaged in. He and a colleague subsisted on careful rations of rice, they were so poor. One morning his friend was so hungry, he ate the day's supply, and Grandfather wouldn't speak to him for the rest of the week. The friend apologized profusely, but my grandfather turned a stony ear. Years later, the friend married the daughter of a poet, and he asked his father-in-law to write a sonnet on a single grain of rice dedicated to my grandfather. My grandfather had the rice grain framed, and to this day, it hangs proudly in the house.

My mother adored my grandfather. She told me all the time about the good things he did. Even though his son-in-law had childhood polio, he never let him feel bad, so to this day, Uncle Darshan is the jolliest man we know. Grandfather married my mother off to a scholar who drank far too much espresso, who had too much brilliance for India, so he sent him to America. He was part of a crowd of men accused by India: Brain Drain! Sons abandoning Mother India! But even though Kennedy, a young, smart man who once had said, Ask not what your country can do for you—ask what you can do for your country, did not govern America, he had once, and that spoke of hope, even if they had killed him. He was an American who was as good as Nehru perhaps, but maybe not as wise, "for really, who could be as wise as Nehru and Gandhi, Mina?" My aunties loved to tell me about Indian history, about Asoka and the Pallavas. My head swam with story, lived for story—"Then what? . . . Then what?" I'd ask. In my school, my teacher said she could not continue the lessons, for I would constantly erupt with questions. She gave me a notebook so I could write them down to ask her later, but instead, I began to draw.

10

Meterling stood in an archway. She saw the sunrise in bits—bright orange low in the sky. She saw the clouds grow purple, saw the sun loom large, awake. She saw the sun loom large, loom large and become round, filling her view—making her round, filling her view of the sky. She walked in the path of the sun, thinking of her son, and smiling and grimacing at once at the interplay of words, at the poor pun, but then her mind calmed again—she saw in the sun's progression her own limitations and saw also her son's possibilities. She knew she would have a son. She saw the possibilities for her son, who, like the sun, would turn from round orange to transparent yellow to a blue steel—a silvery steel, climbing high before she knew it. Her son would see the world, travel through the sky. And with a mother's intuition, she held him strong in the womb, and gritted her teeth in anticipation of the childbirth months away.

She greeted the day each morning by walking her coriander coffee to the herb garden. The tulsi in the pedestal was lush; the thyme had begun flowering too early, because of the spate of recent hot days. The oregano stood tall and full. Only the lavender was slow, raising perfumed leaves to herald the still-green buds. The burst of lavender had always been significant to Meterling, ever since as a child she weaved wreaths from the flowers to shape into crowns. The day was overcast. A thundery day might well ensue. This time, she did not think of Archer for a full ten minutes. Her fingers were growing plump. She had long taken off the rings, thinking she would give them to her son to give to his bride. What would Oscar grow up to be? Would he have his father's white skin, his blond hair? Would he be ridiculed in school? She placed her hands protectively over her belly. She would protect him, she would surround him with such love, and it would shield him from taunts and cruelty.

Nalani also spent a great deal of time in the garden. She liked to walk deep into the backyard, where there was a small clearing under the lemon tree. There, she could lose many minutes just staring at the green grass and breathing in the heady aroma of lemon blossom. She placed a small chair and table there, so she could sometimes sit with her feet up. One day she noticed a papery wasp nest deposited neatly on the table. It was so light and carefully constructed—a honeycomb of networking. As she tossed it away—it looked like there were some waspy remnants inside—she wondered how it got there. Three days later, a small bird's eggshell was on the table. Two halves actually, beautifully oval and colored pale green. When the small strawberries arrived nestled on a mat of leaves, she knew that someone was leaving her presents. She wasn't frightened. She didn't feel as if she were being watched or stalked—no pinprick of fear or agitation to suggest anything out of place. Only a sense of peace and a calm happiness. Soon, they would arrange a marriage for her, and she knew to whom it would have to be.

It was Sanjay, whom she finally caught in the act. Something to do, he shrugged.

Meterling was four months gone and ready to give birth any day. But Dr. Kamalam had said there were four months and twenty-eight days still to go. She wanted to take off all her clothes and float in cool water, anything to feel less weighted. She did not want to wear the bangles at the bangle ceremony when all the women would crowd around her and offer baby advice. She wished she could take a plane to England, run among those violets Archer always spoke of. She wished she could drink a martini. She had seen a picture of one in *Punch* and it looked cool and inviting.

Instead, she ate sugared sweets, round halvahs made of carrot and ghee; small balls of farina studded with almonds. Everything round to remind her of her round belly, her round baby. When she wasn't eating sweets, she felt cross, magic Meterling, ready to break sticks, throw rocks, anything to get it all over with. Why had she been so hasty to sleep with Archer? Did she really think she could fool the gods? How could the baby brave a life with no father?

"Come to the concert with me," coaxed Nalani. "The loud violins might please the child."

"Can violins really be that loud?" wondered Meterling.

It was a local Carnatic group practicing for the winter music fests in South India. A flute player was supposed to be especially good, having studied under the great Mali. Forty violins would accompany her.

As it was, it was only four violinists, not forty. "Would that it were true, madam," sighed the ticket master as he counted out their change. "What a celestial chorus that would be!"

The aunties had wondered if it were wise to bring Meterling to the concert, but Meterling was twitching. Uncle Darshan suggested she go to a scary movie, but Nalani thought violins would give more grace to the birth. "The child inside can probably no doubt hear everything," she said, and then blushed for the frankness of her expression. Smitten with a college boy named Rajan, whom she secretly named Goat Herder, and no one else, Nalani knew that she was not wise in anything to do with the heart.

"But a baby, Nalani," said Meterling, "has to do with the body, and sometimes—yes, only sometimes—with the heart as well. Archer and I didn't think twice; we were caught up in the moment—there I was in his bed, with my sari coming undone. Who could have predicted it? Of course, we knew we were to marry—he'd asked already, but I hadn't said yes, you know. I said yes only three days later, shocked by it all, of course . . . "

Nalani blushed at Meterling's frankness, thinking of Rajan, whom she met at an intercollege outing. She could bind herself to him in one breath, after all.

"What does that mean?" Rasi would ask if she could hear her thoughts. What would it mean to bind oneself like that? Bind like a vine? Like a knot?

"Like a love knot," I would reply, "like a love knot." But those adult conversations were not part of our privilege, so I make them up now as much as I can.

They came back late from the concert, and Meterling was again in good humor.

II

Meterling said we are all of us braver than she could ever be. I didn't understand, because to me it was Meterling who was the bravest of anyone I knew. She was the one in the family who went outside tradition, the one whom the aunts scolded, the one who gave rise to so much talk. But Meterling said we were young and therefore would always be able to do more than her.

"I can't even drive a car," she said, "but you girls will drive as soon as you are able."

"Why can't you drive, Auntie? Aunt Shobana can."

"I fear crashing, Mina, of hurting someone else with my hands. I fear panicking between choosing accelerator and brake. Perhaps I fear making mistakes. I worry about forgetting how to drive while driving. I worry I won't know what to do at intersections. I know I need more experience behind the wheel to gain confidence, make left turns, merge into traffic, but I get scared. So if someone makes fun, says, 'Take the bus,' I think okay, yes, I'm not too proud to do that. But you, my dear, you will drive, and drive well, in all sorts of weather, at night, safely, securely."

"I will learn to drive a motorcycle," said Rasi.

"Of course," laughed Aunt Meterling. "And why not?"

What she didn't tell us: that with Archer came her chance to travel, that without him, she was moored, unable to drive, fixed.

Aunt Meterling herself had a friend, Chitra, who rode a

turquoise blue Vespa scooter, always with her hair in a braid, tossed like a scarf around one shoulder.

"Every girl has a friend like Chitra—even I had a friend named Chitra," grumbled Grandmother, and I knew she loved Chitra. I suppose Grandmother meant there are always girls who test the borders of every life. I wasn't sure if I had that kind of mettle. Rasi did—she did for sure. But me, I tended, even at a young age, to be more cautious, to be the follower, not the leader. If we lied as children, it was my palms that would break out in a sweat, my eyes that widened slightly for fear of being caught. To this day, I can't tell lies very well.

"What is it?" Meterling asked, putting down her knitting.

"Here, it's from Archer's estate." Uncle Darshan smiled, handing her the envelope. Meterling saw the letterhead of Archer's solicitor. Opening the note, she read swiftly.

He had left her three fields: one for rye, two for spice. He'd left her a house. He'd left her his legacy in England.

Rasi whispered, "She's going to tell us that old story about the golden mango."

But Meterling shot us a piercing look, and said, "This is also a story about family."

And Nalani would tell us more later. Nalani would tell us to remember that Aunt Meterling was always thinking tenderly about her parents.

And we knew the story by heart. One day Shiva and Parvati held a contest between their two squabbling children, Ganesha and Murugan. Whoever spun around the world three times first would receive the prize of a most special golden mango. Murugan was the older, and more prone to quick action. He sprang on the back of his peacock, laughing at his brother, and sped around the world. But Ganesha, slower, smaller, more compact, simply folded his hands together in a gesture of respect and circled his parents three times. Delighted, his parents presented him with the golden prize. When I first heard this story, I felt sorry for Murugan, because I too would have chosen to fly fast on a chariot. I thought that this was a story told by parents to keep their children home and safe.

"They gave you life so you spin this way and that. Sideways and upside down, like an astronaut, so you can see the world."

"I want to be an astronaut!" shouted Sanjay at once.

"An astronaut?" said Rasi.

I was mad because I wanted to be one too but Sanjay said it first. In our games, he would get to do it then.

("You dolt, Mina—of course, you could have been an astronaut," he said years later. "What were you thinking?")

Meterling spoke again:

"Your parents are the people who let you dream. Your parents are the ones who taught you how to fly. Spin. See the world. Come home and report, then fly out again."

I dreamed of an enormous cow walking through a field of grain. From the cow's belly grew stalks of grain and rice mixed with barley. The grains mixed freely as the cow swished her tail.

She wore a yellow headdress, with rows upon rows of bells, sewn with green and red thread. The cow's feet danced, and I dreamed of anklets tinkling silver with sound. The cow's eyes were unfathomable and reminded me of Meterling's (which is strange, because, of course, her eyes were always dancing or deep or dark) and I woke up.

12

Meterling, our goose. Our giant. She sat in the sun and looked at the ocean. First she climbed up the banks of shifting sand, where fragrant pink roses bloomed. Beach roses. Then, there was the sight of the sea. The sea, the sea, it slid toward us, then slid back. All that water, all that rain. Meterling drank in the ocean, lay back on the sand, and felt the sun's heat. The water roared and sounded, crash after crash in the soft broken swish glass shatter of water. "Auntie Meterling," we cried, "come splash us with the water, come play with us!" But Meterling lay on the beach, and took in the sun full blast. Only for fifteen minutes, because we were all warned against its rays—all the aunties told us again and again to stay out of the sun. It will darken us and burn us to a crisp, make us faint, and create vomit, headache. Go to the ocean when it is dawn, evening, they say, soft twilight, the in-between hours. For the most part, we listened, but there were some times when we sneaked off to play in the sun, wanting to turn darker and darker, and Meterling once in a great while joined us. She splashed her feet at the water's edge, but brought out an umbrella when the sun became too intense. In truth, our aunties were right, we could only stay a short while before the sand painted out feet with fire and we ran for the shade of the trees, laughing and screaming all the while.

Grandmother spoke:

"I remember when Meterling was born. Her mother was a scrawny thing when Tharak married her. Quiet and abashed by our noisiness, she still found ways to assert herself by wearing jangling earrings instead of heavy wedding gold. We so love gold, don't we, in our culture? Melted down and reshaped—how often has Roshanji come to our house to remake us new jewelry? But Asha wore jangling earrings, and was always abreast of fashion in the cut of her choli sleeves, in the fabric of her saris. That was the way she had her voice among us, I sup-pose, in her clothes.

"And Tharak. My middle child, who was always reading and working. A great scientist, they said, readying for the Nobel, but who knew his life would be so short? Thirty-nine only, and a car crash got them both. And Meterling only six years old.

"It was Tharak who named her, and yes, we all protested. 'What kind of name is that,' we asked, 'and for a girl?' But he said it was special, it would give her strength. We thought it was a name from one of those German textbooks he was reading at the time, about fissures or fixtures or something. Something about test tubes. 'Meta' we knew, there are so many families named 'Mehta,' after all, and someone said it was a diminutive, like the way we shorten 'Shubashree' to 'Shuba,' 'Shobhana' to 'Shoba.' But this 'ling' had a German sound to it, or Malaysian, perhaps. And then the *r.* I never could understand what Tharak was doing with the name. Asha said it had come to him in a dream. She was eight months gone, and he woke her up, shouting, 'Meterling!' But sometimes I think that's just what she told us. Meterling. We got used to it, you know, and of course, it fits. Meterling. Sometimes I swallow it, so it becomes 'Meta-ling.' And of course, we all call her 'Meti' now and then.

"My Tharak. A joy, you know. An absolute joy."

And we kissed our granny's tears away just then.

There were many beaches on Pi. The most popular were crowded, with "Hot peanuts!" and "Lassi here!" sellers and fruit vendors, carts full of pinwheels and streamers, beaches full of kurta- and pajama-clad women, or women in saris, fully clothed men, all walking arm in arm, chatting and laughing, and children shrieking. The sea! The sea! Everything happened at the sea.

There was the Gandhi statue, just like in Madras, garlanded with fresh roses and chrysanthemums. Across the Pacific, on a beach in California, it was a Hawaiian surfer so garlanded, and farther on, in Rio, Gandhi again, only not at the beach. Elsewhere, on beaches around the world, there are statues of Madonnas, some who weep real tears, and Imanjas, gods and goddesses to herald the power of the earth and water. But on Pi, at Madhupur Beach, Gandhi's eyeglasses merely glinted as the sun sank into the water, and all around, children cried out in joy at being at the beach.

But there was another kind of beach on Pi as well, the private beach, where only the privileged could wander, where wealth or status opened the barred gates, where miles of smooth soft sand folded toward the sea line. Once a beach pass was in hand, pure bliss awaited the lucky who walked on its sand.

Oh! The sea! The sea as it shines on the horizon, the sea as it leaps toward the shore, the sea as it sucks back, all foam and spray and salt and wind.

And here is Meterling at the shore, piling small pebbles into a circle. Sometimes she takes twigs and sticks them straight upright near the stones on the sand. She is building prayer circles, she is building miniature Stonehenges, she is creating rock gardens, tiny, small, temporary memorials to Archer. Little shrines to her large, overpowering loss. Her hands work ceaselessly, blue-green pebbles and glittery rocks shaped into circles and left on the sand.

Rasi and I like to build castles. We like to pile sand into soft mounds and dig under them to form tunnels, so that our hands can meet and shake hello. The wet sand sometimes fills with water and we shout with glee.

But Meterling makes circles to track her tears, makes small sculptures to declare her loss.

13

Meterling was twenty-eight when she lost everything she could lose in losing Archer. And yet at twenty-eight, she had everything she could hope for as well. Three short months, that was the entirety of their courtship, their desire, their hope. Twenty-one, that shiny age, had passed her, then twenty-three. By twenty-five, she was treated tenderly, assumed to a life of spinsterhood. At twenty-five,

Meterling became a warning for marriageable daughters as well. It happens, the elders mused. If, as the gossips say, a daughter can only be so dark, or so poor, she certainly could only be so tall as well. That golden promise of a perfect bride required golden skin, golden height, and the golden means of proportions. And Meterling had nothing—her skin was dark, like amber gone opaque, and she was so tall. Meterling was a beauty in a school all her own, and that's why we flocked to her. She was not film-star material, our Meterling, she was no universal beauty. But she was our standard.

I told her I did not plan to marry, ever. I would be a famous scientist who had no time for cooking and husbands. I would live alone with lots of animals, including a horse, like in the storybooks where children rode on horses and lived with cats and big shaggy sheepdogs. *"Beti,"* Meterling would say, using Hindi, because sometimes in Hindi, the tenderness required to cut through an excess of emotion with a perfectly pitched honesty was available—*beti,* which means "child"—*"beti,"* she'd say, "don't worry. All is possible; all is good in this world." And Meterling would smile. She who had lost her love, her joy, at twenty-eight. She'd smile with tenderness, hoping to ease our pain, even as her back ached.

When someone dies, everything dies as well. At least it seems like that. It seems like the gods are punishing you, and no matter what treasure you might have amassed, it all becomes rot, becomes meaningless. Death changes everything. It changes everybody.

Meterling changed, becoming clouded, becoming worn, withdrawn. A light was quenched in her as her sorrow took seed. But Oscar, growing inside her, moved the seed around somewhat. He didn't let it settle. Life, life, life, he whispered, this voice coming into being, this child, shouting at Meterling not to give in. No, live! he must have shouted, this child in being, live so that I may live as well. And we responded to Oscar, this child in being, as well. We responded to his light, as did the aunties, as did everyone who flocked around Meterling. "Live," we told her, "do not give in to this sorrow, do not succumb to this pain. Let it out, yes; let it out so we can carry it for you." Because that is what people do when they care deeply about someone: they shoulder their pain, put their heart to work, put their mind to the grief. And they carry the burden. And that is how some people live. That is how some people—whose time to die is not yet, because of whatever grace is granted in their life—this is how some people survive.

At twenty-eight, Meterling had discovered the one person she realized she had waited for her whole life.

"No," said Meterling. "That's not entirely true. I just met Archer by accident. All that drama came later, because I lost him. But meeting him was accidental. Loving him was the crux of the matter, a choice I made. I was happy before I met him, though. I wasn't pining for something missing. How could I be, with all of you loving me so?" Her eyes filled with tears. The baby was due in four months, twenty-one days.

Rasi and I listened, and Rasi agreed with Meterling, but then she turned to me. "Sanjay stole my transistor," she said.

"What?"

"I left it out and it was gone."

"How do you know it was Sanjay?"

"He had it this afternoon."

"Oh."

"He said he didn't."

"Did you tell Grandmother?"

"Don't worry; I've got a plan."

Rasi went to confront Sanjay over her transistor.

But Sanjay had found a kitten.

Sanjay found a kitten that was hiding under a banana leaf. Scrawny, white, with pink-tipped ears, it cried when Sanjay removed the leaf.

"C'mon here, kitty," he said, but it tried to scurry away. Its paw was caught in a trap. It lay bleeding, and without thinking, Sanjay reached in, pulled away the leaf, and pushed apart the trap's jaws.

The kitten nestled onto his lap, and that is how the kitten named Scrap and Sanjay became fast friends.

We went to ask Uncle Raj, who was a doctor, what to do next. Uncle Raj tidied up the kitten, and gave a lecture, but Sanjay wasn't listening too much. He was wondering how he could keep the kitten, how to convince everyone to let him have a bit of milk or water—what did kittens eat anyway? As it turned out, it was easier than he thought to keep the kitty and feed her as well.

"I want to pet it, I want to pet it!"

"How come you got to keep it when we couldn't keep the puppy?"

"I still see that puppy in the street sometimes."

"I think Mrs. Shankar takes care of it."

"I wish we could keep a puppy. Who needs a cat anyhow?"

"Look at its little nose."

"Look at its eyes."

"It likes you, Sanjay."

"Let me see, let me see!"

"I want to feed it."

"Not an 'it.' Her name is Scrap."

"Scrap?"

"How do you know it's a girl?"

"Yes, it's a scrap of a kitten."

"Did you think it was a scrap of paper when you found it?"

And Sanjay admitted that he had, that he had been looking for some paper to jot down—

"Jot down what? Jot down what?"

"Nothing. Anyway, you see, it isn't a scrap of paper, it is a kitten."

"Can I pet it again, Sanjay?"

"You don't have to ask permission."

"Don't scare it!"

"Look, it's sleepy."

"Maybe we could sing to it."

"Okay, okay—just take turns."

14

I ntelligence, my girls, is how you maintain yourself in independence," said Aunt Pa one day, out of the blue. "Year after year," she continued. "It's knowing how much to spend at the market so you have something left over to spend again. It's making sure all the channels of cash flow are open, that nothing is caught, creating blockage, creating snags. It's making sure that as well as a way out, there is always a way in. Entrance is as important as that Exit sign that's got you so fixed—oh, I know all about it, how at the movie theater, you spot that sign first. And why not?—it's so lit up, so red, so bright. It's for emergencies, after all, for fires and power outages, for stampedes, any unforeseen circumstances. But the Entrance sign is important, too. That one is green, green for 'go,' green for 'hello.' The entrance sign that lets you in, no matter what color, what class, the thumbs-up in our lives. You girls don't know how hard we fought for your independence. You don't know how it was back then, with the British. You don't know."

And it was true what Auntie Pa was telling us: we didn't know. Rasi and Sanjay and all of us, girls and boys both, we just felt so free and lucky those days. We were nine, and ten, and eleven. The world really was our oyster, ours for the taking. We did like to run, we liked to shout, and we liked to sing at the top of our voices. Grown people like Aunt Pa were mystifying. They liked to drink tea, they liked to talk, they had eyes so creased with tears and fears and trembling. It made no sense to us. But at one time, Nalani says, they were young too, all of them, in braids and rag-tail hair, screaming and running and shouting for the sheer joy of it. But the years made one quieter, in our family anyway, it made for a steadier gaze, a firmer walk. And all at once, we hugged Auntie Pa, who batted us away, like she was annoyed, and told us to stop making ourselves pesky, so we ran off to find Grandmother.

We found her in the garden, Grandmother, watering her plants. A new one had bloomed. She called it Chandra, for the moon, and indeed its white, round bloom looked so soft and heavenly, just like the full moon. But softer than the moon, too, which can appear harsh sometimes, all silvery and cold in the sky. This flower was more yellow, creamier, like we could cuddle into it as if it were a pillow and coverlet, and sleep quite soundly, if we were small like Thumbelina, say, or Tom Thumb.

"There is a saying," said Meterling, "that the gods rain down gifts and tangle up our brains." Why else (she thought but did not say, as did we) would the gods give me such a man as Archer, only to take him away? Again and again, all over the world this happens, this suffering. A baby dies, the parents overcome by grief, overwrought by pain.

Grandmother takes in all of this hurt, all of these questions, and shrugs her shoulders. In that shrug lies the way of compassion, of not knowing. But when one is in the throes of emotion, a shrug is hard to come by. A shrug is ancient; it is a way of acknowledging the pain, of moving past it while acknowledging it, of recognizing that many things are out of our control, that the world is impermanent, that love and loss go hand in hand.

As children, our tradition dictates that we be sheltered from all this pain and suffering, sheltered, as it turns out, from the human condition itself. But kids are smart. We figure it out soon enough. We know the grown-ups don't tell us everything, that their ways and methods are baffling, but they are kidding themselves if they think we don't know about suffering. We see it all the time. But as children, perhaps, at least outwardly, we recover more quickly.

Sanjay, Rasi, and I were a team of sorts, a triad of playmates who took turns helping each other to figure it out. When you grow up in an *extended,* stretchy family, the mothering and fathering is done in batches, but there is also a great deal of freedom. When there are only two parents and one or two children, the attention can be focused, but on the island of Pi, we just ran around like rowdies, like we were free.

Nalani saw Meterling's suffering differently, more tangibly, like a shard of steel or glass in her heart. For Nalani, Meterling's heart was embedded with this sliver, and the sliver, like a splinter, needed to be dislodged. Inside her heart, Nalani believed, Meterling carried her grief, and it was up to us, her family, to help her both carry the pain and dislodge it.

But it was hard to deal with Meterling's pain those first few months. It came and went like a flame on a matchstick. With us, she would be happy, or pretend to, and then when she thought she was alone, it would come pouring out. We knew people who suffered from sadness. That sadness twisted in and out like a knife, making the person double in pain sometimes, and sometimes it was like a path that pointed down. Sanjay, Rasi, and I felt bad for Meterling when we saw her doubled up in pain.

What could we do for Meterling?

"Should we make her presents?"

"A boat that she could use?"

"A boat?"

"A wooden boat."

"What would she do with a boat?"

"Everyone wants a boat."

"*You* want a boat—not everyone does."

"Maybe she'd want to play with Scrap?"

"Rani Mami says Auntie should stay away from Scrap until the birth." Rani Mami had come with Dr. Kamalam to examine our aunt. She would help her when it was time.

"Why?"

"I don't know."

"Maybe we should just bring her tea and biscuits."

"That's what Grandmother says."

Our aunt had a lot of tea and biscuits.

Nalani practiced yoga. Nalani practiced deep breathing and dancelike asanas to help her float and ground, energize and stay rooted. One hundred and eight sun salutations was her goal, but usually she did just ten. Sometimes she asked us to join her, but Rasi and I were not very interested. But Sanjay sometimes stayed with her as she rolled out her mat on the roof, and practiced with her, side by side. Afterwards, Rasi and

I would tease him, but usually, we noticed, for an hour or so after yoga, he remained fairly oblivious to our teasing.

Nalani also tried to get Meterling to join her in her yoga, but Meterling always shook her head.

"It will be so good for you, Meti, good for your bones, good for your skin," she'd say, but Meterling always shook her head no, grasped her teacup with both hands, and walked away to muse.

"Archer—she has to let him go. He has taken her heart and she needs it back."

"I thought she had a splinter in her heart."

"Both. She has it all. The whole kit and caboodle of grief."

And we wondered what a caboodle was, if it was anything like a caboose.

Invoking Rilke, Aunt Pa said, "May her tear-filled face make her more shining, may her simple tears flower," and, noticing us, she said, "Something I read once, long ago," sweeping past us, not allowing us to follow. Oh, what a family we had! But Aunt Pa turned back, looked at us, and said, "What I think that means is to let something good come out of the grief."

Oscar, Oscar was going to come out of the grief, out of her belly, we thought, cheered up once again, although doubt had entered rather sneakily into our hearts.

15

One day, Meterling woke in a panic. She could not recall Archer's face. She remembered what they had done together—their walks, the boat ride, the wedding—but what did his face look like? She had no photographs. His hair, it was silvery, and he had a mustache. He was rotund. What did he look like?

How could she have committed herself to a person she hardly knew? And create a baby with him before marriage? They were so sure. She loved him, she told herself, loved him, but the words seemed in that moment empty.

What if Oscar asked her what his father looked like? What if he wondered what the Y chromosome deposited in his features, the nose, the mouth, the smile? What if Oscar became unrecognizable, the two of them a ludicrous pair of misfits? Could she bear to bring such a life to him? Meterling grasped her belly protectively. It had grown more—as, it seemed, had her feet. Her belly button popped out. Sometimes the baby kicked hard.

Archer had promised her the moon, and she had reached for it, expecting it. They would travel unfettered to Italy, to France, see the coasts of California he loved so. They would travel with sketch pads and charcoals, buy paints and canvas. They would honeymoon with easels on their backs and capture the essence of their adventure in art they would bring back and show us. Archer had planned an itinerary, and she had believed every word. She was mad for adventure, the need to leave Pi and see what lay beyond simple domesticity. Now, all of that was lost along with Archer. She would remain on Pi and give birth to a fatherless child, and if she was lucky, she would be enfolded in simple domesticity to ward off the gossip.

More had happened at that violin concert, we found out.

A man named Akbar came to stand in front of Meterling. "Who is that beauty," he had asked at the violin concert, "from three rows down?"

"That's the daughter of Rajeshswaran, the late doctor."

"What is her name?"

"Nalani."

"Nalani. An angelic name. How far till the child?"

"What child?"

"Her child."

"What?"

And then Akbar's friend understood.

"You don't mean Nalani. You mean the tall one."

"Of course I meant the tall one. She is heavenly," said Akbar, his eyes full of dream and stars. "Who are you talking about?"

"I am—no one. I speak of no one. Do you mean the tall one?"

"Yes," said Akbar, "the tall one."

"I don't know her name."

And his friend was quiet, and embarrassed. A pregnant woman. And a widow, he'd heard, too. Who would want to speak to her?

"Introduce me."

"How on earth—"

"Introduce me."

So his friend took him down several rows to where Meterling stood, with Nalani, at the end of the concert.

"Madame."

Madame? wondered his friend.

"My dear."

My dear? Now everyone was embarrassed, but if Meterling was embarrassed, she didn't show it. She merely said hello, and made small talk. Her disinterest was clear. This Akbar walked away, crestfallen. Meanwhile, Rajan and his sister also joined Meterling and Nalani, and now the group became livelier. So lively, it was remarked upon by some neighbors. Word got back to Grandmother—how could it not? Swiftly, inquiries were made, horoscopes were consulted, hurried consults were held, and a marriage date was settled.

We glimpse such a small part of our lives. Imagine a paper clip attached to a piece of paper—or better yet, three pieces of paper. We pride ourselves on our organization, we congratulate ourselves on our innate wisdom, but in truth, all we ever know at one time is the area contained by the paper clip, while reams of paper reside in us.

What became of Akbar? Whom did he marry in the end? No matter my beliefs about myself, I knew that all islanders had to marry. It was a part of the laws that were set down in ancient times, scratched on palm leaf. To break the laws—for island Christians, it meant the word we weren't to say. For us Hindus, it would be a bad rebirth. We might become cockroaches. Yet it seemed to me even cockroaches must have their happy moments, their families and feasts. Maybe the townspeople were right—maybe something like widowhood was the worst life imaginable. Hunger, too, like the people who sat on the curbs begging for anything, the boys with broken limbs surrounding the tourists. We knew their fathers had done that to their children, to get more money. Then there were the girls younger than me who lived in shuttered rooms, who were sold to men, who never had the chance to simply go to the beach and breathe. One of Rasi's teachers had told her, and when we asked Aunt Pa, she confirmed our fears. I had nightmares, certain that ghosts sat at the foot of the bed, ready to pull me to the curb, to the shuttered rooms.

Archer haunted Meterling's mind quite a bit, surely, but our family only really knew of one—no, two, or three—actual reported sightings. One time in the garden, when the washer maid was hanging up the wash, but that could have been a trick of light; she claimed she could hear whistling. Once by the baby Aston Martin, which was parked sadly in the garage, dutifully polished by the driver, at least for the first six months, then left neglected. Except for the headlights, which for some reason Sanjay liked to polish. Not insignificant, because on turning twenty, one of the first things Sanjay did on arriving at Grandmother's house that summer was go to the garage and set about restoring the car. But someone reported seeing Archer there once. Sometimes he was seen in town, a round man in a white suit, but we thought it must be someone else. Meterling herself said no, there was no ghost of Archer lingering around, there was no such thing. Did she wish there were? Meanwhile, in the garden, deep where she thought no one could see, Nalani sobbed.

16

We asked Meterling once if it was true that there were magicians on the island, like Rasi said.

She thought a moment and said, "There are thirty thousand magicians on Pi, if not more." Who were they really? She said, "Cooks and maids, bricklayers, sages and artists, writers, musicians, architects, outhouse cleaners. The sorcery they practice is a deep one, akin to the healing arts. Doctors, too, and mathematicians. And engineers and carpenters. All such magicians and workers—not a charlatan in the bunch." Gardeners? "Of course." Teachers? "Yes, those too." So they don't wear hats and have wands? "No, not like Merlin from your storybooks.

"These magicians create transformations however they can. Heal a broken bone."

"That's not magic," said Sanjay, deeply disappointed.

"It is. Remember when Auntie Shobana broke her arm, and she wore a cast, and then the cast came off, and the arm was healed? That's magic."

"That's science, Auntie."

"Well, who is to say science isn't magic, too?"

"I don't know," said Sanjay afterwards. "I think Auntie Meterling is crackers in the head if she thinks science is magic."

"Maybe," said Rasi, also doubtful. "But maybe she just means there is no magic in the world except what we make of it."

"Of course there's magic," said Sanjay. "Real poof-wow magic."

"How do you know?"

"I just do."

"What do you think, Mina?"

"I don't know," I said. "I believe Aunt Meterling. She knows everything."

"Not *everything*."

"She does," I insisted, and burst into tears.

"Mina!"

"Mina, come back—don't run away!"

"Mina . . . ."

But I did run away, run from them, and run out of the compound to the pond where women washed their clothes. No one was around, because the heat was so strong. I didn't care, I was upset, but I wasn't altogether sure why. Reaching the end of the road, I planned merely to turn around and go home before anyone noticed my absence, but I saw my aunt. She stood in the middle of the pond, slowly swaying. Joy burst into my heart and I began to run toward her. Then I thought I'd surprise her, and crept up quietly. I thought she meant to bathe her feet. But she sat down, and now my heart began to beat fast. I felt a wave of fear come over me, because something seemed very wrong. All of a sudden, I thought she meant to drown the baby inside of her. I rushed up to her, shouting all the while, my feet splashing noisily. She turned around, and her eyes were vacant. I was afraid she wasn't going to recognize me, but she didn't say anything, merely reached for my hand, and stood up, and together we walked home. I realized that I wasn't quite sure what happened. Could water rush in through her belly button? Was that how it was done? But then, how could she take a bath? In the back of my mind, I knew that it was not only the baby she was trying to drown. I took my aunt's hand, and did not ask her anything.

An auntie of mine once studied with Rukmani Devi at Kalakshetra, that famous dancing institute in India. One year and it changed her life, and charged everything she did with a dancer's touch. She learned Bharata Natyam, the sacred dance. She learned mudras; she learned to tip her eyes and head. Like some girls, I grew frustrated I could not tilt my head back and forth like a true Bharata Natyam dancer. But I danced on the roof, in the kitchen, in the front room in and around the chairs, sometimes even out on the veranda. Rasi and Sanjay and I held hands by turns, trying to spin faster and faster, seeing who would lose their balance first.

A widow needs to grieve a long time before she thinks of dance again. In the old days, maybe one didn't think to dance at all. But if life deals a hard turn, it seemed to me that the thing to do then was to step away a bit, breathe hard and soft, and try to dance again.

One day, we got ladoos from the sweet shop. They crumbled at our touch.

"Enjoy ladoos. At a wedding feast, they are the prize. If you are lucky, you will get two by accident when the server forgets he has already served you, and you sit in the right spot where he has finished one batch from his plate, goes back to the kitchen for a refill, and hurries back, forgetting where he had stopped, forgetting the place, and gives you another. A double bonus. Lucky wedding guest, especially if you traveled from out of town, are tired and a bit weary of the events—look, there is the ladoo, shiny and round, glistening with ghee, in front of you. Your treat. Enjoy," said Shanti-Mami to us one day, as we lingered in the kitchen.

"Remember always to eat well, no matter what you have on your plate," Meterling wrote me, years later. She was transcribing her recipes on paper—writing at last! "No matter what life removes from you—and you know, life also replaces what it removes (like breath, say the yogis, in and out like breath)— remember to eat well. Savor what you have. When we get depressed, we forget to eat. Eat anyway. Eat yogurt, eat rice, eat carrots—anything. Fill your tummy up so that it roars quietly and then roars softly. Fill your belly when you can. Hunger for life," she told us. "Make pancakes. Eat biscuits with tea. Eat noodles in broth. Feed your pain with nourishment, not more pain. There is no use for pain that life doesn't provide already."

In her collection of recipes, she would write, "Watch the ladoo break apart on your plate—just nudge it a little with your fingernail, and see the revealed jewels. Saffron. Whole cardamom. Raisins. A touch of camphor. Golden split pea, cooked in sugar and glistening ghee. The cashew half, nicely toasted, next to a plump raisin, and wonder of wonders, the pod of the cardamom, its seeds dispersed into tiny black bits and ground fine into powder. Yes, place a bit in your mouth. Suck the juice, rejoice, it's the *rasa* that you first experience, what we call *rooji*—the essence of any food's taste, the top notes of flavor. Roll the food particle on your tongue, so you can experience all of the parts, and know the whole. Drink the cream of what remains, the innate richness, the joy, the sensation of sweet, the satisfaction. This is dessert. The finish of a good meal. The start of a wedding supper."

17

Mostly, it was Rasi, Sanjay, and I. Everyone else was too old, in boarding school or college. We three walked to school together and walked back. Sometimes, the bullies troubled us. The loud louts who picked on us and made us afraid. Walking home from school should have been joyous in those idyllic days of our childhood, but it made us nervous. Sometimes, the bullies would purposely ram into us, making our books tumble from our hands. They were rougher with Sanjay, leaving him with scraped knees. They used their slates, which hurt him badly. With us, they pulled at our schoolbags. That's why Sanjay, Rasi, and I stuck together. We looked out for each other. The days they weren't there, I ran as fast as I could back home, safe. We played races and counting games so we could be quick on our feet and outrun those bullies. And when we grew, and imagined bullies all around (and in truth, it was largely our imaginations that supplied us with fresh fear), our first thought was to run as well; whether it was from love or work or pain, we ran. It was a childhood habit that was hard to control and harder to get over, but we did—each of us, in our own way, got over it, or we thought we did.

Sanjay made jokes, and ran quickly. Rasi and I held our heads high, and sometimes held hands, two warriors. What was hard was not to snap out at the girls who teased us about Meterling. Sometimes we did snap back, choking—angry, hurt words that led to hair pulling and shrieks. Once my teacher came home to complain and Grandmother listened gravely, but never spoke of it again to us. It did not make sense.

"Don't worry, my mother will punish us both," muttered Rasi, but Aunt Pa said nothing. The schoolgirls had called our aunt Meterling a slut and a dirty pot in Tamil.

We always had to go to school, though, not like Sanjay who stayed home once after he was beaten up by a pack of boys. It made little sense. Our aunt was pregnant; she had married. Why should anyone care?

On the other hand, there were ceremonies that went with nearly every aspect of our lives. From pujas to holidays, there was always reason to celebrate, no matter how grim the world. During her fifth month, the aunties held a special celebration for Aunt Meterling and the baby-to-be, to help pave the way for an auspicious birth. It was held in another auntie's house, because we were still in ritual mourning for Uncle Archer. For one year, we could only visit other people at their celebrations, have none of our own.

Aunt Meterling's arms filled up with glass bangles as our aunties and neighbor aunties each took turns placing them on her, until they reached her elbow. Laughing, they then removed them, and everyone chose some to take home, different from the ones they had brought. Rasi and I chose some as well. Then, into Aunt Meterling's open sari paloo, held like a pouch, went fruits of all sorts, describing a fruitful birth. Aunt Pa said these were ways to distract a pregnant woman, because she might feel restless, or even sad.

I wondered what it must feel like to have such a big belly. Sometimes, Auntie put her hand on her lower back, as if to help carry the weight. Once, Rasi and I imitated her at the mirror, stuffing pillows under our skirts. When we heard someone approach, we quickly tossed them away and jumped on the empty bed, giggling. Rasi did not play with dolls anymore, but I still did, in secret, at night. I'd hold my doll and rock her. She came with a bottle, which I could fill with water, and then she would pee, only, it was from a hole on her behind. She had beautiful black hair that was painted on, and her eyes would open and shut. Sometimes I whispered, "Good, good baby," over and over in her ear.

In school, we were reading *A Christmas Carol.* I'd pretend that my doll was Tiny Tim's sister, and I would hold her tight to keep her from shivering. I asked my mother if she was shivering in America in my weekly letter. No, she replied, she had a warm coat, and wore lots of sweaters. I knew she meant she had lots of sweaters to choose from, but for a minute, I imagined my mother bundled up in sweater over sweater. In her class, Rasi was reading *Treasure Island,* and she wanted to be a pirate. She made treasure maps, and buried toys that Sanjay and I had to hunt for. Sanjay said they were reading Asterix comics in his class, but I knew that couldn't be true.

• • •

In her sixth month, Meterling became more beautiful, as if lit from within. The morning sickness had passed, and it seemed she had made peace with her situation. The baby moved inside her, and we felt it twitch. In a few months, she told us, we might be able to see a foot. I didn't know if I wanted to see a foot.

My mother, writing from America, enclosed photographs of snow. I missed her, missed my father, but they seemed abstract, like sketches. They had been gone two years, and each day, it was easier to accept. In some ways, it was like Rasi without her older sisters or Sanjay without Appam. Yet they both got lots of visits back and forth, and it didn't seem like a loss. No one clucked their tongue and shook their head at them as they did when I proudly told friends of the family that my mother and father were doing very difficult studies in the States. My grandmother told me to never mind them. I wondered if she missed my mother, but when I asked her, she said my mother had my father, and they were both working hard to give me the best life.

It was easy to hero-worship Meterling. She was our hero because she was brave enough to marry Archer; brave enough to say no to the not-so-great part of old culture, the part that asks women and men to walk a certain path. Meterling strayed away, and she married Archer. She was a freak of nature, people used to say, encountering her height as a child for the first time, and so was Uncle Archer. It was easy enough to wander into each other's lives, some said, because like likes like and kind marries kind. And maybe that was the case. But it seems to me that Meterling was so fortuitously cast on a stage that was fast changing, born as she was in a time of shift and great disturbance. Even as islanders and Indians fought for the British in World War II, Pundit Nehru saw the hypocrisy. Gandhi believed the oppressed must fight for the oppressed. Meterling's mother was five when Pi got its independence, and died before she saw thirty. Meterling naturally relied on herself when she was orphaned so unexpectedly, and she grew a lot taller than the girls around her. She was never really a freak of nature. No, she was just capable of change, which scared some people. She was still a dutiful daughter, they said, for don't you know, who can ever really escape that bondage except with another kind of bondage? She sought security and she sought to fill in the blanks of the life that she had.

18

Then, just like that, Meterling retreated into sadness. The fire quenched in her eyes. Give her time, said Grandmother. We did, and the day Meterling woke up from her darkness, it was as if the moon came out. For two weeks, she had been veiled in absolute despair. ("Like Absolut vodka!" cried Sanjay, still trying to make jokes, in near-equal despair to see our favorite aunt all choked and clouded and alone like this—but no vodka was involved, sad the luck and more the pity, we'd later think.) She would not speak to us, keeping to her bed, not even letting Grandmother minister to her. She stopped bathing, which made Grandmother mad, because that was one of the top ten don'ts in the household. On the fifteenth day of relentless grief, Meterling emerged, not as bright as a full moon, but more like a half-moon on the way to becoming whole again. The darkness, her hunger moon, her moon madness, her mood shift, her mad moon passed, and we all breathed a collective sigh of relief. The half-moon remains a beautiful moon. It is a midpoint moon, best viewed after twilight, but really even better when dawn is a few hours away, surprising you with its presence.

At the same time Meterling emerged from her darkness, Rasi found her transistor. She had felt lost without it. No one had taken it. It was where she had forgotten she put it.

"Now," said Auntie Pa, "I once lost a hat that was precious to me."

"A hat?" We tried to picture Aunt with a hat and couldn't.

"I had a hat like that," said another aunt. "A party hat given to me by a friend."

"A party hat!"

"A straw hat with a grosgrain ribbon—"

"What kind of ribbon?"

"You know, those ribbons that are striated."

We stared, but Rasi shook her head. "They're talking about ribbons, and I'm talking about my radio."

"Hats, ribbons, radios, all the same," chirped in a third aunt, who we didn't even know was listening.

"No—" said Rasi.

"Child—" said an aunt.

But we ran away before they could impart even more wisdom.

One day, Meterling turned to us and said, "You know, being tall was never an impediment in my life."

We stared at her. We all knew that Meterling was accustomed to shrink a bit when she encountered other people, feeling her gait awkward and out of place. She'd hunch her shoulders; wear only flat-heeled sandals, hiding her strength.

"No, I never did feel bad. If I did, I tended to look at all there is in the world that goes right. The world is a strange and marvelous place. And there might be much that is wrong with it, or with how you are feeling, how this might hurt, or that . . . Anyway, I don't know what I'm trying to say . . ."

We waited.

"What I'm trying to say is that being tall never stopped me for too long. It's who I am, after all. When I was little, I didn't like being the tallest and the biggest, while everyone else—all the other children—were so little and cute. And children can be mean if they want to, make fun."

We looked at her. I suddenly felt my heart grip a bit as I imagined her longing to be like everyone else, the teasing she must have received for her height. She squinted a bit and continued.

"The thing is, the thing is that at some time I accepted who I was and started to grow into myself. I mean, I knew I was unusual for this town—and you know, children, we are really just talking about Madhupur itself, and not the whole island of Pi—but I knew that in this whole world there are lots like me, and in fact, probably in the whole wide world there were so many like me that I wasn't even the tallest anymore for my age, and possibly, in some places, the smallest. Do you see what I am telling you?"

We nodded—except, of course, we weren't quite sure.

"What I am saying is that we just grow to like ourselves and become who we are." She stopped here and looked at us, vigorously nodding, and shrugged her shoulders.

"Auntie. Would you like some water?"

Her sanguinity did not last long. Again, a mood appeared: Meterling with her anger. Sitting day after day, swallowing it all. So painful her throat ached. Until one day she exploded, and let out a scream. Then she quietly put herself back together again. Sometimes you can see the cracks where a shell or a pot has been mended. Some value the cracks even more and paint them gold to honor the impermanence of the world. Or perhaps because the gold makes the cracks striking. Meterling, when she cracked, just a little, patched up fairly quickly, no scar. But how could there not be scars? To lose so much: parents, husband; then to gain so quickly: a child.

19

Nalani's bridegroom's family was to pay a visit. Everyone fussed to prepare, and Nalani herself tried on several saris, supervised by Aunt Pa. Shanti-Mami made carrot halvah, and in addition, sweets from the Chandigar store were bought, along with some savories. She also made idlis and sambar, and prepared two vegetables—a small luncheon feast. We were also told to dress and mind our manners and behave. When Aunt Pa announced, "They've come, they're here," we ran to the gate. A group walked in, taking off their chappals. Rajan's parents, we saw, looked like distant aunts and uncles, and his sister wore pretty glasses. Rasi whispered to me that she did not like her sari, and I began to giggle. Imagine our surprise when we found another man walking in behind the sister, instead of Rajan, hands in a namaste for our aunts and family. Was this Rajan's brother? Where was Rajan?

This was how we met Ajay. He was the fiancé, Nalani's fiancé. Rajan's horoscope did not match Nalani's. So they found someone more suitable, with prospects in the U.S., who had completed his master's degree.

He had brought Nalani a necklace, and brought us sweets from

Grand Street that first visit. Sanjay had on a Beatles T-shirt that he refused to change. The fiancé remarked on it, saying it was really "cool." He seemed to genuinely mean it, too, and Sanjay glowed. Rasi and I were more withholding of our praise. Meterling peeked in, but stayed away, not wanting to cause confusion in his parents. Everyone knew about Meterling's condition, but it seemed everyone walked carefully around it, too. The marriage would take place after the birth of Meterling's baby, in an auspicious time. Nalani was quiet, and later went up to the roof—to meditate, she said, which meant we weren't to follow.

The next day, the poet visited our house. Her name was Neela Chandrashekar, we discovered, and she had a strong laugh, and arrived with vegetables from the market. She took Meterling for a stroll, and when they returned, arm in arm, Neela said that what Meterling needed was a doula.

A dollar? we wondered. We thought she needed a lot more.

But the word was "doula," a person who helps the pregnant woman in different ways than a doctor or midwife. Meterling met her the next week. A Belgian woman, with a robust face, she had been in India and Pi for decades, and delivered babies for expatriates and hippies, when the flower children wanted natural, loving births, and now some islanders trusted her to help deliver their own.

She came on Tuesdays and Thursdays, armed with massage oils and therapeutic sacks filled with seeds and hulls. The latter she warmed on the stove to place over Meterling's shoulders. She spoke to Meterling about what to expect in the final months, how important it was to walk every day, and feed herself nourishing foods, not just halvahs. Anyway, the halvahs and sweets had been mostly in the first three months. She explained that grief was part of the pregnancy, even in women who had not lost their husbands. Meterling's life would change, and she needed to gently prepare for it.

Meterling at seven months was ready, ready, ready to give birth. Ready to lie down, feel less pregnant. But she was very pregnant. Round and pregnant, told to take walks, keep up her spirits. The doula repeatedly advised healthy eating, what Grandmother had been urging from the beginning. Meterling still wanted to eat round foods as round as her belly to deliver a healthy child, Archer's child, hers. Eating rice and dal with lots of ghee, mild vegetable curries, drinking lots of water, and waiting, she imagined sensual meals, tiny eggplants stuffed with curry, long pieces of purple okra dripping with flavored oil, saffron-scented pilafs. She wanted to suck on her food-laden fingers, let her tongue slowly catch the drips of thandai, close her eyes as the cumin broths coursed down her throat. Were her nipples becoming hard, was this kundalini brought on by dreams of food? She shook her head to clear her thoughts.

20

The cousin from England called again. Archer's cousin. He asked Meterling to come to England and see the fields Archer had left her. This time Meterling took the receiver. "I can't," she said, hesitating, and then saying, "I'm pregnant." There was silence on both ends for a while.

"Then I'd better come see you," said the cousin.

He did not waste time. He arrived one morning at the house, dressed in a beige kurta and nicely pressed pants. He didn't look much like Archer, being younger, taller and lanky, like someone who didn't know what to do with his limbs. He brought chocolates from Belgium for us. We were all curious to see him, and wondered how our aunt would react to his presence. I wondered if his family's snub still hurt. Grandmother, pursing her lips, led him to our front room, where we had some charpoys and chairs. I loved this room because of the mirrored red coverings on the pillows, and the low table made of a dark wood that held an elegant silver tea service, one of my grandmother's wedding presents. Only a few years ago, Rasi and I would hold tea parties with our dolls. That was when Rasi too played with dolls. Sanjay was not allowed, "only girls," we said, but Sanjay didn't care anyway. He practiced cricket with some boys in the street, batting nicely, he'd tell us later.

This man looked like he might play cricket. He had an open face, and since he had shaved off the mustache he wore at the wedding, he no longer looked so funny. He seemed embarrassed by our frank stares, and Grandmother was on the verge of scolding us when Meterling entered. The cousin, whose name was Simon, blushed, and stood up. She calmly walked in, eight months of pregnancy in front of her, wearing a pale-rose sari. She had placed jasmine in her hair, too, because he was Archer's cousin and had come all this way.

Shanti-Mami had made some pakoras, and Aunt Pa brought them in. Greedily, Rasi, Sanjay, and I reached for them, ignoring Auntie's pointed looks. They were hot and crispy, and we tried to be careful about them crumbling and leaving oily stains on our dresses and shirtfront. Receiving Simon-Archer (for that was what we called him in secret, though Aunt Meterling, overhearing, corrected us and told us his name was Simon Peter Harold Forster) was different from receiving Nalani's intended bridegroom. There was an awkwardness, created perhaps by color or gender. Our grandfather had worked with white men, and frequently brought one or two home, his supervisor mainly, but sometimes the younger engineers, who came for a good home-cooked meal. Uncle Archer had been made welcome, too, after the wedding was announced. Once a wedding is announced, tensions ease somewhat. After a wedding, there's much hearty laughter and joking.

Simon was unmarried. He was a journalist, and traveled a good deal. No, he'd never had anything in the *News* or the *Accent*, but he had published in the *Lincolnshire Post*. He covered local fairs, and garden shows, and wrote theater and book reviews; abroad, he wrote travel pieces. Meterling mentioned Neela, the poet, but he didn't know her works. He mentioned the works of Indian poets he was familiar with, and for a few minutes, he and Meterling spoke easily about them. But perhaps fearing they were leaving the others out, they began to speak of the weather, the unusual rain. Uncle Darshan, who by this time had come back from his college, and was seated with a hot cup of coffee, said the pollutants we released into the atmosphere mixed up nature. Icebergs, he said, were melting, but Aunt Pa said that was nonsense.

Simon-Archer was offered a second cup of coffee, but he stood up, saying he had already taken up so much of our time. He was staying in a guesthouse, and the proprietress would have dinner waiting for him. Then he blushed once again, looked at Meterling, and asked if she would meet him for dinner tomorrow. At once, Grandmother and Aunt Pa put up a fuss, saying that she was in her eighth month, but Meterling, to everyone's surprise, accepted. The doula had not wanted her to be bedridden, but also to be sensitive to her fatigue. Later, Aunt Pa and Grandmother decided it must have to do with the will.

. . .

While Meterling waited for Simon-Archer to call for her, Aunt Pa told her to be very careful of what she ate. Under no circumstances was she to eat deep-fried foods. And the minute she felt tired, she should come home. Meterling looked pretty that evening, wearing a soft georgette silk that had small red blooms on a cream background. She had put up her hair, and used a decorative comb in the bun. Again, she selected jasmine to wind around it. They smelled especially good, since the blooms were just beginning to open.

Simon-Archer arrived and they set off. Ajay came over a half-hour later. He had been visiting regularly, and he and Nalani took us to the movies. We argued over James Bond or Disney, and we finally settled for Disney, a showing of *Snow White*. It was much scarier than I thought, with the wicked queen. Sanjay and Rasi made fun of me afterwards, teasing me with "How about an apple?" until Nalani told them to stop. Ajay asked if we wanted ice creams, and Nalani laughed, saying, "As if there's any question!" They seemed to like each other more. He was funny, cracking jokes and breaking into bits of film song, trying to win Nalani's heart. He drove us to the beach, which was crowded as usual. The vendors were busy, and groups of people sat together eating and laughing. Carefully watching out for dog droppings, we walked to the midnight-colored water as the waves crashed. Walking to the right, we soon left some of the crowds behind, aside from the occasional family or lovers who had the same idea as us. It wasn't an entirely crime-free area, especially at night, so we didn't go far. It was a good thing Aunt Pa wasn't with us. Sanjay, Rasi, and I looked for good, gleaming shells and rocks, but the water was too rough to seek them, and it was too dark. Nalani was still laughing.

We made our way back, and found a café that sold ice cream in a dish. We each had a scoop topped by a sugar wafer, and Nalani and Ajay had coffee. They were talking about France. It seemed Rajan was forgotten. Maybe they had just been good friends, and not in love, as Rasi said. I hoped he would come to the wedding. Already, Rasi and I had been fitted for new clothes, even though the wedding was a long way off.

Simon took Meterling to the Tanjore Hotel restaurant, renowned for not only its food but also its cleanliness. It was completely vegetarian; the cooks trained in Madras, and then had to pass additional tests in Madhupur. The Tanjore was full; lively couples poring over menus, family groups celebrating birthdays. The women were draped in soft silks and vibrant prints, ears full of gold and silver, cholis cut fashionably low. The waitress, who herself was fashionably outfitted, led them to their reserved table.

"Archer and I used to come here, when he first moved down. I stayed for about a month. I was on school holiday," he told her as they sat down.

It began simply: "Tell me everything about him," she asked.

The cousin told her about Archer's childhood, his parents who died young, as had Meterling's parents. He told her about the school they both went to, the games they played. All through dinner, he talked and answered questions, and asked some of his own. Over coffee, he told her Archer liked pickle-and-cheese sandwiches and Cadbury's Fingers. "Cadbury's," whispered Meterling, "I like those chocolates, too," thinking of Archer as a boy, how Oscar might grow up like him. All she knew of Archer was so brief, so slight—his humor, his kindness, his patience. His gaze, as he looked at her, had

said: "Would you marry me?—and hers had replied, "Yes, yes."
Thinking that the fates had been kind to her for once, thinking that she too would have a chance at happiness. And a few
months later, the wedding and that dance. But the cousin was
talking again, not letting her mind go down its familiar path.
Instead, he said, simply, "Let's take a walk, Meterling." And she
was startled to hear her name in his mouth.

He paid, and offered his arm. She took it. Next to the Tanjore
were the famed Narati Gardens, a park that was often used for
films and weddings. It featured hundreds of varieties of flowers in continual, orchestrated bloom. The jasmine was heady.
A few couples, just-marrieds most likely, walked hand in hand.
Meterling was embarrassed, but there was still so much to learn
about Archer. How had he been at school? Where did they go
for vacations? What sports did he play besides the cricket he
had told her about?

The cousin was patient, and told her as much as he knew.
They had left the gardens and were going to get a milky drink
for her and a coffee for him before they noticed the time. Meterling wondered that she didn't feel tired, but happy, somehow.
Still, she'd promised to be in before ten.

When he left her at the door, Meterling asked if they could
talk some more the next day, and he agreed with a smile.

"I'm glad you came out to dinner."

"I'm glad you asked."

Not sure how to take her leave, she hurriedly kissed him on
the cheek, and quickly went inside.

21

They spent the next weeks talking about Archer's habits and his character. Meterling felt she knew more to tell the baby, and the cousin said he felt more settled with Archer's death.

"It's good to talk with someone who knew him now, not in the past as a boy. Susan won't talk. She just went on holiday to Scotland, and refuses phone calls. She's very upset, but can't bring herself to accept it."

"She must blame me."

"She shouldn't." Simon hesitated. "This is unrelated, but Archer also had a heart condition."

"He never told me!"

"That's why he was at a desk job. He was supposed to lead a quiet life, which is hard to imagine."

"He was dancing at the wedding, exerting himself, drinking—" Meterling faltered.

"And happier than I'd seen him in a long time."

"I wished he'd told me. I could have done something."

"He would have told you later about the heart. But no one can prevent an aneurysm," said Simon.

They were quiet in their embarrassment. Simon wondered if their lovemaking had been too exuberant, if that was why Meterling was blushing so deeply. Then he wondered why on earth he thought that.

"Susan—she'll be an aunt soon. I wonder if the baby will inherit her characteristics," said Meterling presently.

"Stubborn, fiercely loyal, and smart. She's head of her company, you know, and will probably receive an MBE."

Meterling hadn't known.

"I'm joking about the MBE. Their mother died young. She had just wanted both of them to settle down, have children—oh, God, I'm sorry—I didn't mean—"

Meterling's eyes had filled with tears. "No, it's not that, it's just that it's all so confusing," she sobbed.

And Simon, stricken, just enveloped her in his arms.

We came to like both Ajay and Simon-Archer more. We felt bad for Rajan, since there seemed some injustice there, but we couldn't put our fingers on it. Ajay was smart, funny, and handsome, too, in a way. He seemed to be concerned for Nalani's welfare. It could be a show, although I didn't know how to put that into words. He always asked her if she was chilly, or needed water. He played with Scrap, who was larger now, with sleek fur, and a habit of needing her belly rubbed often. He drove well, too, and unlike Uncle Darshan never cursed at the other drivers. Was this what it meant when my aunties spoke of "suitable boys"? But did Nalani long for Rajan? She didn't show it. A bride would be chosen for Rajan as well. It was just horoscopes.

Our family didn't believe in horoscopes. Regularly we went to temple, and every morning we chanted at the kitchen shrine. We had favorite gods and goddesses. But we left some of the trappings behind, the ones that said sect must marry within sect. Uncle Darshan, especially, was vocal about modernity. He could, and did, orate at length about women's rights, and the capacity of female brains. Aunt Pa sometimes rolled her eyes, because her female brain knew that brains had no gender, they were simply brains, and no one used his as much as Einstein had.

Rajan's family did believe in horoscopes, and they were the ones to say no to Nalani. Theirs was an orthodox family that required the women in the household to isolate once a month, eat separately, and not let anyone, except for babies and toddlers, touch them. Auntie Pa wouldn't explain why, but we found out from school friends that one day, both Rasi and I would bleed, and need some bandages, that it wasn't that anything was wrong, but something that just happened. For months, I feared that day, expecting the worst, until I forgot about it. We couldn't use something called tampons like my mother carried in her purse, because then we'd no longer be virgins, and being a virgin was important, like getting good marks at school.

Ajay's family did not believe in the isolation laws, and were on the fence about horoscopes. They didn't particularly want Nalani to work after marriage, but would not stand in her way. Nalani had decided to become a doctor, and after the wedding would go to medical school. She would have more degrees than Ajay, which only bothered Ajay's mother, but Ajay's father thought they would be lucky to have a first-class doctor in the family.

My parents were modern as well, but theirs was an arranged marriage. From America, they sent me photographs, taken in parks and from their car, and they looked happy. I had become so used to their absence. Sometimes I wished I could ask my mother things about marriage, about Ajay and Nalani, about all our strange old customs. In my letters to her, I usually said I was fine, the weather good, and what I was reading. She was a great reader herself, and sent packages of books for all of us to share. That was how I got to know *Ramona the Pest,* and *The Four-Story Mistake,* and Encyclopedia Brown. Sometimes a strange disquiet would come over me at bedtime, and perhaps that was when I missed my mother the most, but reading usually made the feeling go away.

22

How strange it is to record what I saw and knew at ten. There was so much I learned later. The Puranas advised that women marry quickly. The very sensual nature of a woman's body was feared, and I learned it was not just that a man's thoughts might be, well, *inflamed,* but that it was the woman's yearning that was the trouble. Without marriage, sex was merely for pleasure, experimental, thoughtless. With marriage, it was for offspring.

Maybe that was why their families gave some destitute widows to brothels. She could be either virginal or experienced; either way, her body, if not her soul, was ready to be bought, as maybe it had in marriage. Perhaps a family had given a dowry of a milch cow to the groom. When the groom died, they lost the cow and gained a widow. Other widows seemed so taken with the idea of purity, wearing white, changing saris throughout the day, white for white, bathing several times a day as well. There was also the custom of *madi,* a holy cleanliness which pervaded a person after a bath, and after fresh clothes were donned, lasting until prayers were completed.

My own grandmother wore green, and her hair was silvery, thin, and long. She did not move in with Auntie Pa but kept the house my grandfather built for her. She tended the gardens, supervised the servants, heard the weekly discourses by visiting pundits at the local temple. She played Parcheesi in the afternoons, swept out the stray goats from the kitchen, and put up sour dried mango pickle in Ali Baba jars. The idea of remarriage to her would be preposterous, if not scandalous, and to be honest, I could not picture it, either. She had married young, at fourteen, and took up residence with my grandfather at seventeen. In the pictures, she looks skinny, with wide eyes, next to my grandfather, who wears a suit, and in later ones would sport a Nehru cap.

Her children came quickly after she turned nineteen: Tharak; Pa; Nalani's mother; my mother; Sanjay's mother. I heard there might have been a child who had died at birth, a son, but this subject really was off limits for us. In my grandmother's day there could not be an intercaste marriage without extreme consequences. Couples fled the island if they had money; some committed suicide. Some were killed in the name of family honor. As girls and boys went abroad for studies, they often chose their own partners. And of course, there had been a time right after independence when intercaste marriage was politically encouraged, but only for a short time.

Now it was month eight and a half. Soon, soon, said everyone. The monsoons would begin in September, but the intermittent rain had already begun. The cat played on the veranda, sometimes with string that I held above her quick paws. Sometimes she would meow silently, other times softly, or fiercely. She seemed to have forty different kinds of meows. I wondered if her heart opened like ours did to her, if she felt safer knowing her humans were inside, or if she felt that somehow, she was protecting her humans.

Meterling often met Simon for walks. At some point, hardly noticing, they began to speak of themselves.

Simon described the small garden he had in his London flat, and how the plants paid no attention to his ministering. Mostly, he put up his feet and read the *Guardian*.

"I was a regular twit growing up, you know. Mocking my elders, completely loafing off at school. I don't know how I passed my A levels."

He went on to Cambridge, and after obtaining a first in philosophy ("largely because I can memorize quickly, but the funny thing was, once I actually cracked open the books, and put pen to paper, it was as if I'd discovered a door I never knew existed"), he became an intern to a publisher's associate. The firm published books on Italy. Once they did a book on coffee machines.

"Did you know Balzac was supposed to have consumed forty cups of coffee a day to keep writing?" he asked Meterling.

She smiled, and said, "I studied home science, learned a little economy, nursing, it was all included at my college. My father was brilliant, but I did not have that kind of ambition."

"I can't imagine you as being anything but."

"That is because you are a kind man, Simon, and hardly know me."

Her friends Chitra and Neela visited her too, bringing gifts. Chitra brought her twins, just two years old, and we played with them. They really were cute, their skin so soft, and they could be made to laugh so easily. All we had to do was cover our eyes and they would go off in a fit of giggles. Neela brought poems, and belly oil. With a twin each at our hips, Rasi and I stood at the gate of our compound, looking out. For a moment, I glimpsed my future, a young mother with a child.

"What do you want in your future, Meterling?" Simon asked her, a few days later.

"What an odd question. I want the baby to be safe, strong. I'll always be protected here, with the family, but . . ."

"What?"

"I wouldn't mind seeing a bit of those places I dreamed about as a girl. They are probably ordinary for you, but I'd like to see Paris, and Italy."

"They are in no way ordinary. I will take you there."

It was so simply said, with such quiet assurance, that Meterling saw it as a certainty, not a possibility. She was already in love with Simon. Now, they had somewhere to go.

They were walking in the Narati Gardens. It was Friday, and the grounds were still quiet. In the late afternoon, the weekenders would arrive. A light drizzle had just stopped; the rolling lawns were slightly wet. Their sandals made slight sounds as they walked. The rain had brought up the scent of the green around them, and the air felt washed. The baby kicked, and Meterling wondered if happiness could produce a premature birth. He seemed so eager to get out. She'd already shown us how his tiny foot pushed out at the skin, a sight that mesmerized us. She wished she could place Simon's hand on her belly to let him feel the baby, and realized she wanted to feel Simon's hand rest against her belly. She blushed.

Simon took her hand.

"Meterling, will you marry me?"

He said it quietly, not knowing her response. He had thought about it for weeks, even from the moment he first sat in the living room. He chased guilt and desire away, but companionship remained constant. They had been able to lift the burden of grief together, bit by bit, and with it, guilt for being alive when Archer was not. Meterling pressed his hand.

"I am pregnant."

"I know."

"And you would get both of us."

"I know that, too."

"I get moody."

"I will hold you."

"Tightly?"

"As tightly as you need."

"Of course, I will marry you. I never thought otherwise."

23

We worried Simon-Archer would take Meterling away. They would marry, and what then?

"A widow is supposed to die after her husband dies," said Sanjay.

"That's the stupidest thing you ever said."

"That's what they did in the old days."

"We are not *in* the old days."

Then, families sternly guided love, if love was even thought of as much as land, money, children. After Meterling told us she would marry again, the word leaked out. Some people thought it was scandalous. It was much too soon, and she was seen as fickle. Plus, widows didn't often remarry. Some assumed the baby needed a father and thought Meterling was being pragmatic. Some thought a white man was most appropriate, since the baby would be half-white anyway. Some thought it was for the money. "What money?" asked Aunt Pa, rolling her eyes with anger, then with laughter. And that indeed was a sea change for Auntie Pa. To go from anger to laughter is like going from debt to understanding what debt is—that is, not just the money but also the value. The value of money, and the value of anger, she would tell us, is important to learn. More learning, we sighed.

I knew, more than even Rasi or Sanjay, that Meterling was in love with Simon-Archer. "It is as if I have come alive all over again," she said, laughing, thinking I wouldn't understand. But I did. I had seen Meterling fade a little bit every day after Archer's death. And with the cousin, I saw her come back to bloom bit by bit.

It was like the dawn after the wreck. When something catastrophic happens, like a shipwreck, people gather together after the storm, assess the damage, blink into the light to grasp something that is too big to grasp at that moment, that first look. Some grab a cup of coffee from the folks next door; some squint at the way the shore is littered with effects without coffee. The deep sorrow, the deep pain overcomes, but then they begin to pick through what's left, say prayers in thanks that it was not worse.

I saw them kiss. They melted into each other. At first, I didn't understand what they were doing, but they fit. I'd never seen Archer and Meterling kiss like that. In fact, I'd never seen anyone kiss like that. But it looked just right. They looked just right.

His family didn't agree, because it seemed unseemly. To throw himself away on a pregnant woman, an island girl, a brown-skinned widow, his cousin's wife, for godsakes, said the distant relatives. As he expected, Susan was not supportive, although his parents were. His mother said she'd worried about the widow, and the child, but said they should wait, in deference to Archer. The adoption process could start immediately, however.

But Grandmother was upset. She did not think Meterling should remarry so quickly, although we knew of widowers who did, some within a month of the death. There were laws created specifically for the right of widows to remarry. They were instituted for the number of very young women, sometimes children, who were left widowed and unwanted. Their hair might be shaved off; they might have to forswear garlic and onion to spice their food, and wear only pure white; but that was only the beginning. They were to look as unattractive as possible, because men, it was said, lusted after widows like vultures swoop in on flesh left on the ground. Some widows spent their lives in cities by the rivers, waiting for death.

Aunt Pa kept saying ours was a progressive family; she thought Meterling should marry whomever she chose, especially now with a baby due. Yet Grandmother fretted. She increased her prayers. No horoscope had been drawn up for Archer, and none was needed for Simon, if he was to be accorded the same respect. Yet, maybe a horoscope might help, but most of the family disagreed.

Nalani was happy for Meterling; glad the baby would have a father, and Meterling a husband. For thousands of years, brides were selected for grooms and vice versa; and traditions rooted in strong belief were slow to let go. Love marriages were looked at with great suspicion, for what did children know about what was best for them? And they *were* children, sad to say, in not-so-long-ago times, though householding would only begin after puberty. Even now, at weddings, silver toys are brought out as part of the ritual so the groom and bride were kept amused. Living in another age, I might already be bespoke at ten.

· · ·

We began to call Simon-Archer "Simon." He wanted Grandmother's blessings on the union. He said that Meterling had
already suffered so much that it would be cruel to cut her off
from her grandmother. When the publisher of the *Hindu* long
ago in India arranged for his widowed daughter to remarry, his
relatives refused to attend the ceremony, which they thought
scandalous. Grandmother was father and mother both to
Meterling. So Simon began quietly to campaign for approval.
Like Uncle Archer, he brought flowers and requested to see
Grandmother. They sat down for tea, and first spoke about the
weather. At last, he spoke directly.

"I will take care of her and Oscar for the rest of my days."

"Do you too have his weak health?"

Simon offered to have a medical checkup.

"And if you have a child, what will happen to Oscar? Will he
be treated like a stepson?"

"You know I would not do that."

"But that's it, Simon-ji, I *don't* know you. Archer lived among
us for many years. But you live in the UK, where you could
have girlfriends and indecent clothing and rum punch. How do
I know you won't run off with a girlfriend when you get bored
with Meti?"

Simon would object, promise, and the discussion would
close until the next day.

My grandmother, I think, feared the upset of social order and
that turning away from the gods would ruin my aunt's remarriage. The neighbors would forever snipe and not cover their
mouths discreetly, and the gods would throw darts. She would
be gossiped about as well as the couple, but what she feared

most was Nalani's future. Would Ajay's parents recoil from the match?

It was around this time that Dr. Kamalam came around for a talk with my grandmother. Everyone walked around the house in long faces. Uncle Thakur, Uncle Darshan, and Auntie Pa were all upset with Grandmother, although, as they frequently said, it was pure medieval thinking that had got them into this situation. We believed for thousands of years in astrology, the stars under which you were born, the family you came from. A Brahman could trace his ancestry to one of thirteen original saints. Marriage matches were an art and a science, dependent on oral histories and priests; even after a match was made, the search for an auspicious time for the ceremony began. Ours was a culture that deeply respects elders, that watches its collective tongue when words like "death" or "sex" are intimated.

Dr. Kamalam was cut against the grain from the same cloth. Brahman as my grandmother, she spoke her mind quickly and to the point.

"What you are attempting, Usha, is antediluvian. There is no reason for this nonsense, except that it has been the way too long. Where would we be if we blocked every new idea that came into our way? Motorcars, airplanes, computers?

"Meterling is not old. She has a right to happiness, married happiness. Her child could have a fine father with this English boy. Don't be foolish."

But Grandmother was adamant. The social censure would be great and could even touch my marriage, and Rasi's. It was not done, it was simply not done.

24

We played with Scrap outside, went for pistachio ice cream and saw movies with Nalani. We had had weeks of mild weather. Meterling looked very sad to us, Grandmother worried, and Auntie Pa was exasperated with us for getting underfoot.

Uncle Thakur intervened.

"What does it matter what people think, or even what the Vedas say? We live in modern times."

Maybe he could have convinced her, but Meterling herself thought it was wise to end things with Simon. It would be too much for Grandmother to bear. Simon argued with her, but to no avail. He believed, like we all did, that Grandmother would come around.

"When does love just turn to possession, Simon? We want to be together, but is it just the want we want?"

"Logic in love, Meti?"

"There has to be logic in some things. I don't mind if we appear monstrous or grotesquely comic to others, but I don't want Grandmother to crumple inside. She's been through too much suffering and loss."

"So have you. Don't you feel you deserve happiness?"

"Maybe it's too ingrained in me, the way my ancestors thought."

"But with Archer?"

"You sound like a boy, now. I'm about to be a mother. There's Oscar to think about."

"He will need a father."

"Imagine him at school, getting teased. His mother marries his father's cousin, like . . . almost like *Hamlet*."

"I don't understand this."

"I can't, Simon, I mustn't marry you."

She was crying now.

Rasi and I discussed her decision with frustration. Although we were banned from seeing it, even if it was an old film, we knew that in *Silsila* Amitabh Bachchan marries Jaya Bhaduri (who is his real wife, anyway) because her fiancé dies in a plane crash. She is carrying the fiancé's baby, and asks Amitabh to marry her, even though, unbeknownst to her, he loves Rekha (who in real life was his mistress, according to the gossip magazines we weren't allowed to read).

"But by marrying Jaya Bhaduri, he makes a big mistake, ruining their lives, and the baby dies anyway. Then after he runs away with Rekha, Jaya Bhaduri becomes pregnant with his kid."

"How is that possible, if he doesn't love her? Did she have an affair, too, out of revenge?"

"I don't know. I think husbands can have sex with their wives even if they love someone else. Anyway, he's her husband; he can do what he wants. That's the rule."

"It's a stupid rule."

"I know. And poor Rekha, she doesn't love her husband, either."

"Rekha is married in the film?"

"Of course. How could she run off to Paris with Amitabh if she weren't?"

"Do you think Simon has a secret love in England?"

"Maybe that's what Grandmother is afraid of. After all, she saw *Silsila*, and *Kabhi Kabhie*, in which, you know—"

"I *don't* know—you give away all the stories!"

"It doesn't mean you can't enjoy them anyway."

"What happens in *Kabhi Kabhie*?"

"Well, there is a girl whose mother also had a fiancé who she isn't married to—"

"Enough," I said, covering my ears with my hands.

"Anyway, it's not like we'll be allowed to go see these movies anyway."

"I want to see *Cinderella*."

"You know what happens to the mother there? She—"

"Rasi!"

But what if Simon did have a secret love in London? Someone who looked like Sally Potter, one of the English college students who lived in town to study at the ashram. When she first arrived, she wore vintage go-go boots and a short skirt and a see-through top. Now she wears brightly colored kurtas and long skirts, her hair scraggly and short. I think she looked better when she first arrived, so exotic and foreign, with long, straight brown hair that was probably ironed, Mary Angel told me, who'd heard it from her mother. Ironed or not, it fell like silk.

What would Simon's secret girlfriend's name be? Something English, like Lizzy or Pats? We had Pinkys and Dimples.

"Maybe her name is complicated, like Constance Adelaide Adele."

"Do you thinks he loves her?"

"He might have gotten her pregnant, just like Uncle Archer got Auntie pregnant. Maybe she is really poor—or maybe, he's already married to her!"

"He can't have two wives!"

"Of course he can. Or maybe he really loves Aunt Meterling, but his other wife won't let him get divorced, and maybe they already have kids, but there's nothing to feed them, because the cupboard is always bare—like Mother Hubbard!—and maybe she has to work in a factory, and her chief officer is really mean, and threatens to take away their home, only Simon-Archer refuses to listen, because—because he wants to marry Aunt Meterling for her money!"

"No! She doesn't have money."

"She has three fields and a house. That's more than Adelaide and her children have."

"But he wouldn't just leave her like that."

"Maybe she threatens to kill herself if Simon doesn't leave Aunt Meterling."

"She wouldn't know about Auntie."

"Well, maybe she threatens to kill herself if Simon-Archer doesn't return to England and make it right—or maybe, she will go to the police!"

"Why would she go to the police?"

"Maybe Uncle Simon poisoned Uncle Archer!"

"He died of an *aneurysm*. And anyway, none of this is true. Uncle Simon loves Aunt Meterling, and there is no secret love in England."

"Probably. Look, there's Sanjay—I think he has my transistor again."

25

Week thirty-eight arrived. All morning Wednesday, Grandmother kept dropping things. She liked to grind the coffee beans herself when the tin ran empty. This morning, as she opened a fresh package from Kaladi, a few beans scattered to the floor. I helped her pick them up from under the stove. Then, after the grinding, as she transferred the powder into the tin, her hands slipped and powder spilled. For some reason she began to smile.

Shanti-Mami arrived to begin the day's cooking, and Anitha for the day's washing-up. Anitha was just a few months younger than Nalani, with a broad smile, even as she squatted among the vessels to wash in the alcove off the kitchen. Her husband drank too much, and Sanjay said he beat her, too. That's why some mornings she arrived late, no smile. Those days she would have long talks with Grandmother after the dishes were done. There was a litany of life in her words, involving a sister-in-law, a brother-in-law, a sick mother. Usually, Grandmother gave her extra money, while Aunt Pa railed against the system of police who turned their eyes away. This morning, Anitha was fine, as she had been for several weeks, her husband working in another town. Grandmother discussed the day's menu with Shanti-Mami, deciding on idlis for tiffin. This was no big surprise, as we usually got idlis for tiffin, though we would have been happy with just a sweet and milk.

"The baby's coming."

Nalani had run into the room with this announcement.

Startled, we rushed out of the kitchen. Meterling was ready, and Grandmother agreed. Meterling smiled wanly at us, and asked Sanjay to fetch Simon. Chitu-Mami, the midwife, and Dr. Kamalam had already been sent for. Soon, she lay on her side as the doula, who was already there, massaged her lower back. Grandmother said a quick prayer. Our aunt would smile, then pain would cross her face, and then she'd let a breath out. The doula counted the time between the groans. She cheered our aunt along, as if we were at a cricket match. How in the world would a baby be able to be born out of her body? I imagined Aunt Meterling stretching a hole as large as a small head, but that was like magic, a universe's expansion. A bicycle jingle let us know Sanjay had arrived with Simon.

We didn't see the actual birth, although we wanted to, sort of. Men and children still were not allowed. We heard words like "dilation" and "centimeters." We hung out at the doorway, with Simon. He looked so worried.

"It won't hurt for too long," he said, wiping his forehead.

"How long does it take?"

"I'm not sure. My aunt Patricia delivered very quickly, but she's very athletic. Rode horses and that sort of thing."

"How quick is quick?"

"Half-hour?"

"How long will Auntie take?"

Simon shook his head.

It took five hours. Later the doula said that was because it was the first time. We heard Meterling shout with pain, which Simon kept repeating was perfectly normal, keeping us from running inside, although it looked like he wanted to do the same. After a while, we heard a baby cry. Finally, Aunt Pa let us go in. There, in her arms, was a tiny baby. It was very red, but had soft black hair. The eyes, when open, looked very big. I was surprised to see its skin was brown. Somehow I imagined the baby would be white with blue eyes, blond hair. I wondered if everyone was thinking the same thing.

"Meet your cousin," said Aunt Meterling.

Simon hung back until Meterling smiled at him, and said, "You, too."

Grandmother nodded at him.

He entered bashfully.

"How are you feeling?" he asked.

"Tired."

"Eight pounds, three ounces," said Dr. Kamalam.

"Ten little fingers, ten little toes," said the doula, also smiling.

Both Aunt Pa's and Grandmother's faces were streaked with tears, and Grandmother looked radiant, the happiest I'd seen her in so long.

We cooed at the baby, who was very red and distraught.

"He's feeling the air—it's all new to him," said Nalani.

"He looks just like Tharak," said Grandmother, breaking into a wide-toothed smile. I hugged her, my grandmother. I looked at Simon, who was crying as well.

Maybe it was at this moment she decided Simon could marry Meterling, if she still wanted him.

Now we all had to troop out to let her—*them*—rest.

Eleven days later came the naming ceremony. We all crowded around the crib where the baby slept. Aunt Pa whispered the baby's name in his ear. "Oscar" was official.

Later, someone wrote his name out on a layer of unhusked rice that had been spread out just for this occasion, and the aunties put anklets and bracelets on him.

"Won't it hurt?" asked Simon, to which everyone laughed. What do men know about babies? Or new mothers, either? It was the aunts who bathed the baby. They stepped in and did nearly everything. Meterling fed him and rested, fed him again and rested, and we hung around her bed. They both slept a great deal.

Would he have a Sanskrit name as well? He would. Ramana. Oscar Ramana Tharak Forster. That too was written on the grain.

The anklets and bracelets were unhooked and slipped off after the ceremony. Around his waist, he wore a simple black cord, tied with turmeric root. He constantly ate from my aunt's breast, and then slept, contented.

"I think Archer must be watching him, too," she told us.

I wasn't sure, because perhaps he was playing carom, or was a baby in a new life. Once my grandmother told me my grandfather became a fly after his death, so he would always be in our presence. My mother says I got the word wrong, that my grandmother meant gecko. But I think she believed my grandfather went straight to Vishnu, and I think Aunt Meterling thought the same of Uncle Archer.

And just like that, she agreed again to marry Simon.

26

We were right. Simon was going to take Meterling and Oscar away. They had already decided to move to London, after Meterling assured him she would not pine for our family on Pi. Simon wanted to get back to work.

"I'd like to return to editing, Meterling. There's a job at one of the smaller houses, and they've been wanting me to join."

"But won't you miss writing? The fast-paced traveling?"

"Covering garden shows isn't exactly fast-paced, and travel pieces are not as much fun as it might seem. I wanted to try my hand in it, that's all. I want a change."

"I want *you* to be happy, Simon. And you have been through an awful lot of *change*."

"I *am* happy—probably happier than I've ever been."

"When do we leave?"

"Why don't you stay here for a while, while I get us settled? You could spend a little more time with the family, and you could use the help with the baby. The kids will be upset at your going at all."

"In the villages, the brides spend more time with their parents sometimes than with their husband the first year," said Meterling.

"Ah, but not us," said Simon, hugging her.

It was decided. Simon would go on ahead in a couple of weeks, begin his new job, and return for Nalani's wedding. Meterling and Oscar could have more time with us.

. . .

"Why is it that when we add to the family, the family goes away?" asked Grandmother.

"The world just becomes bigger," said Meterling. "Imagine how it just used to be villages, then cities and kingdoms, everybody contained."

I wished they were moving to the USA, but Simon had his family in London, and Oscar had his roots there, too.

"But it's not impossible. And there are planes," said Meterling.

"We can visit you in London, and go to the U.S." added Nalani cheerfully, though she would miss Meterling terribly and everyone knew it.

"There's your wedding to plan," said Meterling. "It may be months before I leave, and there will be no question of not attending your wedding, if that's what you were thinking."

"You'll help choose the saris and jewelry?"

"Would I really miss any of it?"

"But Meterling, what of *your* wedding, what will you do?"

"We'll just get a registered wedding. Simple and quiet."

Six weeks after Oscar's birth, Aunt Meterling and Simon went to the high court building to marry. Mrs. Gupta, in black robes and a wig, was the presiding judge. Rasi could not stop staring at her, and the degrees framed behind her in the office. A black fan was motionless above our heads. We were back in the rainy season, having survived the heat of spring and the lesser heat of summer. As a family, we were all there, and brought garlands for them to wear, and threw rose petals when the marriage was formalized. We ate at a hotel, which was nice, because if I looked down the long table, I could see most of my family. Simon's parents had come over, too. They stayed at the Tanjore, and seemed a bit overwhelmed. Simon's mother probably

imagined an English bride in a beautiful lace gown with a veil
for her only son, not Aunt Meterling, who wore a dark-red sari,
not nine yards, just six, but a sari nevertheless. At the table,
Aunt Meterling sat with Simon's mother, and slowly, softly,
began to talk with her, but it looked difficult.

Simon seemed to enjoy seeing his parents. He went on walks
with his father, trailing a stick in his hand. His father was
friendly with all of us. Simon got him to try our coffee, and
the hotter foods. His mother stuck with tea. I liked them well
enough, although they made me shy. They kept asking what
standard was I in, never remembering the answer. His mother
had once been an accountant, and his father worked for the
family company. In the evenings, they sat with Meterling and
Simon and Oscar, as the trees rustled with the breeze, and the
perfumed jasmine wafted across the veranda. Simon's mother
held Oscar in her arms, cooing. At first, she seemed afraid of
him, but later told Grandmother, "Well, a baby is just a baby."
Still, I noticed that she looked at Oscar, *stared* at him, really, and
her face crisscrossed with vying emotions. I overheard her crying, asking Simon, "But you will have children of your own,
won't you?"

It didn't make sense to me, this obsession that children had
to be born of the mother and father, that adopted children were
somehow less. Our family had it, and now it seemed Simon's
family had it, too. Simon's father seemed to mind less. "I'm a
grandfather, and you can't take that from me," he said, softly
humming, boarding the ferry that would take them back to the
airport in India.

In a week, my mother would visit. It had been a year since I had seen her, and I was excited. Now she would get to see how tall I'd grown, and my school projects. Maybe she would come with me to school. She would be able to meet Oscar and Simon, too. Then again, I wondered if she would want to do any of those things. As it turned out, Simon was in England when she came. After the registered wedding, Simon still lived in the guesthouse, and Meterling with us, where the aunties, despite their teasing, were still taking care of Oscar. It seemed a perfectly fine arrangement. But now Simon was scouting their new life abroad, and my mother was to come scout out mine.

We met my mother at the harbor: Nalani, Uncle Darshan, Uncle Thakur (who was on leave from his office), Rasi, Sanjay, and me. I wore a nice frock, which came with shorts attached that my mother had sent to me for my birthday, and my hair was painfully pulled back in two braids. Every now and then, I'd tug at the ribbons to loosen them. From where we stood, we saw the boat dock. Crowded with people waving and shouting to us on land, the small boat was majestic in a way. Soon the passengers descended. There she was! My mother, in a very bright green sari, holding a big purse. Uncle Thakur kept me from running to the door to meet her. At the arrivals building, then, we waited for her to clear customs, and finally my mother swept me up in her arms. She hadn't forgotten me, as I secretly worried; she knew who I was.

While we waited for her luggage, my mother told us about the flight. She described the meals they had been served, the passengers next to her, and the hard candies the stewardesses brought in trays. Opening her bag, she distributed almond cookies wrapped in beautiful paper from the Italian airport. She described the way the plane rocked through a lightning storm, which was called "turbulence." All the while, I clung to her, as if I were five years old instead of ten.

We crammed into the Ambassador van Uncle Thakur had hired, and drove home. Outside, green rice paddies flew by, and silvery lakes. Coconut trees rippled their fronds lazily, and my mother pointed out a man climbing up one, using a small piece of rope to help him ascend.

"There is nothing like this in the U.S.," she said. "All the coconuts are in supermarkets—but at least there are coconuts! But no fresh coconut water. I miss that."

So Uncle Darshan immediately asked our driver to stop at the next roadside stand, where a woman hacked off the tops of green coconuts, scraped the soft white flesh inside, and handed us each one, with a straw and a scraper. The driver said he didn't want one, and went off a ways to smoke. Happily, we drank and ate. Once we finished, we handed the nuts back to the vendor, who scowled and smashed them into a pile behind her.

"Everybody wipe your fingers—no stickiness in the car! Okay, now let's drive fast, because they will all be watching the clock," said Uncle Darshan as we got back in.

Everyone was waiting on the veranda. Aunt Pa rushed toward the car door as we spilled out, and hugged my mother fiercely.

"*Vare-va*, look at your hair," she said, smoothing my mother's short pixie cut.

My mother grinned, and touched Grandmother's feet.

"Finally, finally. Why did you take so long to return?" my grandmother said as she held her foreign-gone daughter.

"And look at you, my dear," said my mother, turning to Aunt Meterling, who was really her niece, to hug her. "Look at you. And look at this darling boy."

. . .

The entire month she was home, I slept in her bed. My mother cuddled me, but morning usually found us facing out, back to back, deep in our own separate dreams. I asked her what her school was like. She told me the brick walls were covered in green ivy, which made me think of Sleeping Beauty. She was studying astrophysics, and said that her team was building a telescope better than any before. Sometimes, her team worked all through the night, taking naps on couches. She was helping with the lens, creating mathematical formulas to make sure the dimensions were right. She smelled good, like perfume and powder. She gave me extra kisses and hugs from my father, who was hard at work, she said. She let me wear her jewelry, but not her marriage chain ("One day you'll have one of your own"), and showed me the clothes she'd brought for all of us: T-shirts and jeans, more dresses, and, best of all, sneakers. When I laced up mine, I felt I could run as fast as I wanted to, that anything was possible.

During the day, we went to temple, visited all the relatives and friends nearby and far, went to see silly movies, and, every day, got an ice cream at the beach. My mother laughed a great deal, and with her, both Aunt Pa and Aunt Meterling looked like girls. Or at least, they looked less auntie-like. We played with Oscar, who was fatter now, sturdy, and happy to cry whenever he felt like it. My mother brought him a stuffed tiger, the mascot of my father's university school, with which he was delighted. She also brought baby clothes and soft rattles, and teething rings. My mother met Ajay, and promised to return for the wedding with my father. She squeezed Nalani's hand, hardly believing, she said out loud, that Nalani was already marrying.

Late at night, she spoke with Grandmother and Aunt Pa about America, encouraging Auntie and the uncles to move to the States. She said we'd all get a good education. Aunt Pa was not that interested, but Uncle Thakur was. He was eager to see Rasi get an education in the U.S. Aunt Pa wondered if it wasn't risky to leave a good job for one that didn't exist.

"Life is an adventure, Parvati!"

"Life also means providing for your children."

As they began to argue, my mother told Grandmother about my father. He was working on his dissertation, and would be going on job interviews. We would likely settle in New York or New Jersey, she said.

I was not certain of the move. If Rasi and Sanjay moved as well, it would not be so bad. Everyone wanted to go to the U.S., everyone. But what about Pi? What about Madhupur, and the beach? No coconut water—what else would there be none of? Already Meterling was going to London, and Nalani would be going to medical college while Ajay applied for jobs in the U.S. I worried my grandmother would feel lonely, for we would be abandoning her like a sinking ship. Why couldn't she come too? But Grandmother had no desire to move. She liked Pi, her world, as she had known it from birth. Yes, the house might be quieter with all of us gone, but she would not move in with her daughters. Meterling begged her to come to London, but in the end, Grandmother said if she had to live with anyone, she would take on boarders. The house could be rented, providing an income, and kept open for us when we all visited.

27

An auspicious day was selected for Nalani's wedding. Our family had spent months getting ready, securing the hall, the musicians, caterers, sending the hundred-plus invitations. Everyone was coming. Oscar was now almost three months old. I was so excited to see both my mother and my father that I could hardly contain myself with anticipation. Sometimes I just jumped up, feeling my skin would burst.

By now, the baby could roll onto his stomach. He seemed more and more a person. Simon brought all sorts of baby gear back with him from England, including soft little knitted socks from his mother. Oscar would get a tiny snap-on kurta for the wedding, with gold embroidery. Every time we saw it, Rasi and I would exclaim, "So sweet!" But far sweeter was Oscar, who gurgled happily and kicked his hands and feet for no reason. My grandmother had feared that Simon would be nonvegetarian, but he surprised us all by revealing he had been vegetarian since his college days.

Simon had located a flat within walking distance of his new job, with a small garden. The subletters of his old flat had decided to stay on. He showed us photographs. The building it was in was of a yellow-white stone, and you entered through a small wrought-iron gate. There were geraniums poking out of tiny pots behind the railing, and a gray cat snoozed nearby. You walked down the stone steps to a door painted green. Inside, there was a kitchen we eagerly pored over, it having a refrigerator, and a stove with an oven, a round wooden table with two chairs. There were two larger rooms, and a Western-style bathroom with a big tub that stood on claw feet. From the kitchen, another door led into a small rectangular garden, growing roses, herbs, and some flowers we could not identify in pots. The street was above the garden, so it felt secret. Meterling liked the whole place, but I liked the garden the best.

There were more photographs of the street, of an Indian takeaway, a large grocery store called Waitrose, a pub, and a park. There was also a picture of Simon's office, and some family pictures, including ones of Simon as a boy. He looked pretty cute, we had to admit.

Would Meterling like England? We played a game called L-O-N-D-O-N, but we didn't know much about the city. Uncle Darshan brought us a picture book and we learned about various buildings, the Globe Theatre, Buckingham Palace with the Changing of the Guard, and the Parliament buildings. We all liked the map of the Underground trains. When we visited, we would use it a lot, we decided. Still, it was very different than Pi. There were no bullock carts, no motor rickshaws, no temples, no beach. No us.

"Sometimes I think he is too perfect, and wonder how I am blessed enough to have him in my life," said Aunt Meterling, to which Grandmother always responded by saying that Meterling always deserved the best in life.

Simon finally met my parents, who hoped to go to a postdoc conference in London one day. They spent a long conversation about the city and its restaurants. We were gathered to see the saris Meterling and Nalani had bought for the wedding. They had bought saris for the groom's family, as well as silk and gold thread dhotis for Ajay, his father, and his brother. They were appropriately appreciated, but what everyone wanted to see

were the saris for the aunties and Grandmother. Here was the
real show. Auntie Pa received a lovely dark-brown gold-shot
Banaras silk, with an extensive mango-design paloo; Meterling received a beautiful blue Banaras silk, the color of twilight when just the faintest hint of sun is on the horizon; and
my mother and grandmother received Kanjeevaram saris, one
red and gold, the other heavy emerald green, while Rasi and I
received long silk skirts with matching tops, yellow-gold and
pink, respectively. Our skirts had already been made, so we
rushed to try them on and twirl. They didn't flare out like our
Western frocks, but billowed like bells.

Nalani had four saris: one six-yard in orange for the formal
engagement; one six-yard in red for the wedding; one tissue-silk
gharara in pale pink with an all-over pattern in silver thread
for the reception; and one that would be presented to her by
Ajay's parents at the wedding itself, a nine-yard one into which
she would change for the final ceremony. Ajay's parents would
also present her with a sari at their home. Nalani had chosen
the first three. When coaxed to try on the gharara, she came
out looking like a film star. All of a sudden, I felt like I was
going to cry. I didn't want Nalani to get married, go live in
Ajay's house, even if she did like him. My mother must have
noticed, for she gave me a hug, and told Rasi and me to take off
our new dresses before we spilled something on them.

All day and night, women sat stringing flowers together with
needle and thread for the garlands. Cooks had been hired to
make the wedding feast. Men who were champion sweetmak-
ers set up shop with a seriousness that would have seemed
almost funny if they hadn't given us tastes when no one was
watching. The man who made murukkus was famous throughout the town, because he could coax enormous spirals out

of the most delicious chickpea batter dropped in hot oil; his sons helped him make small ones for the reception dinner. A man delivered glossy plantain leaves that needed to be kept moist. Coconuts were being broken and shredded, vadas being fried, sambars and rasams were simmering, vegetables cut and peeled. A very strange concoction resembling mini-volcanoes were shaped out of sugar; they'd be present at the wedding ceremony, but would not be eaten.

First was the official engagement party. The next day would be the wedding, beginning at seven a.m. That evening, after we had stuffed ourselves with sweets, we sought out Nalani. She looked so small. Yesterday, she had henna applied to her feet by Auntie Shobana, who was born in Lahore and relocated to Madhupur. The designs she drew were intricate, spirals and flowers, which she also applied to Nalani's hands. We had been shy around Nalani in her engagement sari and all the gold jewelry and flowers, but now she wore a simple blue chiffon sari. Tomorrow her hair would be transformed into an elaborate style with jasmine flowers and tassels, but now she wore it in a simple braid. Again, I was overcome with a sadness I did not understand.

Rasi was curious about the wedding night, but Nalani batted away her questions. She lay full length on her bed and stared at the ceiling. We lay beside her. We used to lie like this on our roof, looking at the stars. Nalani had once told us that each of us was born under a special star that connected us to our ancestors, that heritage was never something to throw away. Now she told us when it came time for us to marry, our parents would choose wisely, that they would match family, education, outlook as well as stars. I didn't tell her I was going to live alone.

"Rajan?" I asked.

"Will always remain my fond classmate," she replied.

If she doubted herself, she hid it well. I wondered if it really was for the best she was not marrying Rajan. I had read enough Mills & Boons to know that the road to true love was a rocky one. Maybe they would have had a lovely wedding, but so much could happen afterwards. Rajan might have died like Uncle Archer. Maybe the horoscopes were right, and the stars knew more than we did. I remembered Aunt Meterling asking me if I understood why Nalani could not marry Rajan.

"It has to do with his family not wanting her in the house during her monthlies."

Aunt Meterling looked at me.

"Beti, it was because his parents wanted a rich bride, and Nalani is poor, but worse, an orphan."

"She's an orphan?"

"Yes, that what the word means. No mother or father, and some people are very particular about family."

I didn't tell my aunt that I thought you couldn't become an orphan; you just were one, like being poor, or short. I realized I hadn't really thought it through and felt embarrassed.

"She's better off with Ajay," said my aunt. "Imagine having to live with the kind of family Rajan must have."

Maybe Aunt Meterling was right; maybe Nalani was truly at peace, as her paper fortunes predicted, trusting in the future she and Ajay would have. She would become a doctor, and both she and Ajay would have jobs in the U.S. I thought of how many different ways stories are told, how many lies and truths. I resolved to tell the truth, no matter what. I felt fairly proud about that.

Nalani rolled over onto her side, and looked at me.

"You must marry when the time comes, Mina. It is your duty," she said.

Rasi smirked, but I felt as if my destiny had been written then and there, only it troubled me.

"Of course I will," I said.

At five a.m., Nalani bathed, and dressed in the first wedding sari, as centuries of women had done before her. We made our way to the marriage hall, in our silk and flowers and jewelry. The hall was completely decorated with flowers, as the priests tended the fire. Nalani looked like a princess, but also a stranger, with her makeup and jewelry. Ajay arrived with a fan and ceremoniously pretended he wanted to live the life of a brahmachari, and Uncle Darshan interceded with him, saying that married life as a householder would be equally fulfilling. Ritual after ritual was performed. For some reason Rasi dug her nails into my hand, and I could tell she was crying a bit. Nalani and Ajay exchanged heavy garlands of flowers as they were raised up in the crowd. Then the muhurtham, when Ajay tied the marriage thali around Nalani's neck as we threw handfuls of rose petals, and the drums and horns played loudly. Done! Nalani was married.

Nalani was to spend the night at Ajay's home, where his mother and father presented her with another sari. Their neighbors visited, and we came over for a big dinner. I had eaten so many sweets and snacks by this time that I eyed what was on my plate with trepidation, but I dutifully held out my hand for the wedding payasam and then the wedding ladoo. Meterling leaned her head on Simon's head, then laughed as he attempted to scoop the rice and rasam with his hand. There had been banana leaves provided for the lunch, but Simon was served on a plate then, too. Always, he was asked if he wanted a spoon, and always, he shook his head no. Finally, half-asleep, my uncles singing *filmi* songs, my aunties looking tired and happy, we wandered home. The stars were bright in the sky, and I looked for constellations. Behind us, the house was quiet, just Nalani and Ajay and his parents, maybe some cousins, too. How good it must have felt to Nalani to finally unwrap herself, and slip into her nightgown. And if it was Ajay's presence that awaited her, maybe that was good, because together, they could sleep, exhausted, and married.

PART TWO

Time Passes

But what after all is one night? A short space,
especially when the darkness dims so soon, and
so soon a bird sings, a cock crows, or a faint green
quickens, like a turning leaf, in the hollow of the
wave. Night, however, succeeds to night. Winter
holds a pack of them in store and deals them
equally, evenly, with indefatigable fingers.
They lengthen; they darken . . .

—*To the Lighthouse*

28

She had dreamed of him again. Sitting jackknifed on the new bed she shared with Uncle Simon, her heart racing, my aunt Meterling woke with panic. For seven consecutive days, she had dreamed of her Archer dying in seven different ways. In her first nightmare, she pushed him over slippery rocks in water; in the second, he walked backward off a cliff. He clutched his heart only once, falling to his knees, wearing a yellow tuxedo; that was dream number six. In dreams four and five, he was shot by an assassin and stabbed by a knife. Only in the first was she directly responsible for his death, although in all, she was implicated. In this seventh, the latest, her hands slipped from his as he tumbled off the Middle Tower of the Tower of London.

All she told me years later was that she had nightmares; as always with my aunt, I embellish the stories. I was not there. Had I been there, I tell myself, maybe I could have prevented them, and though I had desperately begged at the time, the idea of sending an eleven-year-old to a foreign country while her own parents already lived in another one, and her extended family lived on Pi, was dismissed.

"I could be an opera girl!"

"What's an opera girl?" asked Sanjay.

"An ayah."

"You have to be old to be an ayah."

That was true. One of Mary Angel's cousins had an ayah

because her mother worked, and that cousin was much older than me.

"But you don't have to be old to be an opera girl!"

We knew of an American family that wanted to hire opera girls from Madhupur; they would pay for room and board in exchange for looking after children. Grandmother wrinkled her nose at the idea, and said these girls, whom she called O-pairs, would have no rights, and on top, would pine away. She used the Tamil phrase for "pine away," but in English it sounded awful, like living in a tree without company or food.

I complained loudly, but I did not go to England with Aunt Meterling, and she continued to have nightmares. She told me how those first months had been when I was older, but I imagined what she chose not to tell. Isn't that who we are at heart, a species that tells and doesn't tell, keeps the heart and brain hidden, complicating our lives for the drama, so we don't have to face the night?

In the mornings, my aunt read the newspaper with utter concentration while Uncle Simon played with the baby. A woman aged a hundred and one had died. My aunt had lately grown fascinated with obituaries. The newspaper reported it with a caption under a photo of the woman celebrating her last birthday, her mouth beaming, a paper hat on her head, with balloons and cake nearby, and a column describing her life. Does the life ahead seem longer when you are elderly? Or does it merely seem a continuation of what you know? If one were to sit and examine each decade, count the measure of one's life, maybe it would seem long. "Every day, you know," said the centenarian-plus to the reporter, "I wake up surprised I made it another day."

The woman had been married to the same man for sixty-seven years. She had seven children, beginning in 1909, nearly all of whom were still living, plus sixteen grandchildren and six great-grandchildren. Meterling stared at the paper. Only a year ago, she, Meterling, was twenty-eight, pregnant and getting married. Now, she was a widow, wife, and mother. She looked out the window. There beyond the garden view was more of the English world, more dazzle, more drizzle, and black bare limbs trembling with raindrops. It was beautiful and it was England, and she, my aunt Meterling, was here. Despite the state of the world, despite the bombings near Underground stations, despite the unworldly ferocity of soccer fans, despite the fear of unexpected public violence—here was my aunt, in an England she still considered beautiful, new, and full of possibilities. But where were the sketch pads and easels, where was the travel that was to have lit her days, as Archer had promised her a year ago? They hadn't known about Oscar, of course, they had merely planned around what they knew; but would she be as happy? I was convinced of my aunt's ability for survival, provided she was looked after. As for the dreams of travel, they grew in me, like a seed sprouting in the stomach of a sage to turn into a tree as he meditates.

From the first, she liked the flat. She liked the cozy kitchen, with the clean-swept floor and a picture of a rooster on one of the walls. Because she had seen the photographs, she had not expected to be surprised, but she was, opening and closing the doors and looking out the windows, sitting on the plump gray couch the landlord had provided. It was semi-furnished, but she did not see any need for more furniture; freshly painted, it had an air of beginnings, new starts. It was so different from island homes, from *her* home. No dark, heavy colonial furniture or mirrorwork hangings, no twenty-five foot ceilings with metal fans, no wooden swing. It felt like the twentieth century, not the nineteenth. Spacious, bright, *and,* thankfully enough, she *fit.* Younger, she told me, she used to think of herself like Alice, who drank the bottle that made her arms and legs and head thrust out of the Wonderland house she was in.

She had seen so many illustrations of English homes, cottages with teapots and chintz, but the flat was streamlined, with a wall painted a light brown in the living room. Ceiling moldings from the Regency townhouse the flat was ensconced in remained to add character, as did the thick doors that led to the bedroom and to the garden. The kitchen opened onto the living room, and the bathroom, painted light blue, was off to one side. Because it was tucked under the main townhouse, it felt protected from the street it fronted. Cutting flowers from the fairy rosebush, which would brave on for another month, she could see people hurry past on their way to work. There was a bakery around the corner, and the sweet fragrance of buns and scones drifted delightfully, wending its way past an old plane tree whose mottled bark Meterling first mistook for disease.

The first day there, she drew out from the suitcase her Ganesha, carefully wrapped by Grandmother in an old sari, and a small silver Lakshmi and infant Krishna. She had told Simon that she needed to travel with her faith, to set up her shrine and not lose her connection to Pi. There was a bookcase in the kitchen, and there, she arranged the small statues. Grandmother had also packed her a silver diya lamp, and had even rolled some cotton wicks for it. They had landed at Gatwick on October 6th. From the plane, looking out the window, she was surprised to see how green England was. The grass seemed springy, freshly cut, verdant like spring. Where was Keats's season of mist and mellow fruitfulness? She longed to see the apple trees as much as she longed to see snow.

Through customs and the taxi ride, Meterling held Oscar, and leaned into Simon. He narrated what they were looking at, but the words flew past her. She looked at the view, seeing Austen, seeing Dickens, seeing Eliot. It was only when they had stopped in a store to purchase milk, butter, coffee, and other sundries, that she spoke.

"Oil, Simon—we need oil for the lamp."

At the flat, lighting the oil lamp, bowing her head, her palms pressed together, she prayed like Grandmother would for good fortune in these new beginnings. Then she put a small pot of milk on the boil, let it nearly boil over, and prayed for an abundant new start to their new life, an overflow of fortune. Simon made coffee, and they used the now-sacred milk to lighten it. Meterling gave a few drops of the cooled milk to Oscar as well. Their new lives in their new flat had begun.

29

Those first weeks were filled with a kind of wonderment, as Meterling and Simon settled down together. They did not have much to unpack beyond clothes and books. Simon left for work around eight, and on her first solo trip outside, Meterling with Oscar in a Snugli walked to a flower market to purchase some blooms for the flat. A day at her disposal. The air was fresh with autumn, as people hurried by. She listened to the noise of the traffic, looked at the red buses go past, and bought a newspaper. She compulsively consulted the map Simon had drawn for her, but she got lost anyway. She had wandered off the perimeter, toward the arrow on the paper marked Chelsea, or was it Millbank? There was a pub on the opposite side of the road she was on, with doors spilling open onto the sidewalk. Looking both ways, crossing carefully, she walked toward it. A man sitting just inside the door looked asleep as she went toward the bar to ask for directions.

"C'mon, let's go," said the man at the door. Heaving himself off the chair, he walked outside. The bartender indicated she should follow him, so Meterling did. He looked like an old sailor with his grizzled chin and cropped gray hair, and he was silent. After depositing her on her street, he lumbered back for his pint. Krishna, Meterling thought, watching him go back—she had been rescued by Krishna.

Mrs. Vickers, a woman of few words, came on Wednesdays. Simon hired her to clean, because, he said, "we can afford it, and you're not used to this," which was true enough; when had she had to do anything out of need in terms of housework? In Madhupur, she cooked only because she wanted to, mended only when she felt the inclination. At home, there was a servant for each task; Grandmother looked harried only because she needed to organize, or maybe because there were so many underfoot. Plus there was Oscar to look after, also on her own; but Meterling felt a twinge of guilt. Still, it seemed to make Simon happier, and she would be kidding herself if she protested too much.

"I've lots of Indian and Pakistani clients I do business with," Mrs. Vickers said curtly that first day, hanging up her coat and bag. Immediately, Meterling felt rebuked. Mrs. Vickers had a fat zippered Filofax full of clients. Although used to women cleaning around her, to lifting her feet for the broom, Meterling found that in London, she needed to leave the flat on Mrs. Vickers's days. She found herself feeling embarrassed, wondering if Mrs. Vickers in her white skin resented working for "the Indians and Pakistanis," whereas, she reflected, outside with Oscar, they had far more to resent. She tried to tidy up before Mrs. Vickers came: piling the laundry into baskets she had bought from an open-air market, tidying up the toys, washing the dishes. It was not enough, but Mrs. Vickers never said a word, and was brisk, nearly scientific in her cleaning, and what Meterling came to appreciate most was how the flat looked and smelled after Mrs. Vickers left: clean, smoothed out, renewed.

Simon gave her a Barclay card, but Meterling insisted that she get her own to draw from the interest on Archer's estate. This was easier than both had anticipated, since the transfer of money had occurred months before, and what was required was a new account created under her own name. The bank issued her a credit card, a set of checks, and a safe-deposit box. Together, she and Simon stored her wedding jewelry in the bank's vault, under the kind of quiet courtesy exhibited by the bank employees for the wealthy. For she *was* wealthy, my aunt Meterling, an heiress who had married money, twice.

Simon had introduced her to the neighborhood, taking straight routes she could memorize. They walked to Waitrose, which was larger than any shop she'd ever imagined. How did the British make choices: single cream; double cream; full fat; less fat; goat milk; soybean milk; kefir? In Madhupur, the milkman brought fresh milk on his bicycle, warm from the cow, and she received it in a vessel from his jug to take inside to boil. There were so many lights in the store too, so that everything gleamed. It was such a *white* country.

But pockets of green were scattered everywhere. No matter what part of town they were in, it seemed, there were neat squares of garden full of fall growth. When the pace got to be too much, or she became overwhelmed by all the buildings and street signs and roads, she studied the tulips, which were putting on their final show before winter. Purplish-red shocks of leaves as well as dark-orange berries clung to the tree branches, which held a certain enchantment; Meterling had never witnessed an autumn before. She snapped pictures, which she sent to us. ("All she does is send pictures of trees and flowers," complained Sanjay.)

> To bend with apples the mossed cottage-trees,
> And fill all fruit with ripeness to the core.

Simon took her on the Underground, which thrilled her, because she had studied the station map back in Madhupur. So now she actually stopped at Oxford Circus and Paddington, Tottenham Court Road, minded the gap, held tight to husband and child. They sampled chum chums and other milk sweets somewhere near Fitzroy Street. She bought jars of mango pickle to accompany the ones Grandmother had made and packed for her. Meterling's excitement was tremendous those first weeks—to see what she had read about, to experience what was in Dickens, in the *Spectator*, all the readings at school. Simon took them to his work, where he introduced his colleagues. They smiled, shook hands, fussed over the baby, and went back to work. She had not expected an editorial office to be messy, but it was, with lots of people moving in and out of cubicles and doors, holding bits of paper, while bookshelves bulged with manuscripts and books. Simon's own office held a half-dozen coffee cups, stained and forgotten, breeding mold, as well as a neglected plant of some species—a palm? A jasmine? Giving the baby to Simon to hold, she cleaned up his office, threw out the plant, tidied his desk somewhat.

Had he wanted to talk of Archer, or did he hope that she would bring the topic up? To think they had made it to England so easily, so conveniently. Archer was buried in the countryside, but Meterling hadn't asked to see his grave. Perhaps she still smarted from being so cruelly left out of the funeral plans. Simon winced, thinking back to how quickly he and Susan had acted, how thoughtlessly, how selfishly.

He showed her the food court at Harrods, the Koh-i-Noor diamond at the Tower of London, and the Sword of Mercy, with its tip cut off. They toured the British Museum, walked through Bloomsbury, and looked at Dickens's house and the Old Curiosity Shop on Portsmouth Street. One day they took the ferry to Greenwich, and the tour guide on the trip pointed out the places around the docks where the pirates, the rogues, the rebels were hanged. Snippets she remembered that she hardly knew were stuck in her mind kept coming to her: "Shakespeare answered very badly because he hadn't read his Bradley"; "Waterloo was won on the playing fields of Eton"; "Once more into the fray"— so much history, too much history.

"How will I learn it all?" she said later, on their return home.

"Learn what, Meti?"

"All this English."

30

At night, she woke up, her heart racing. Once again, out of nowhere, she had dreamed of Archer. Always in the dreams, she failed to save his life. How could she have saved it at the wedding? By refusing to dance? Avoiding a splashy wedding, so his aneurysm could explode in a quiet setting?

She didn't know whether to tell Simon. She resolved to go to the library and learn about dreams. But she put it off, and decided if she had another nightmare, she would both tell Simon and go find an Indian doctor. Simon's arm draped heavily across her body, and she welcomed its anchor. Sometimes she felt like she wanted to be pressed with his sleepy weight on top of her, so that he became a shield, a force field, warding off memory, warding off the flickering thought that somehow perhaps she had willed Archer's death, that however unlikely, a part of her subconsciously protested their marriage. Surely, though, that was afterthought, after Simon, after all that happened.

How much could they bear to speak about Archer? How large was their guilt. How it crept, if left unchecked, into their lives almost constantly. What they had done was not unusual, after all. Cousins, brothers, even uncles married widowed relatives to keep the bloodlines, the inheritances, the name, and though the church for years decried unions of affinity, a 1921 act allowed the marriage of a deceased brother's widow with her brother-in-law. Perhaps in feudal times such a marriage prevented the younger son from marrying well on his own, or going into the clergy; then there was also the pervasive idea that if a man and woman wed, they were united in blood, and all relatives became blood by default.

It was the scandal, the gossip that people loved. How merciless was she to wed so quickly, how tactless of him! How practical of her to want a father for a child, how foolish of him to squander his life! How deceitful of both to marry outside their own color and culture, to hurt both families in the bargain! How complicated, how unnecessary and undignified and selfish! It was the sheer selfishness of love that people minded, that refusal to think of the feelings of others for what—sex? This was what Grandmother feared, the censure of the neighbors and distant relatives, the outright stares of strangers. This was why she did not protest as heavily as she might have to keep them on Pi. In England, they could start a new life, she thought, finally coming to peace with the parting.

Yet she must have known the difficulties that were within Simon's family. The gin company had a reputation, but in the end, maybe the tribulations of family had little effect on the business. Gin making had long been associated with notoriety, Simon told her, despite its beginnings as a medicinal tonic in Holland, condemned by Henry Fielding as poisonous and pernicious to the soul of England, causing the country to succumb to a perpetual state of drunkenness. They looked at the Hogarth prints of Gin Lane, where the drunken figures lolled about, mothers ready to kill their babies as a result of the spirit.

"No wonder you didn't want to work for the company."

"It's lurid. Gin was responsible for thousands of deaths, abandonment, the ruination of families. People paid wages in gin. Saved the extra step, my grandfather said. People used to line up just to nurse themselves from the spigot, and when they built the palaces, it became fashionable and aboveground to sip their drinks with their pinkies up."

"Where's the family palace now?"

"The family palace—that was the joke. Forster Gin Palace. It burned down during the Blitz. It was supposed to have been beautiful—it had a bas-relief of Greek maidens chased by satyrs and gods, and these ridiculously ornate mirrors, eight feet tall. My great-grandfather was shellshocked, and wouldn't rebuild. So the company relied on its northern distilleries and the one on Pi."

"Who's running the company now?"

"An uncle of ours. Ruth-Sidney. Archer was to run it himself, but he refused. I didn't want it, and neither did Susan. My father was never in the running. He likes the production part, not the sales meetings and negotiating with lawyers, the flying about. But they make a good team, Uncle Ruth-Sidney and Dad. It's complicated—the whole damn company is riddled with complications."

Simon looked so troubled that Meterling did not press for details.

Simon took Meterling to the site of the original factory in a town on the outskirts of London. The main factory was up north. The original factory had been torn down after a fire, replaced by a microdistillery responsible for artisanal blends sold mostly in private auctions.

"Where've you been, Simon boy?" asked a man whose ruddy complexion was accentuated by a squint and a grin.

"Larry—thought you'd be retired."

"Nah, there'd be nothing for me to do, then."

This was Larry McGuire, who had run the place for the past forty years, before, as he put it, "it went designer."

Simon quickly made introductions, which led to more appraising looks at Meterling and the baby, and the foreman led them through the rooms containing copper stills, the purification processor, and, finally, the room of botanicals. Here, they were experimenting with bearberry, bayberry, and coriander for a Christmassy blend. The scents were strong when oak cask lids were lifted.

"Take a whiff of this, lass," said Larry, offering a handful of coarse brown seeds, which he crushed in his palms. His hands were nearly as brown as the seeds, Meterling noted as she inhaled the fragrance. They reminded Meterling of something on the edge of her memory—not merely the coriander, but the scent of wood and fire. Was this smell familiar to her even in childhood?

They were offered gin mixed with bitters in the sampling room, and Meterling and Simon, with Oscar, took their drinks to a patio that overlooked the Tittleton River.

"When I was pregnant, I craved to taste a martini."

"Hmm. You're sure you can drink while feeding?"

"In moderation, and I'm only tasting." She took a second sip. "This is delicious, Simon. I had no idea. I see now why people want to drink."

"It's good stuff."

"I could live here," said Meterling. She took another sip and pushed away her glass a few inches. "Oh, I know I can't really, but this is so lovely, Simon, the beauty here."

She looked at the river rushing past, the meadows beyond.

"You do have three fields."

"And a manor house somewhere."

"And a manor house somewhere," repeated Simon, "that you haven't yet seen."

"Not yet, darling." She sighed. "Not yet."

"Why not?"

"I'd feel I was trespassing. Let's wait a while longer."

31

Nearly every fine day, Meterling packed a small lunch and took Oscar out in his pushchair to the Serpentine, where they watched the exotic ducks. She ate her cheese sandwich with chutney on white bread neatly, while Oscar gurgled with delight, his belly full. There were other women with children, and at first Meterling was enchanted, thinking how multicultural England was, with so many black and brown women birthing white children. It dawned on her pretty quickly that they were nannies, working like ayahs to feed their own children left home with a grandmother. She supposed she was taken for a nanny, too.

She remembered in her first week, struggling to take the stroller up the stairs, and closing the gate behind her, an elderly woman walking by the building had answered her smile by inquiring brightly, "Do you own or rent?" Meterling had stammered out the truth, the resentment dawning later. Other women might have handled it differently—lied perhaps, or asked what business it was of hers, or pretended not to know the language. At the Madras airport, she had seen a woman who had cut into the line at security by stealthily shoving her Louis Vuitton luggage with her foot. No one had said anything; airport security would remain lax for two more decades. The woman left her place, wandered away, and returned to claim her luggage in the line. When confronted by a guard, she claimed blithely, nearly theatrically, not to know the language, any language, and maintained a face of innocence. Everyone knew she was lying, but what could be done?

She finished her sandwich carefully. She watched as businessmen and women walked briskly by, perhaps from the Mall, using their lunch hours for errands or assignations. One or two glanced at her, but most walked quickly, striding in the way those who needed to be *somewhere* did. She had never known such a place for speed, aside from the loitering teenagers, tourists with cameras, and women like her watching their children. She sighed. Too much English. Maybe she should have stayed in Madhupur. Maybe Archer's spirit would have been appeased, and she would not be dreaming of him at night.

She wondered if Oscar, too, missed Pi; if he was aware of the change in environment; if the way Grandmother's sari smelled like old silk and cardamom, the scent of roses from the garden, and the jasmine she always wore in her hair had already faded from his memory. Could babies know nostalgia, as she did, deep in her bones when she was alone or in the park sometimes, nearly brimming over with those wretched tears? Could he understand that this place was thousands of miles from where he was born, that the very salt in the ocean, and therefore the very air, was different?

When it began to drizzle, she held out her tongue to see if she could taste hedgerow and lavender, but quickly pulled it back, realizing she might taste the urban grit. Then she stuck it out again. Big Ben, the houses of Parliament, the curried eggplant someone was cooking, the river Thames—was this what was being caught on her tongue? The myriad of urban greens, in a country where not one inch was spared cultivation, where even the wild was carefully planned? She loved England, the idea of it, but the reality of England? Where did she fit when it was just she and Oscar, without Simon? She was censured in Madhupur, she knew, but she felt censured here, too. Because she was trying not to think about it, she thought about it. So many glances tossed her way, men staring into her eyes. ("Those are merely poor sods, Meti—don't look at them," Simon advised.) How could strangers know what she had done? Bringing to life a child conceived out of wedlock, marrying her late husband's cousin? A cousin close enough to be a brother? And Archer—no, she would not think of Archer, it was ludicrous.

Oscar was "such an easy child," which was the phrase Simon's mother had used. Meterling kissed his belly lightly. At four months, he gurgled and sounded "ba" at different pitches. Meterling and Simon had hung black and white geometric discs above his crib, as a baby book advised. They read and sang and whistled to him. But too soon, too soon, because to leap five and a half years was an easy enough thing to do, Meterling thought, he'd go to the nursery they passed on their walks, where they'd teach him new words and songs. He'd wear a little uniform—at least, she thought he would, or did they do that in kindergarten? Soon, he might start saying, "I'm British," refusing all other prior heritage, all family back home.

She had so much family who would gladly take care of Oscar, family who would not confuse him because their skin color and hair color would be like his. He would not feel too different on the outside, like she always had. Moving to the UK made her more aware not only of her skin color, but of her deeply submerged feelings of patriotism. Every time she saw a South Asian woman, she wanted to catch her eye, but no one did. To be South Asian was not an anomaly to these women. Mostly Meterling saw white. Yet London was a world city, so why was she seeing only the majority white? There were all around her South Asians, British Africans, Middle Easterners, and Asians, but she saw white. It was hard enough being tall; now, she was prominently brown as well.

Anyway, Oscar was not simply island, he was Archer, too. But if he were on Pi, he'd learn Tamil songs, pick up Hindi, not just English, always English. When he was old enough, four or five years old, he'd undergo the rite of Vidyarambham, the official start to his studies. Wearing a silk veshti under his freshly ironed shirt, he'd hold a palm leaf, inscribed with Sanskrit verse, ready for his first day of preschool. Of her own vidyarambham, she remembered the school floors filled with puffed rice—but that could not have been true. The teacher must have distributed some, and maybe she spilled hers on the floor. She was already tall, although they had been sure she'd stop growing by age twelve. What they hadn't counted on was her height at thirteen, fourteen, fifteen. The tailor kept having to sew strips of cloth to the bottom of her skirts and sleeves. She ran around in flip-floppy thong slippers, those being the easiest to buy every six months. How proud her grandmother had been, standing her against the wall, to measure her, Grandfather, too, before he died. He'd wanted her to be a pilot, but Grandmother hoped she'd be nicely settled and not have to work at all. What had been her parents' wishes for her? How short she must have fallen from their expectations!—yet this was what she chose: Oscar, Simon, London.

It was the silence in the flat that unnerved her while Simon was at work, the lack of trivial questions and comments constantly around her, the way Rasi, Sanjay, and Mina would be on her heels all during her pregnancy with a favor, a demand. They once had wanted to know if she practiced magic—so seriously they stood in front of her, waiting for her answer before scampering off. England lacked homeliness, that particular South Asian word denoting not plainness but coziness. They made her into a tall tale, sometimes, the way the family had a habit of doing with everyone. Here, too, as she looked around the park, stories could be made about the rheumy old man wrapped up in his red scarf, walking his schnauzer, erupting with great coughs, the skinny woman in a nurse's uniform checking her watch, smoking a cigarette. She was inside a Beatles song, "Penny Lane," all around her British and calm. She, Meterling, was in Britain. She, Meterling, was in London. Again and again, she surprised herself with this thought. Her heart ached. Of course, Simon and Oscar—here she scooped him up to her lap where he reached for her breast—made all the difference, *were* the difference, but why could she not keep the blue away? Think pink, she told herself, think pink. Her toes began to tingle.

"You look beautiful."

She started, and looked around.

No one.

"You have to actually think of me to see me."

The voice was too familiar.

"Ah, here I am." He materialized, because that's what ghosts do, appear into view without preamble. White suit, pink tie, sandals. Fat and sweet as he had looked at their wedding.

"Archer." The name stuck in her throat like a piece of gravel.

"Yes, darling. Look, you can see me even better. And that's my boy . . ."

She held the baby tight.

"But—I don't mean to upset you," he said.

"What are you doing here?"

"I just wanted to have a look at you and my son."

"You're dead—you died, Archer."

"I'm sorry, my love, I didn't mean to," he said, sounding pained.

"They buried you."

"Ah, but it was too late. I'd already fled the body, just to have one last look around the island. By the time I came back, the ship had, well, sailed."

"I'm imagining things."

"No, I'm here, in the unflesh, so to speak."

"Why are you here?"

"I told you, to see you. Make sure you are all right."

"I'm fine."

"Are you?"

"Of course I am."

"I would never have brought you here. London is cold, it's ruthless. You belong on Pi, with flowers in your hair, eating mangoes."

"That's patronizing."

"I'm sorry, but Simon—Simon doesn't know you like I do."

"Of course he does! Simon knows me better, Archer. He loves me and I love him. That's enough. If he wants to live here, I don't mind. Oscar can be with his grandparents . . ."

"John and Nora? My parents are his grandparents, Meterling, not John and Nora."

"It doesn't matter. Don't be angry with Simon. We helped each other. You died so suddenly."

"That's why I'm here now. Those who die unexpectedly with unfulfilled desires return."

"Is that a British belief?"

"No, Hindu."

"But you're not Hindu."

"There was a cultural breakdown somewhere."

"I must be mad."

But just like that, he disappeared.

Had she really seen what she thought she had? Had she really had a conversation with him? For a long while she sat staring at the space where he'd been. Oscar's mouth had detached from her nipple, and he was fast asleep. Waking him, she burped him, and let him drift back to sleep. She must have been more tired than she realized. She resisted the temptation to pick up Oscar and go back home immediately. What if Archer followed her home? She shook her head. She must be dehydrated, and it made her delusional, that was all. She did not believe in ghosts.

She purchased some Fanta at a kiosk. A peeling poster advertised a Nostalgia Ball. "God Save the Queen all over again," it said.

"How elegant!"

Meterling stood still.

"Exotic. Like a bird of paradise."

The voices moved away, and Meterling was relieved they had come from two well-dressed women walking arm in arm. Had she been the subject of these comments? It unnerved her how many people felt emboldened to comment on her appearance aloud; but mostly, if they felt so moved, they addressed her directly and told her about their last trip to India. They spoke of great-grandparents and such who used to live there and had developed a taste for kedgeree. Meterling didn't know what kedgeree was, and never corrected them about where she was from. What use to say "I come from Pi, not India," when they really just wanted to talk of their travel or great-uncle—or, as she had recently experienced when she did assert her nationality, a woman just tipped her head and said, "That would be in the Maldives, wouldn't it?" before launching into a story about her daughter? She had expected the British to be stand-offish, stiff-upper-lipped, and all she had heard, but strangers flocked to her. Strangers and ghosts. When she complained to Simon about the strangers, he laughed and told her to accept the compliment. He said it had to do with her magical attraction, a beam of light in a storm.

"Your height is a radio tower, attracting the lonely," he said.

But she didn't want the attention, and wondered if she should dress in more sober colors. Her saris were bright, pinks and greens and blues suited to the tropics. Maybe she needed colors to match the English sky.

Archer must be lonely, too, she thought. He had spent one night with her, promised his life to her and had it removed from him. Maybe this was why the old customs did not allow widows to remarry—to keep the ghosts away.

The sun had begun to go down, and she had hardly noticed. Hurriedly, she slipped Oscar into his pushchair, and headed home.

At the flat, she tried to write letters when Oscar had his longer afternoon nap. "Vivekananda lived near to our flat," she wrote to us. Her neighborhood was called Pimlico, which cheered us up; it was such a strange name. It reminded Nalani of "Pimpernel," like *The Scarlet Pimpernel*. It didn't remind me of anything, but I liked saying it aloud, "Aunt Meterling of Pimlico." But it didn't make her leaving any easier for us.

Most days—for she tired easily, she discovered—she put Oscar on the big bed and curled up right beside him. At first, she did not want to ask Simon if Oscar could sleep with them at night, wanting to spare him squeamish thoughts about Archer. But one night, he simply said, looking at her tired eyes, "This is what adoption means. Other people's babies in your bed, and there's nothing wrong with that."

And that was how she grew to love Simon even more, wanting to engulf him without drowning him. But the spaces to occupy herself without him stretched long, hours spent talking to no one but Oscar, who was more often than not content to quietly play with one of the toys Nalani had sent him. Briefly, she worried if he was autistic, and if it was her fault, for shouldn't her depression before meeting Simon mark him somehow, cloud him unfairly in pain? Didn't she deserve that? The doctor said the baby was fine, that she ought to be glad that he wasn't fussy, launching into a story about another child. Dr. Morgan. She was efficient, composed, and looked Anglo-Indian. She only raised one eyebrow when Meterling walked in with Oscar, though the receptionist appeared startled at her height. She had thought she'd blend in more easily with the English, who were known to be spindly and tall, but it wasn't always the case. Simon came to her forehead, but she still remained a half or full head above nearly everyone else she met face-to-face.

She wondered if she could tell Dr. Morgan about seeing Archer's ghost. She wondered what the doctor's response would be, if she would merely shrug and say it was part of diasporic distemper, a common result of living abroad. She had been dehydrated, she reminded herself.

32

Soon it would be Diwali. Of course, she shouldn't be celebrating Diwali; she was still a widow. Yet, she was also a bride, and a new mother, she wasn't in Madhupur, and it would be her first Diwali with her new family. Simon was going to get sparklers, and she had bought tiny clay pots to fill with oil and wicks to line their terrace. She missed the children—Sanjay, Rasi, Mina—their voices, their brightness. She missed everything: little things like the clatter of the morning sweet-bun delivery, the way Grandmother lined them up for handfuls of spiced curd-rice, into which children and grown-ups alike dipped a thumb to create a well, to be filled with glorious spicy tamarind sambar. In the very same way, they'd pop a hole into a gol gappa, so that it could be filled with a thin sauce, before tossing it into their mouths.

Stop, she told herself, stop, this was dreaming and living in the past, and what good did it do her?

On Pi, Simon would . . . Simon would . . . Simon . . . Here her fantasy always stopped, because what would Simon do? Would he be as alien there as she felt here? And was it fair to him, he who had literally found her at the last moment, he whom she loved with both passion and devotion? And didn't that Indian writer say no one could ever go back to his or her homeland again? That nostalgia by its very nature is imagination? In her letters from New Jersey, Mina's mother, Jyoti, did not mention nostalgia; but then, her days were filled with science—that was how Meterling saw her, in a lab coat, peering into telescopes and test tubes, solving mysteries like Quincy, M.E. She was here, in London, with her two boys, and that was the reality.

Her two boys. Simon did seem boyish, grinning with excitement as he lay underneath her, like a kid with a Christmas present, and if truth were told, he made her feel like a girl. That sense of tingling hormones that were allowed breathing space in Western dating and teenage coupling, the frantic stolen kisses as well as the we-don't-care-who's-watching near-copulations she witnessed on the streets, were not easily available on Pi. When Meterling's impulses and desires were released, it was like a wave of rediscovery. With Archer, she had been shy, curious, nearly studious as she watched him examine her body, poring over her like a patron of the arts, murmuring soft moans of appreciation. Eyeing his body had filled her with apprehension, and she was certain they wouldn't fit, that *it* wouldn't fit in *it*. She didn't mind so much that what they were doing was desecrating the ancient laws that forbid premarital sex, but she minded her apprehension. She didn't fully understand his wonder over this coupling, until he released her pleasure, leaving her both surprised and shocked. As she felt her body softening, he—intercoursed—and she had gasped at the pain while he, breathless, withdrew, but not quickly enough. They had only done it that once, that impossible one-in-a-million chance of sperm meeting egg—result: Oscar.

In London, though, desire blossomed in Meterling, quickening desire. In amazement, she found herself in a state between sleep-deprived torpor and acute sensitivity. Mostly, they lay together skin-to-skin, hardly moving, happy in the weight of one another. But other times, she hungrily sought Simon's kisses, twining her arms around him, pulling him toward her.

Weren't new mothers supposed to transfer their desire to their infants? But Simon wasn't the father, so maybe that need to repulse the father came from the subconscious knowledge that he was responsible for childbirth pain. There—a new psychological insight. But whom could she ask? Dr. Morgan? Pa would know, and Pa might even tell, but Pa wasn't here.

One day, she was late returning to the flat. The sun was coming down as she strolled Oscar back home. It had been raining earlier, and the wet made the asphalt shiny. She breathed in the air, but caught nothing, no surge of freshness, no increased negative-ion activity. The store lights weren't yet on, but in an hour, as teatime neared, they would be. She stopped in front of a store that sold beautiful cashmere sweaters, hung on steel hangers like artworks, in pale pastels and varying shades of gray. Looking up, she had seen for a moment her own face superimposed by the window's reflection onto one of the headless mannequins wearing a wool lace miniskirt and boots that stretched over its thighs (did mannequins have thighs, or merely legs?). The breasts were bare and pointy, because either that was the fashion or the store clerk hadn't finished dressing it and had popped out for a cigarette. The mannequin's skin was stark white, and Meterling saw herself hovering over it like a ghost wearing its clothes. She pulled her raincoat closer to her body, wishing she'd mended the torn pocket, sewed the button. It belonged to Simon, and the lining smelled like him, which comforted her a bit.

They were in Kensington, and Pimlico wasn't that far. Looking up, she noticed a black Mercedes pull up to the curb in front of the familiar green awnings of Harrods. The driver got out, and a woman in a burka emerged, wearing sunglasses. Why would she need sunglasses at dusk? She strode swiftly past Meterling and entered the store. On a whim, Meterling followed. She and Oscar could always take a cab home.

The woman headed for a set of elevators, quickly navigating among the crowd of people buying food for dinner. Smiling, she entered the elevator with the woman, joining a few other women. No one said a word as the lift ascended and the woman got out at the third floor: gift wares and bedding. She followed the woman, curious to see what the woman would buy. Sheets upon sheets of linen, it turned out, prettily packaged, deeply expensive, and forming thin, flat packages. Was she buying for a hotel? That would be a job done on the phone. No, it must be for her own boudoir. She must be the wife of a Saudi prince, or maybe she was an executive, a president of a company that didn't mind women presidents. There were so many sheets. "Thank you, Ms. Mirazi," said the clerk, handing her two dark-green bags. If she was someone so wealthy, wouldn't she have a servant to carry her bags? And at the same moment Meterling thought this, a man stepped quietly from behind—where *had* he come from?—and took the bags. Her servant, or her guard, had been watching Meterling watching the mysterious woman. The pair headed back to the elevator.

Checking on Oscar, Meterling wandered a bit on this floor, until she came across tiny pottery figures of English houses. This was more like the house she had imagined, with a thatched roof. Oscar stirred.

"Do you think you'd like to live here?"

Oscar blinked at her.

"In a thatched cottage somewhere in the country, so when you grow, you can run around?"

Oscar made a spitball and drooled on his chin.

"Well, I guess you are a city boy, then," she said.

"He should be eating sugarcane and running around barefoot," said a voice near her ear. She flinched, but did not speak to Archer.

33

The sky was moody, a palette of grays and blues, darkening quickly. Without the lush green color of the tropical island greenery, rain in London fell miserably, creating damp, depression, chills. No wonder the English loved their English teas, their English scones with double cream, which they called English even though in reality the latter had been used in Indian cuisine for thousands of years while the British tore at roast beef and hunted deer, drowning all with ale. My aunt wrinkled her nose; she would not fault the English for their ignorance, she resolved. Still, what did the women drink before the East India Tea Company? Cider from North America? Punch? She knew that when English women first tried to serve tea, they had no idea what they were doing. They served the leaves, boiled like potatoes, in tiny plates, tried to eat it, and wondered what the fuss was about. Yet these same English learned to make tea, and serve sweets to go with tea, little cakes with lemon glaze, and buttery biscuits. On Pi, she had devoured Jane Austen's books like chocolate, imagining the sprigged muslin dresses, the crowds at Bath. She didn't recall teas in the books, but she remembered the dinners. *Persuasion* was her favorite—and it was at the table Austen brought together the surprises and catalysts for plot, she remembered Miss Shanta impressing on the tenth standard. Real dinners were not like that; if violent emotions were felt and hidden, it was because a train was late, or there was less pocket money for the monthly budget. Conversations were unremarkable in her life, unless good spirits and humor were cause for notice. What had George Eliot said—that it was the unremarkable people who made for the equanimity of life in peacetime? Something like that.

Simon had bought her a cookbook that was full of vegetarian British food. It had beautifully photographed terrines and timbales, cassoulets and soups. She leafed through it, and tried to make a tart with leeks. The vegetables were hard to clean; she forgot to blind-bake the pastry and reduce the temperature of the oven. A burnt pie resulted, the smell lingering in the air for days. She cried as Simon laughed.

When she first tried to eat pizza, ("pete-za," she reminded herself, not "pisa") slicing across the cheesy top with a knife, Simon had had to convince her the tomato sauce was really vegetarian. Didn't Americans eat pizza with their hands? The British used fork and knife. It was tasty, if chewy, but the red sauce was disquieting. What would Darshan joke? They put meat in their pies, plugged in their water to boil, and made coffee from a jar. They traveled in tubes. English people, she discovered, spoke very fast, even on that television show with the Indians. They had a secret vocabulary, it seemed, and she wanted subtitles to follow. She resolved not to call the British "they." She drew her shawl closer to her body over her sweater, because she was home now, having gone out to purchase milk, raincoat dripping by the door, rubber boots off, groceries inside, and having made herself a cup of tea.

She wondered if Susan would share a cup of tea with her if she telephoned. But Susan was so distrustful, so wary, as if always working to bite back her resentment but not always succeeding. I am the woman who killed Archer, thought Meterling, the woman who made him dance. It was Archer who insisted on the dance lessons. Couldn't she tell Susan, "Look, could we just start over?" But then, why should she be so conciliatory toward Susan? So her brother married me; so her cousin married me, too. What did it matter? Susan was Oscar's aunt—wasn't that enough?

Simon appeared, interrupting her thoughts, tousle-haired, as if he had awakened from a nap. He needed a shave. He treasured his Sundays, and would wear his pajamas all day. Buried under the newspaper or under the covers, he emerged to coo to the baby, eat, and make love to his wife. This is what they meant when they, whoever the wordsmiths were, coined "a month of Sundays." Absentmindedly giving her a kiss, he walked to the window and rested his head on his arm against the pane.

"Damn. Does the English sun ever appear except in its former colonies?"

"Imagine contented Englishmen at home in sunny gardens, with no need to plunder and pillage."

"Ah, plunder and pillage," said Simon speculatively, but Meterling waved him off and went to make him a cup of tea. She liked Yorkshire tea best, strong and good, able to stand hot milk and sugar. She discovered that tea could be satisfying to the end, and wondered if it had to do with the weather. Just as she was to take Simon's cup in, she heard a plaintive cry. Oscar? But this sounded more like a cat, a *meow* that sounded distressed. Opening the back door, she found a small black kitty, now mouthing its mews silently. She stared in amazement, not having witnessed such a silent appeal since seeing the street widows on Pi with their begging bowls, who were so exhausted, so tired, they could only mutely ask for alms. Hurriedly, she opened the screen and scooped the cat in.

"Simon, we've got a visitor."

"Oh, dear God," he said when he saw the cat.

"We have to take care of it. Go get me a towel."

"What about my tea?"

"Don't be an idiot."

Soon, wrapped in a once-white towel after being gently but thoroughly rubbed down, the grateful cat softly purred.

"And it might belong to someone else. The landlord won't let us keep a cat, darling."

"Well, we'll have to move."

She was kidding, of course, but Meterling's insistence on keeping the cat caught Simon by surprise. He hadn't witnessed her stubbornness so completely before. Maybe in this strange new world, she needed an ally. They put out flyers and an ad in the paper, but no one claimed the cat. He found himself liking the creature that came running to him after work as he removed his coat. It stood on its hind legs, trying to greet him as people do, and flopped over onto its back, waiting for its belly to be rubbed.

"A thoroughly domesticated kitty," he said, "aren't you, Pibs?"

"Pibs?"

"Puss-in-Boots."

Pibs took to guarding Oscar, who liked grunting into his face. At first, they worried that Pibs would bite suddenly, but Pibs and Oscar seemed companionable. Evenings, Pibs lay contentedly on a pillow by Oscar's bouncy seat, while Meterling and Simon read by lamplight beside the fire. Simon taught her to twist newspaper, layer kindling and finally a log; and on drafty days, she liked nothing better than the fire. They had found an old hearth toaster in an odds-and-ends market, and she sometimes heated chocolate between slices of bread.

But despite this warmth and affection and food and love-making, there were still long stretches of day which found her doing nothing at all, long stretches when Simon was away and cat and child asleep, days where she often just stared out the window. This was when the blue slipped in, even as her thoughts became full of lush color and strong images, when she remembered sitting on the veranda with tea, the kids beside her, or Grandmother. She thought of Archer, his innate kind-ness, his joviality, how they began to trust one another. She stopped herself—what if his ghost were to appear? But her thoughts ran on. If only Archer had known Oscar—that was the thought that climbed its way to the top of her thoughts. If only, if only—that terrible trap of the mind. But wasn't the darker thought that she felt grateful he'd died, if only to have Simon? That was why she disliked these large spaces of day: it made her examine what she didn't want to examine. It left her ragged.

"But I feel it too, Meti. It's horrible. It's almost as if I killed Archer with my mind. When I first saw you at the wedding, I was lightning-struck. I couldn't believe Archer's luck, and I'm sure I instantly wished I were in his place," said Simon when she approached the subject. He bit his lip. "My father said it's things like this that you don't question, you don't torment yourself with, and I have to agree with him."

Meterling had to agree as well. It was pointless to pick over the past; yet why did the past creep up on her when she found herself lonely? As if on cue, Oscar began to cry, and she went to feed him. Maybe she should be grateful for what she had;

and really, this feeling, Oscar gently sucking, was so lovely, she didn't, she *must not*, want more.

One Saturday, when Simon asked her where she wanted to go, she said she was exhausted and wanted to stay put.

"I feel like we've opened all the presents at once, Simon, and now there's all this debris, the boxes and the strings and ribbons and wrapping paper that needs to be put away."

"There are still some boxes left."

"Can't we just hang on to them a bit longer, wait to open them?"

"London isn't finite. No city is."

"Let's just stay in bed with the baby and eat toast."

"Or let's just let Oscar play a bit more in his bouncy seat."

"Where did Asian women learn to lean their cheek on their hand? Is it inborn or learned?" asked Simon.

"Learned, obviously, but surely Western women do the same."

"Not as often. They play with their hair."

"Honestly, Simon, where do you get these stereotypes?"

"I think it must come from a natural and historical sense of contemplation."

"Your prejudices?"

"Women and their cheeks and their hands."

"There are all those paintings of women looking out of windows. The miniatures always show that. Queens or handmaidens, but sometimes I wonder if they aren't just prostitutes displaying themselves?"

"Like in Amsterdam?"

"Simon, where *are* we going for the long weekend?"

"Amsterdam? To sample the wares?"

He played with her hair. "I was thinking of France."

But the conversation was already being left behind, as they engaged themselves more seriously with hands and cheeks. Later, they lay next to one another, panting. It was usually at this point that Meterling went to sleep, even as Simon felt ready for another go. Now they held hands, idly stroking one another, waiting for Oscar to cry. Pibs did, but they ignored him, knowing there was food in the bowl, water in the dish.

"Do you think Pibs needs a companion cat?"

"Is that a way of asking if I want another baby?"

"No, I meant—that is, I really was thinking of Pibs. But do you want another baby?"

"Do you?"

"Well, yes. In a few years. Wait, you're not pregnant, are you?"

Meterling laughed at his stricken face, and reassured him that she wasn't. But she agreed that in a few years, they might think of another baby. They began to talk more seriously of where to go for the long weekend.

34

They went south, getting an early start to beat the traffic, or at the very least, avoid gridlock. They drove toward Craywick, while Oscar squealed every time they passed sheep. They stopped once for lunch, admiring the countryside, exploring two churches, and ate cheese-and-pickle sandwiches at a local pub. By the time they reached their hotel toward dusk, they turned in, skipping dinner. They woke to the sunlight drifting into the room through the lace-covered curtains and a racket of birdsong. It was chilly enough to light a fire, but instead, they wrapped themselves in quilts and ate breakfast on the terrace, slathering butter on hot toast, and drinking steaming cups of coffee.

"Let's live here, Simon."

"Okay," he said, trying to feed Oscar mashed banana. He refused it. "Did you know birds macerate food for their young?"

"I mean it . . . one day. And yes, I thought everyone knew that."

"Oh, really? Everyone?" he said, trying to feed her the banana and kiss her at the same time.

They explored the town on borrowed bicycles, visiting the pond that boasted enough ducks (that is, more than none) to cheer Oscar. Nearby, they stopped at a used-book store, which featured books cozily housed on wooden shelves, with the scent of lavender-honey tea permeating the air. Round tables held displays of local works and photographs from a time past. A vase of roses, anemones, and dahlias was next to the cash register, where a ginger cat was sleeping. The owner, Lucia, welcomed them, and offered them biscuits.

"I'm having my tea anyway." She said this with a mysterious smile, murmuring something about Jaipur, about Udaipur. "And when I was a girl," she continued, "I had a crush on Raj Kapoor. My name is Italian, but I grew up in France, and we watched all the Indian movies!"

So they had sat on faded upholstered chairs, drinking hot tea in big white cups, dunking biscuits like old friends. Lucia had owned the place for thirty years with her partner, she said, sounding almost surprised. Her smile was broad; this was what a successful woman looked like, thought Meterling, leaning back against the crochet headrest. Later, humming "Aawara," Lucia wrapped their purchases up in paper, while Meterling took a last look to see if by some strange coincidence she would find Neela Chandrashekar's work. There was a selection of works by Indian and British-Indian authors, but most were the household names. As they said goodbye to Lucia, she reminded them to get an early start the next day.

"Where are we now, Simon?"

They had followed a trail and now stood in a meadow, wild with weed and bramble. Trees edged it in the distance. Some sheep grazed in the distance, too.

"Won't the owner mind we're on his land, Simon?"

"I think we're okay to walk. Come, I'll take Oscar."

"It's so peaceful."

The sun was out, and unlike in town, it blazed bright. Meterling took off her shoes and socks to feel the cold, damp earth. It was packed tight, dormant.

"What do you see in the distance, Meti?"

"A house."

"Your house."

"My house?"

"Your house. Why wait any longer?"

"I don't know. It holds so much story, you understand . . . past lives. Archer's life, Susan's—yours, too."

"Only for the holidays, really. Shall we take a look? Dispel some ghosts?"

"Don't joke, Simon. I feel as if I've received something I was not meant to have."

They stood in the fields, her three fields. She wondered what the gardens looked like. Squeezing Simon's hand, she wondered if it was time after all to look. A slight wind stirred the grass around them. She would not plant rye, she reminded herself with a start.

They returned to the car to drive up the gravel road to the house. It really was a manor, run-down, with boarded-up windows. Large stone Ali Baba pots holding overgrown boxwood and autumn leaves and pine needles flanked the shallow steps to the door, whose knocker was an incongruous elephant's head.

"Ganesha," mused Simon, as he tried the key he drew from his pocket.

The old house had good bones, built in 1770, a classic Georgian with eccentric touches added in the 1900s. One such touch was the Corinthian columns that acted as decorative balconies over the second-storey windows; another was the cupola, added as an afterthought, with a widow's walk that looked out over the fields.

Sheets had been thrown over most of the furniture, and the uncovered ones were hideously threadbare. Mice must nest amid the stuffing, thought Meterling, gingerly making her way through the rooms. A staircase, thick with dust, led upstairs, but Simon cautioned her against exploring it, citing safety. Nevertheless, giving him the baby, Meterling went up. Bedrooms and bathrooms and studies, each filled with a scent of damp and discard. The windows caught her attention, large ones that provided views of the fields, of the trees and sky. She could imagine us—that is, Sanjay, Rasi, and me—lounging about during country rainstorms, reading on the window seats, Pibs curled up against our feet.

The staircase felt solid as she descended, the wood thick with dust and grime.

"A place for dreaming, for dreams," she said.

"I'm surprised no one's squatting in it," said Simon. "It's been empty for years. There were tenants for a while, but not for a decade at least. Hard to believe, isn't it? It's like a mirage, really."

" 'Squatting'?"

"Living illegally."

"I wouldn't blame them. This big old house needs people in it."

"What do you think?"

"It would take an awful lot of work."

"You could have a garden. You could invite Mina and the other kids to come stay over their holidays."

"You've thought about it."

"It's here, and it's yours. It's the one thing immigrants never have, land and property. It's what leads to all the feelings of inadequacy and trespass."

"What about your job?"

"I could commute. I could even stay in London four days—"

"While I am a kind of house widow, your paramour in the country, hidden from view while you batch it up in the city?"

"Meterling!"

"I'm sorry." She flushed. "I want to live with you, Simon, not in a big, drafty house that's full of ghosts."

"Of course we'll live together. You can sell the house, get rid of it."

"I wonder if we could exorcise the ghosts?"

"What?"

"If we do keep it, I mean, do you think we could get a priest to come and bless the house?"

"Why not? I knew an Indian family who bought a house and had a ceremony with a cow. A farmer lent them a cow."

"The cow represents prosperity, so you need it at a house blessing. There are farmers around, it seems."

"So what do you think? We could easily borrow a cow."

"I don't know. Simon, I think I see—"

But at that moment, Oscar began to cry lustily, and if Meterling were to confess to Simon that she was visited by Archer's ghost, it would have to wait for another day.

Traffic caught them. What they had missed on their way in held them fiercely on their way back. Well, traffic—you may as well enjoy it, there is nothing to be done about it. Simon was one of those rare men who were unbothered by waiting, because, he said, it was out of their control. If one was going to be delayed, then so be it. Meterling was glad she had packed apples and cheese, and had tea in a thermos. They unfastened their seat belts and listened to the odd bursts of car horns.

Oscar began to fuss, and Meterling quickly got into the backseat to change him.

"Simon, did you ever think this is the way it would be, back when you were twenty-one?"

"You mean nappies and traffic and you?"

"Oscar and traffic and me."

"You do know 'nappies' is code for Oscar? In fact, maybe we should change his name. Nappies Forster. Or better, Diapers Forster—that's a billionaire's name for you. He could support us in style in our old age."

Getting no reply from Meterling, Simon added, "It couldn't have turned out better, for me, because I'm in this, all of it, Oscar and traffic and you."

The cars began to move again. In the other lane, they saw a row of policemen sweep away the glass slowly from the scene of an accident. They reached London in three and a half hours.

35

Some days in town, Meterling and Oscar dropped in at Lyle & Assam's Cafetiere. Mostly, they sold fine cigars, but a sign advertising Italian coffee led her in the first day, stroller and all. It didn't smell like cigars inside, exactly, more of wood. Behind glass cases were the cigars, from Brazil, Colombia, Mexico, everywhere but Cuba. Beautiful wooden boxes lined with more wood held the smokes, while the discarded boxes were scattered about. Ever since childhood, Meterling loved cigar boxes. Grandfather had a supply of them, and she would run her hand over the smooth wood and the fragile paper labels, imprinted with names like "Royale Jamaica" and "Arturo Fuente y Cia." She used to store shells and treasures in them, later pencils. While Grandfather had a rare smoke, she'd sit by him, a pencil in her mouth, imitating him and keeping out of sight of Grandmother.

An Iranian man with a curious tilt of his head and a kind smile looked at her and Oscar from behind the counter.

"You have coffee?" she asked, hesitantly, thinking that maybe the sign was a code for something else. She had not yet got used to the advertisements for prostitutes in the friendly red telephone boxes. What did "coffee" stand for? Hashish? Arms?

It meant cappuccino, in a small porcelain cup, with cinnamon. Gratefully, she warmed her hands and throat, as the man came around to coo at Oscar. This was Assam, a thin man whose business partner was named Lyle. Lyle was American, and was largely MIA, a silent partner, being an alpine skier whose father financed the store's start with money from his dry goods stores in Peoria, Illinois. Assam ran the business, Lyle visited six times a year, and they were the best of friends.

They could not afford to call the place simply Assam's, he said. "Half the people walking by already think the store is a front for arms traders," he said as Meterling blushed.

"Not you? Come on, you're Indian."

Island, she corrected, thus beginning a lasting friendship, her first in London.

Lately, though, Assam had become more voluble in his speech, bemoaning the lack of clientele, speaking of closing the shop.

"This country eats you alive, Mrs. Forster. Sometimes I just want to get out."

"But why?"

He didn't reply, and she did not know what to say except cheerful things that rang false.

"Assam-ji, why don't you come to dinner this weekend with the family?"

He smiled ruefully. "We're going to visit my wife's parents in Northumberland. But you must throw a party, Mrs. Forster. It is Diwali, after all, and it will lift your spirits. We like to entertain and eat, we Easterners, and if we don't, we will wilt like flowers."

She finished her coffee and paid, checking on Oscar and readying to leave the store.

"Don't wilt like a flower, Mrs. Forster!"

36

She *would* give a dinner party. It would give her something to do. She left a message with the receptionist for Dr. Morgan to call her. A simple Diwali supper (for it was in four days), she decided, four at the table, for Dr. Morgan had a ring on her finger, not counting Oscar. When the doctor accepted her invitation, Meterling began to plan. She went over a dozen menus in her head, knowing she was overdoing it. Whenever this much overwrought thought went into cooking and planning, the meal was bound to come out unspectacularly. So, she switched to ironing the red cloth napkins from the Sarasti factory on Pi, and then the tablecloth. She polished the silver Simon's mother had given them, and checked the glasses. Her mother-in-law had also given her candlesticks—what was she thinking? A supper for four? She had to invite Simon's parents—why hadn't he said anything?—and she would invite Susan, too. If Susan brought a date, that meant eight at dinner, not counting Oscar, who would be fed beforehand. Eight! Why not? Plus Assam and his family . . . but no, they were going out of town, to visit Niloo's family. A party! Well, what had she been doing, after all, getting acclimated in this new land, but to throw a glittering dinner in appreciation? Semi-glittering. Casual, really. But it was Diwali, so semi-glittering it was.

Did she have enough matching napkins? She found herself getting excited and at the same time slightly ashamed. No, not enough, but she could mix the red with the gold vine-patterned ones Rasi and I had given her. We had selected them because they were bright and bold and big, just like our aunt. Only foreigners bought napkins; we rinsed our fingers and mouth at the sink after eating, but foreigners must not have enough sinks. We worried about our aunt going off to a country without enough sinks and bought her napkins to take with her. If we could have, we'd have rolled ourselves right up in the red-and-gold vine cloth and gone too.

"She needs to be protected," I said.

"Uncle Simon will protect her," said Rasi.

I wasn't sure. Uncle Simon was too thin to be a warrior, I felt, too soft and easygoing. If our aunt needed protection from baffling foreign ways, would he be able to cope? Uncle Archer seemed a better choice, it occurred to me; he was so solid, so capable. Aunt Meterling needed Uncle Archer to help her out in London, we decided; but of course, Uncle Archer was dead.

There was enough silverware, Aunt Meterling decided, but the glasses would be an assortment of juice jars and wine tumblers, some plain, and others featuring bold bubbled surfaces. Simon had brought boxes of odds and ends as well as books from his old flat, and she burrowed through them.

"You could always borrow some from Mum," Simon had said.

But Meterling refused, wanting somehow to do this herself. If she asked her mother-in-law, she'd get beautiful napkins and advice.

"I can give you plenty of advice," said a voice, but when she turned around, she didn't see any sign of Archer. Had her toes tingled? She wasn't sure. Shivering slightly, she rubbed her arms.

A simple pulao, following a delicate lemon rasam, with Brussels sprouts and sweet potatoes in a curry stir fry, red moong dal, spinach and potatoes, naan or parathas for Simon's father, who much preferred it to rice; and for dessert, in addition to the Indian shop sweets, a tea cake.

Now, she had things to do. Since it was Diwali, she needed to purchase new clothes. She made her way to the Indian shops where she felt like she was in Delhi, entire streets full of desi shops, selling everything from dishes to food to clothing. Hindi, Gujarati, and the occasional Malayalam filled the air in quick streams, as shoppers haggled over the prices and the quality of wares. She looked at rolls of sari material in one cart, but went into the store opposite, which sold good Mysore silk. She could have been back on Pi. The store was quiet, and saris were stacked neatly against walls in vivid colors. A plump matron eyed her height warily at first, but came forward quickly. Soon she was suggesting colors and silks, tissue versus heavier cloths. There were even old-fashioned prints, borders that seemed ancient, handloomed and outrageously expensive, even for London. These beauties were displayed behind glass. Meterling fingered a pale-pink georgette sari and thought how nice Nalani would look in it. For herself, she turned to a muted blue with a border done in silver thread. She had the option of buying a readymade choli or being measured for a blouse that would be ready in two days.

"Two days?" asked Meterling, surprised at how quickly it could be done.

"This is London," shrugged the proprietor, apologizing for the delay.

But the days of tailors stitching up a blouse in an hour for their clients were nearly gone, even on Pi. Grandmother used to make her own, on an old Singer, her feet rhythmically pedaling as her hands fed the cloth. Meterling, followed by every other grandchild, used to thread the needle for her. In school, they had learned to sew, embroidering handkerchiefs with tiny rosettes, and unraveling the hems to tie them up neatly for a pretty edging. Nalani used to say that was the best thing about the convent school she'd attended: everyone could hem perfectly.

Meterling got measured, protesting that the front should not be so low cut as to upset her in-laws, and the back needed to be more than two inches.

"Then, madam, you will have an unfashionable choli," said the tailor.

As she and Oscar made their way to the bus, she noticed a small sign: S. D. Shakur, Ayurvedic Doctor and Specialist— Walk-in Consults Available. Taking a breath, she walked in. She found herself in a small, musty room without a reception- ist, although there was a desk facing the door. To one side was an electric kettle, with paper cups, tea bags, instant coffee pack- ets as well as sugar and powdered milk. She was tempted to make herself a cup when she noticed another door off to the side. She knocked, but received no answer. They must have left the outer door unlocked by accident, and she sighed, preparing to leave, when a slight man entered the office. He looked sur- prised to see her.

"Yes?" he asked.

"I'm looking for Dr. Shakur."

"I am he. Do you have an appointment?"

"No, I—"

"Well, you are lucky. My three o'clock canceled—come on in."

My aunt was about to protest she was already "in" but instead followed him, rather bravely, through the side door, which he left open. She doubted he had a "three o'clock." She sat down on a wooden chair and he filled in a few lines on a chart at his desk.

"So, what seems to be the matter?"

"I have a friend."

"Ah."

"She lost her husband, but remarried. Now she imagines"— she began, shifting Oscar to her other shoulder—"that she can see the ghost of . . . I'm sorry—it sounds ridiculous."

"Your friend sees the ghost of her dead husband?"

My aunt nodded.

"How did he die?"

Meterling told him.

"He died without fulfilling his life's desires. He cannot rest because he was neither burnt nor old enough to die. I suspect what he wants is not your friend, Mrs. Forster, but her child."

"I—"

"But don't trouble yourself, Mrs. Forster; ghosts seldom get what they want. That's why they are unhappy. Now, I need you to return so I can do a complete history, medical, physical, including temperament calculations."

"I could ask my friend."

"Yes, by all means, come back, Mrs. Forster."

Two days later, when she picked up the blouse, she saw the tailor's decisions about the back were correct, and was grateful that the front was more modest than fashionable. She picked up a nice shirt as well as a kurta for Simon and a little kurta for Oscar. She looked for Dr. Shakur's office. She went in.

This time, a receptionist in a green sari and cardigan greeted her, and offered her a cup of tea. My aunt sipped from a cracked cup with a painted rose, and waited. Oscar waited as well in his sling pouch. The receptionist smiled at Oscar and then went back to work. Presently, Dr. Shakur ushered them in. The receptionist, who was a nurse or perhaps a doctor as well, took her blood pressure, her height and weight, and listened to her heart behind a screen. Oscar was placed in a cloth baby hammock that was hung from the ceiling, as on Pi. When she was done, she closed up the screen, and Dr. Shakur took my aunt's wrist and listened to her pulse. There was no mention of her "friend."

"Where do you live now?"

My aunt told him.

"Where are you from originally?" He questioned her about her diet, her preferences for temperatures, her bowel movements, and her sleep patterns and any resultant dreams. Aunt Meterling told him about her nightmares.

He took notes, and then told her that her humors were out of sorts.

"This is why you are having these kinds of dreams. You do not want the Bhuta to interfere with your present life, so even before you met it, you tried to kill it. That is good."

"I didn't try to kill him—I just didn't help him survive, in the dreams."

"I want you to eat ghee every morning, and refrain from any food after seven o'clock in the evening. You need to eat cooling foods, no chilies, spices, no caffeine, everything room temperature so the Agni will be soothed. You understand? The Bhuta is bothering you because it is angry it is not having a life with you. Do not encourage it. Do not engage with it. If it wants to speak, don't respond."

Dr. Shakur gave her some tiny moist pills in a packet.

"This is to strengthen your blood. Come see me next week."

Meterling said goodbye to both the doctor and the woman in the sari.

Together, with Oscar in the Snugli that her mother-in-law got them, the brown pills in her purse, she boarded a bus to buy sweaters at Marks & Spencer for the rest of the family, and then, with all their purchases, took a taxi home.

37

Simon ate crisps out of a packet at the kitchen table, looking at the paper. She put down her packages, transferred Oscar, who was already asleep, to his cot, and returned to the kitchen. Sighing, she slid into a seat and hungrily ate the crisps Simon offered. She liked to douse hers with hot sauce, which Simon complained made them soggy. But Meterling liked her snacks hot. For now, though, she would stay away from spicy foods. Archer appeared almost casually, reading over Simon's shoulder. Salt. She had forgotten about salt.

She fled to the bedroom.

"Meterling, what's wrong?"

But Meterling cried harder into her pillow, her skin damp, her wild, unmanageable hair sticking to forehead and pillows.

"Please, let me in, tell me what's wrong."

For a moment, Meterling lifted her head, but she could see him beyond Simon, smiling. With some force, she embraced Simon, kissing him, thinking that if she were to make love passionately to Simon, Archer would have no choice but to go. "Forgive me, Simon," she said silently, undressing quickly.

"I don't understand you," said Simon, later, buttoning up. "Why won't you tell me what's going on?"

"I went to see an Ayurvedic doctor."

"Why? What's wrong?"

"I can see him, Simon."

"Who, for godsakes?"

"Archer. I can see him. He is always there."

"Archer."

"I know you must think—but I'm not imagining things."

"I've seen him, too."

Meterling stared at Simon.

"At first, I thought I was dreaming, but there he was, opposite me on the train."

"And then you realized it was someone else."

"No, it was Archer. I thought he'd tell me something, bless our marriage, get angry, anything."

"You were on a train."

"Even when I got out at the station."

"What was he wearing, Simon?"

"The white suit he had on at the wedding, with the pink tie."

"Do you think Oscar sees him?"

"I don't know. I've only seen him that once. My scalp started itching."

"My toes tingle before he appears. It's eerie."

"My great-grandfather on my mother's side saw ghosts. He claimed several lived in his house. He said that they were friendly. When I was six, I once visited him with Archer and Susan. He was dying then. He asked me to come close to him. I went near, thinking he'd tell me about them, give me a secret, but all he did was tweak my ear."

Simon rubbed his ear as if it hurt still.

"Archer, Susan, and I combed his house, but we never saw the ghosts."

"He wants me to live on Pi and eat mangoes."

"Archer?"

"Simon, maybe I should invite him to the dinner party, but the doctor said not to interact with him."

"I don't think he needs an invitation."

"I think he wants Oscar."

"Well, he can't have him."

Meterling wiped her eyes. "Mrs. Vickers might leave us if she sees Archer's ghost."

"Mrs. Vickers hasn't seen him."

"Am I being rude, Simon? He left me the house and the fields. Maybe he's lonely, maybe he just wants company."

"His inheritance actually brought us together, Meti. Don't feel guilty about that. The expected hardship for an heir is the estate tax, not the ghost of the deceased."

"Maybe we ought to sell everything."

The next day, Meterling woke rested. She threw back the covers, upsetting Pibs, who had nestled by her ear. It was Diwali and she had not had a nightmare. Maybe Archer's ghost had decided to go away at last. The pale sun lit up the curtains. Her first Diwali with her husband—a tremendous thing. A buffet was the perfect choice. That would be easy. Simon started to laugh, but agreed to help. Mostly that meant chopping vegetables and then staying out of the kitchen. By the time all four burners were on, he decided to take Oscar out, "to get from under your feet."

Having made his escape, my uncle Simon wrapped his scarf closer around his neck, and made sure Oscar was sufficiently bundled but not suffocating. Navigating the buggy, and listening to Oscar's delighted squeals, he remembered how worried he was that he might accidentally drop the baby. Or go to a supermarket and forget him in the car. He had never once dropped him or forgotten him, but the thought plagued him in the rare nightmare. He would then get up and make sure Oscar was breathing.

He missed Archer. The shock had hit him with such force. Archer had been his older brother, the genial advisor. His parents let him do anything if Archer was around, even if they recognized that the latter was more often co-conspirator than chaperone. Archer would keep Simon safe. Archer did keep him safe. It was Archer who introduced him to the first taste of the family gin, and bought him his first packet of condoms. It was Archer who insisted that Simon keep up his studies, who let him use his flat in London later as a place to crash. Archer's flat overlooked the Thames, and when Simon brought his first girlfriends there, they could hear the water lap as they clumsily unwrapped themselves and learned to make love.

It was Archer who pressed upon him *The Tao of Sex* and Henry Miller and *On the Road*. Those books and others occupied the shelves and the floors of Simon's first flat after matriculation. Degree in hand, he wound up not at the great financial houses like his peers, or the courts, but as an intern for Roman Books, a small publisher of volumes about Italy. *A Hundred Ways to Look at Spaghetti* and *Love in Tuscany with a Picnic Hamper* all found themselves between hard covers, and Simon's job was to read through assorted manuscripts, fetch coffee, make coffee, answer phones, and open mail. Soon, he began to write rejection letters: *We are so sorry to have to return your manuscript. It is just not what we are looking for now.* Then back would go the proposal into an envelope helpfully provided with the submission. In a year, he became an assistant editor, and in two, an editor. In three years, he found another house, one that published travel exploits, trekking guides, and garden books. He began and ended affairs with (or was left by) two women he worked alongside: a girl in marketing straight from university, and an assistant who began to arch her eyebrows at him when they passed each other, as if they were sharing a secret joke. The joke was their brief cohabitation; the joke was he never fully satisfied her. So here were her eyebrows, raised upwards, and her eyes widening in their sockets, in the hallways, in the tiny coffee area, expecting his to respond in kind. She left to work at Faber or Penguin or Bloomsbury, and the university student immigrated to the States.

A series of casual hookups followed, but nothing amounted to much. He resolved to become a bachelor, set in his ways, attached to fuzzy slippers on the weekends and dinners at the pub round the corner. He wondered if he could learn to love a pipe as his father did, and spent time in tobacco shops, looking at displays of wood-grained ware. Tobacconists were solid places, he thought, with a hushed quiet, while their proprietors stayed back, only letting out a discreet cough to indicate their presence. In addition to pipes, one could find miniature chess sets, backgammon boards, and fine colognes (their names evoking another era with words like Bay Rum, Lord's Favourite No 10, Trucfitt & Hill), as well as soft leather pouches, tortoiseshell mustache combs, and, of course, an ample selection of cigarettes and cigars. In the end, he decided he wasn't a pipe smoker, though he still liked to stop in the shops for a heady whiff.

Archer wanted him to visit Madhupur, set up a publishing company with island bookbinders. Instead, Simon stayed on in publishing in London for ten years, until he'd had enough and walked away. Now was the time to write his book. He would freelance for local newspapers, but that too became steady. He became "Simon Digs Up," the roving horticulturalist, with a weekly nine-hundred-word column. Susan took him out to lunch his first-year anniversary on the job. She ordered champagne and told him that Archer sounded almost bubbly in his letters.

"Bubbly?"

"Happy. As if he's taking stock of his life and likes what he sees."

"And that's cause for alarm?"

"It is, when he is living halfway around the world and has no intention of returning home."

"Let him be, Susan. Doesn't Archer deserve happiness? And can't you visit to see him?"

"Pi? I don't ever want to go to Pi."

A month later came the wedding invitation, printed on saffron and red paper, most of it in Sanskrit. Sowbhaghyavati Meterling Marries Shri Archer. Blessings, blessings, and more blessings.

Looking at Oscar, he could see Archer's dimples. He had stopped in front of a tobacconist's. His mother said the baby looked exactly like Archer, but his father said he looked like Simon. Simon's heart had opened to Oscar upon his birth; if he analyzed it, it was a combination of grief and joy and a tenderness he didn't know he could feel toward a baby. He wanted to protect him, protect Meterling. Was he being macho? Male pride blustering up ineptly and uselessly, for how could he protect him from accidents, falls, a world that spoke its frustrations with bombs and violence? Just the other day, there was a bomb scare at Waterloo Station. Just like that, he had transformed from a carefree vegetarian in London to a concerned father and husband.

A stylish woman stooped to peer at Oscar, and then at Simon.

"Simon?"

"Estelle."

"Where have you been all this time? Did you—is this your son?"

"Yes, he is, actually. I've become a dad," adding hastily, "and a husband."

"Well, that's wonderful news! And so brave of you."

"Yes, I suppose it is."

"Really brave of you, Simon."

"So, um, this is my son, Oscar."

"He's adorable, that's why I stopped in the first place. Which hospital?"

"Oh, he was born on an island in the Indian Ocean," he said, retrieving the toy that had fallen on the pavement.

"Didn't your cousin—oh, I'm so sorry, I heard."

"Well," said Simon, without thinking about it, "this is actually Archer's son." *Damn.* Why had he said that?

"Oh, you and your wife adopted his son, that's—"

"No—I mean yes, but he's actually her son."

"But I don't understand—how can . . . ?"

"Oh, it's complicated."

"You're married to your cousin's wife, I see—I think it's—"

"I know, brave of me."

"Noble, really. No—really. Practically medieval, if you think about it."

She laughed—out of embarrassment, Simon hoped.

"Well . . ."

"Yes . . ."

"So good . . ."

"Absolutely."

Damn Estelle. And why did he ever feel the need to say this was Archer's son? Now, the whole damn publishing industry would know. Well, so what if they knew? He had fallen in love with his late cousin's wife. He adopted Oscar. It was simple. God, wasn't it Estelle who used to tease him at Berkham's with

"Simple Simon," how did it go? The rhyme would enter his brain like a worm all day, he thought, and he wouldn't remember the words.

"Oscar, what do you say we go get a slice of pie?"

They went to American Pudding, a well-lit café, and found a table. This was where many mothers and fathers came with their children, and the babble was loud. Then again, everything was loud in London, the buzz of a world city.

From his rucksack, Simon fished out a bottle of breast milk. Oscar was only semi-interested. A few more months and they could start solid foods. He met his pie with relish. Nearby, a six-year-old boy was squabbling with his sister over chocolate while their mother sat wearily in front of her tea.

"You took big bites and Mummy said we were to share."

"She didn't say anything about the size of our bites."

"Mummy!"

Their mother had laid her head down on the table.

At another table, a kind of fathers' group converged with assorted youngsters in nappies whose voices competed with one another.

"If I were back at work, I couldn't afford the time—"

"I know what you mean. Here she's getting promoted, and I'm left at home all day."

"But who can afford the child care if we do get back to work? For godsake, Timothy, give the train to Jonathan!"

Oscar was now sucking his bottle with more interest. A dinner party. Simon had nearly forgotten.

That morning, he had risen early with Oscar, to find Meterling already up. She heated sesame oil in a small pan and, pouring it into a tiny bowl, handed it to him for the Diwali oil bath.

"You could come in with us," he'd suggested.

"Not with the baby. My grandmother would faint."

"We won't tell her."

But Meterling shook her head no, and so together, they bathed Oscar in the sink, massaging the oil into his skin so he gleamed.

"Look, he loves this."

"A born pasha."

Sometimes she felt, Meterling said, she could eat his toes, his plump legs and arms, he was such a dumpling.

They dressed him in his new striped blue onesie (the kurta was for the party) and tiny fuzzy socks. Simon received a shirt and sweater, while Meterling wore the new sari; she would change into something else while cooking. Oil baths, new clothes, sweets and lights for Diwali, Festival of Lights, to welcome wisdom and common sense in everyone.

Now Oscar wore a wool baby coat and baby shoes, a baby scarf and hat and mittens. A dumpling.

"I probably look like one, too, these days, the way your mother cooks," Simon told his son. "Let's go and get her flowers."

38

There was an old florist's off Marylebone High Street, and its bell clanged as Simon and the stroller entered. The woman who ran the place, Birdie Bee, looked like she had decided to remain sixty-five forever. Her silver hair was pulled back, her face refreshed with lipstick, and she wore a smock from whose pockets peered sprigs of something yellow, and green marking tags. She crouched down to greet Oscar with the grace of a woman who had practiced yoga from the very start. Birdie used to sell seashells by the seashore, as she liked to tell people, in a small store in Blackpool. Then she married, moved to Oxford, and learned the city by bike. There was a photograph of a laughing, smiling girl in a tartan tam on a bicycle with a basket in front. After her husband was killed in the war, she came to London with her children to stay at her sister's, and bought the shop dirt-cheap. She still rode a bicycle, with clips and a helmet and a basket in front.

In the center of the store, artfully arranged nosegays and bouquets, featuring dried pods and tight rosebuds, were featured on a table. The *Westminster Watch* described this as the place where the cabinet wives got their arrangements. On the back walls, a profusion of blooms fell from long metal buckets, arranged according to color. Where did one get lilacs this time of year? Yet there they were, cut bunches in water alongside wreaths made of bay leaves and lavender. Roses of every color had their own display, framed by hydrangeas and branches of evergreen.

"Parrot tulips," she suggested at once when Simon described what he needed. "Look at these, just perfect for autumn," gesturing to a row of flame-colored flowers with feathery tips. They were startling, maybe too showy, but it was Diwali, and they resembled lanterns in their way. In fact, Chinese lanterns made sense as well, plus winterberry. Birdie wrapped the flowers in brown paper and string and expertly tucked the package into the stroller, wishing him a good dinner as an early firecracker burst somewhere nearby.

Outside, the post-lunch crowd had thickened as shoppers hurried to the butcher's, the cheese shops, the patisseries. World cities never slept, but they had rhythms, waves controlled by business hours. Two major rush hours, a surge during lunchtime. Other than that, it was open to tourists and the self- or unemployed, who tarried on the sidewalks, waited at the gates for the guards to change or for a glimpse of the prime minister. He waited to cross the street with Oscar; his heart was immense. A year ago, he was miserable, about work, about love, and then the devastation of Archer's death. Now, he had a marvelous life: a wife, a son. At the palace, the flag was up.

39

Meterling kneaded the dough for chapatis and put it under a wet cloth in a bowl: after pinching them into a dozen or so little balls, Simon would roll them out into rounds, or near-rounds, and she would cook each one on a hot griddle. The boiled potatoes had cooled as she was making the dough. She rough-chopped them, and then coated them with a dry rub of turmeric, chili, and salt. Getting out a large pan, she popped black mustard seed in oil, sizzled cumin and asafetida, and threw in the onions Simon had chopped earlier. She added the potatoes, and after things had browned a bit, frozen spinach, and later, tomatoes. She covered the lid; in twenty minutes, she would have a wet curry. How easy it was to cook. In truth, if she did have a passion outside of her passion for Oscar and Simon, it would be cooking. She had met a food demonstrator at Sainsbury's who cooked kebabs on an electric grill. She wouldn't mind being a demonstrator—this is the way to make dosa, this is how to make pakoras. She knew there were Indian and Bangladeshi aunties who offered home cooking to students far from home, naan for pickup, curry to go. Why couldn't she do something like that, after Oscar was ready for a baby minder?

She would give herself time to dress. Last night, she had taken out a seam in her petticoat, thankful for the efforts of Mr. Wali, her family's tailor, who always had the foresight to make three sets of stitches in his clothing, knowing his clientele's need to adjust. She had not lost all of the pregnancy weight, and in London she tucked into more food than was necessary, tucked so it showed on her body. Now, in addition to being tall and brown in London, she was becoming large. She didn't mind. She rinsed the rice at the sink. Still, the only large women society seemed to accept were pregnant ones; all others were seen as incapable of controlling their urges, lacking discipline. Susan went to the gym six days a week, ate a diet of "twigs and leaves" according to Simon, but she did look smashing (what a word, "smashing," Meterling thought, smiling, because it was one of Thakur's favorite words) in her tall boots, slicked-back hair, her artful clothes. Meterling added water, a bay leaf, cumin powder, and lit the gas underneath the stockpot.

"Indian women are lucky—the sari hides all the imagined faults of our bodies," Susan had once said. Meterling hadn't bothered to remind her that she meant "island," not "Indian," because Susan was speaking of her. In Britain, everyone assumed she was Indian, and she had begun to let it go. Auntie Pa would bristle, saying Pi had enough of an identity crisis without its own citizens contributing to it.

Why was it Susan and she were so awkward around each other? Uncle Darshan would say that it was the old way of sisters-in-law, but there seemed to be more to Susan's hostility. True, they had not begun on best terms. What had she said—"Did you have to needlessly ask him to dance?"? But sitting out the dance would not have prevented the aneurysm. It was waiting in his brain, building and readying to burst. Susan had been livid at the wedding, but meeting Oscar had changed that. She was not certain how to act around him at first, but Oscar, bless him, just grabbed her pinkie in his fist and would not let go. She was utterly charmed and then and there became his. Her mother-in-law, Nora, had not been won over so completely. Oscar was Archer's child, and sometimes she made it emphatic, saying to Meterling "your child," which caused Simon to shout, and John to pick up their coats and throw back an apologetic look.

"Yes, he is my child, but why should it bother her so much?" Meterling asked. "He is your child, too. Archer never knew him," which led to tears she blinked furiously away.

Susan generally ignored Meterling, heading right to Oscar when she visited, bearing baby clothes and toys, which she tumbled onto any available surface. How easily women sting each other over men, when they should be embracing one another. Was any man worth the trouble? Yes, she had married Archer, and yes, she had married Simon, and yes, yes, yes, she was still here in the family, she had not gone away. Civility was the thin line between love and hate, was it not? Couldn't Susan and she maintain détente—oh, couldn't Susan just accept and move forward?

She looked at the next set of vegetables. Simon had cut the sweet potatoes into hexagons, and sliced the Brussels sprouts in half. He hadn't complained that morning, singing as he wielded the knife, saying he always wanted to be a sous-chef. Curries in his post-university days meant takeaways, or cheap dinners in places full of plastic tables and luridly colored plastic chairs. Meterling had taught him, among other things, the sensuality of eating, the slow process of letting the fragrance enter the nostrils, the anticipation of the tongue. He learned to take his time. They fed each other midnight samosas while Oscar slept in his crib. "Imagine if the erotic Indian miniatures featured food instead of phalluses," she said, but Simon rolled his eyes. He said, "Sometimes, there are no substitutions, my love." They had argued that point well into the night.

She braised the vegetables, seasoning them with only salt and pepper, a counterpoint to the rice and saag. Maybe they could serve small glasses of mango lassi to start, but they'd have to use paper cups. So they'll use paper cups—the pleasure is in the content, not the container, Grandmother would say. She wondered if she should have invited a friend or two of Simon's, the ones from his university days who hid half their words, so she could never follow the whole of the conversation, or the ones from work. Next year, perhaps.

Meterling turned the rice onto a platter to season with lemon and spice. Turmeric would turn it light yellow; she'd keep plain rice on hand as well, and maybe she ought to do a coconut rice as well—there was shredded coconut in the freezer. People tended not to take big portions at parties, but still, she wanted enough. She was careful to keep aside portions for herself that were bland, according to Dr. Shakur's instructions, and she reminded herself, no wine.

If Archer had to materialize, now would be the time, but the apartment was quiet, and she told herself, she would not be spooked.

Susan. She was far from the point of going shopping with Susan, the things women must do together in this country (well, their tastes would be different), but sometimes, Susan stole out of the office to share a sandwich with her and Oscar in Hyde Park. She even baby-sat one night so Simon and she could see a movie. They had returned, hardly able to watch the film, to find Susan holding a fast-asleep Oscar in her lap, listening to Bach. Susan had looked after them, he and Archer, Simon told Meterling; in the way, perhaps, she, Meterling, had looked after Nalani. Motherless daughters. Meterling had asked Susan to bring a dessert to complement the tea cake she bought at the bakery yesterday. Would Susan bring Tom? She had, last time she was over, giddy in a short white dress and long gold hoops. He was—an investment banker? An equities trader? Something with computers?

She'd need another curry—the takeaway, then. The dal! She'd forgotten the dal. Quickly, she found the saucepan and got to work.

Auntie Pa would be astonished that she had cooked the entire meal herself. Well, with Simon's help. Where was he anyway? She hoped he'd remembered to feed the baby. Sitting down, finished at last, she realized how tired she was. She would draw a hot bath while it was still quiet. It was five o'clock, and dinner was at seven. She looked at the bookcases, bulging with books. She wanted a good novel to read slowly at night, something to sustain her, since she had finished the one she had been reading. When Oscar used to sleep in fits and starts those first weeks before adjusting, they thought, to the English weather, they'd read to one another from a copy of *Middlemarch* Uncle Darshan had presented them.

Wiping her hands on a dishtowel, she took down a book. She hardly had any time to read. Oscar now slept through the night, though the doctor said the pattern might change again. She'd place the book on the nightstand at least, so she could begin after the party. It slipped a little from her hand—was she that tired?—and a postcard came fluttering out. It had a picture of the Eiffel Tower with "Paris" written across it in fin-de-siècle script. She turned it over. It was addressed to Archer. The script was a hasty scrawl. "Darling! Join me! I am lonely for your arms! Mouxx." There was a large heart underneath the message.

She felt a jolt. Of course he had had a life before her, how could he not, but the postcard felt predatory, claiming "I was here first, he was mine before you." Was she French? Mouxx? Was that really a name? Was it Mou, with two kisses? She slipped the book, *"A Study in Scarlet" & Other Stories*, back, but on second thought, took the postcard out to dispose of it later, and carried the book to the bedroom. More importantly, she thought, did Archer go by hovercraft to Paris to this Mouxx's, an overnight bag in his hand? Was he already fat then, and was she tiny like a mouse? Did he lie on top of her, gathering her to him? Meterling's anger, sudden, strong, surprised her. She had never before felt such rage against Archer, leaving her, leaving Mouxx, alone, lonely. Her anger ached. What if Simon hadn't felt the need to come to Pi? What if he had just accepted her silence, written a letter, withdrawn? No more questions. It was the Festival of Lights. A new start.

As she filled the tub with very hot water, throwing Epsom salts in, she noticed how full the Boston fern had become. They had a tiny window in the bathroom that was three-quarters covered by a gnarled wisteria, which let in a little light, but the plant must thrive on the steam. Mouxx. What *did* that mean? A mouth pursed up for a kiss? She suddenly pictured a waggling bottom, a—what were they called?—a feather boa—and thought, I'm jealous of a ghost. She lowered herself into the tub, relishing the heat. Her skin seemed to melt into the water. Twenty minutes would be all she needed.

40

Forty-five minutes later, Simon came in with Oscar as Meterling wrapped a towel around herself, after pulling out the bath plug. Her dark skin glistened. Her hair in a turban, she greeted her family in the living room, Simon undoing Oscar's buttons.

"Look at his rosy cheeks! Simon, where have you been all this time?"

"We ate pie. While you have been luxuriating in a bubbly tub . . ."

"Pie! We have—"

"Dinner, I know. Look, I brought flowers."

She exclaimed over the tulips, bent to give them both kisses, and rushed to dress Oscar in his new kurta. She wondered if the material was soft enough. If he fussed, she'd change him, she promised herself, feeling a little guilty. He gave her a smile, and pumped his arms. She kissed his toes—her *baby*. Simon put away the stroller and put the kettle on. He told her about running into Estelle as Meterling tied her petticoat. The bell rang as she was arranging the pleats on her sari. Simon's parents. Quickly, she brushed her hair and joined them as they surrounded Oscar with their attention.

"I thought I'd bring a little extra food, darling, just in case," said Nora, thrusting a grocery bag in Simon's hands, even as she reached for Oscar.

"But you didn't have to—"

"Just some salads, that's all. Potato and curried cream, and deviled eggs on endive."

Meterling took the food to the table, and unpacked the pretty glass bowls. What was endive? She hoped it was not non-veg. Nora never quite believed she was capable of feeding Simon, just as she was not convinced Simon was truly vegetarian. She had even provided serving spoons. The door rang again, and it was Dr. Morgan—Kavita—and her partner, Lisa. Meterling was surprised both that her partner was a woman and that she was the receptionist from the office, the one who'd shown surprise at her height.

Simon bundled everyone's coats to the bedroom while Meterling served tiny glasses of pineapple juice. They awkwardly sat in the living room, eyes glued on Oscar, until conversation slowly began to build.

"So, are you girls roommates?" Nora asked Kavita and Lisa.

"Well, we're partners, really."

"Partners in crime, eh?" asked John.

"Partners as in common law."

"Ah."

Everyone drank a little more pineapple juice.

"Well, I definitely approve," said Nora, brightly.

"It's not a matter of approval—" began Lisa.

"The weather has been awful, lately," said John, to no one in particular, and Kavita hastily agreed.

Kavita and Lisa had been together eight years, and yes, they lived together almost from the beginning, in North London, near Camden Town. No, they had bought the property a while back, with help from Kavita's parents. Simon's mother wondered if her son and his wife might do the same, while his father said no, it's too late for that, now, they'd have to try farther out, unless they wanted a fixer-upper.

"A fixer-upper?"

"DIY. Hammers, nails, plumbing."

Simon seemed to be excited by the idea, but his father said he ought to just take over Archer's old flat, instead of renting it out.

"Your family will start growing, and you'll need the space," he said.

"But they want to make new memories, John."

"How can you make new memories? A memory has to be old by its very nature. In any case, you can take over the old home, and Nora and I will get a little pied-à-terre in the city. What do you say, dear, we can trip the light fantastic?"

"How is your family, my dear? The young couple that wed?"

Nalani, she told them, wrote often.

"She is happy with the boy."

"Didn't she love someone else?" asked Simon.

"What? Tell us the story," asked Nora.

"No story. She had a schoolgirl crush on a boy in her class. Well, maybe more than a crush."

"Their horoscopes didn't match," said Simon.

Meterling glared at him. Now she would have to explain horoscopes and matches.

"It's difficult for some young women to say no to their family's wishes," said Kavita.

"Some? You mean most," said Lisa.

"Well, yes, most. They're raised to follow their family's wishes, not risk love marriages."

"Your parents didn't object, Dr. Morgan?"

"Call me Kavita. Well, they were upset for a while. Lisa and I as a couple are illegal in my country, you know. But I had done all the other so-called right things—went through medical school, had a job, and lived abroad."

"Didn't they want you to return after the degree?"

"Yes, to look at prospective boys, but I stalled them until I finally told them."

"At first, her parents pretended they hadn't heard. I told Kavi it wasn't that important."

"But I wanted them to know. Maybe I wanted, like all good Indian girls, their blessings."

"You must have received them, if they helped you buy a house."

"That was my father. He came around sooner than my mother."

Susan interrupted the conversation, arriving at the door with gaily wrapped champagne and a plush toy for the baby. Simon met and quickly embraced her.

"How is it going?"

"There's been only one palpable hit so far," he said in a low voice. "And you should try to go in unarmed, for once."

Susan made a face, and moved past him, and presented the bottle and toy to Meterling. She also brought along a copy of Neela Chandrashekar's latest book of poetry, which she'd bookmarked to a poem called "Birth Channel," underneath which was printed "Dedicated to my brave Meterling."

"I found it at Blackwell's," said Susan. "I was looking for Blake, but I pulled this out, paged through it, and imagine my surprise. This is you, isn't it?"

Meterling had never had a poem dedicated to her before and was flustered and pleased. The poem spoke of passage and water and rebirth. Simon said he wasn't quite sure what the poem meant; Susan said his reaction was certainly psychological, since to her, the poem was very clear and actually quite moving. Surprisingly, Kavita knew the poet's work, having found some of her books in a shop in Madurai.

"And to think you know her! She seems very mysterious, very passionate," the doctor remarked.

"I don't read much poetry, or fiction, for that matter. Nora reads novels, but I like history," said John, settling into his chair.

4I

By the time drinks were poured, Oscar looked ready to sleep. This was the tricky part, because she would need a good half-hour to feed him and put him to bed. She never got used to the idea of nursing in front of her in-laws, even though Susan had friends, she said, who seemed to delight in the show. Maybe they were just tired of making it seem so mysterious. She shut the bedroom door. Oscar's wispy head grew heavy with sleep as she eased his mouth away, and put him in his crib. She wondered if she should just put him in his bouncy in the living room, but knew Nora or John would wander in and check on him, if not Simon or Susan. This was her family, after all, who even if they might question her at times, would forgive Oscar everything. He looked peaceful; his eyes closed with baby swollenness, his hair just a little damp. She could not imagine life without him, she thought, bending to give him another kiss.

John forgot the punch line of the joke midway through telling it, but seemed not at all embarrassed. Even Dr.—Kavita—and Lisa laughed at his delight. Seated at dinner—not a buffet after all—she was glad she had made raita the night before. There was her labor before her, in large and small dishes: the lentils, the rice, the two kinds of vegetables, the raita, and the parathas that Susan and Simon must have made—no! It was Kavita and Lisa, it turned out, to her chagrin.

"We had so much fun in the kitchen—please don't mind!"

"I hadn't made parathas in years" said Kavita, adding apologetically that she got hers from Sainsbury's.

"These are out of this world," Susan added hastily, forestalling any more blushes on Meterling's part.

Nora's salads were good as well, as it turned out—she had known that Nora was a good cook, a fact that always had intimidated and slightly irritated her, but now she was grateful her salads and eggs were on the table. Everyone dug in. Later, there was quite a bit of lemon rice left in its bowl, though, and she wondered if she had added enough salt. Only John filled his plate with it twice, while Nora remarked on his delicate stomach.

"Thank goodness Simon was a good eater," she said. "I'd serve feasts for the three of them—back when even you liked to eat, Susan."

Susan delicately forked some Brussels sprouts. Simon hid a smile.

"Don't laugh, Simon. It's true; I'd make Christmas dinners and cook for weeks. The pudding alone took a month, and when the children were little, we'd have lovely roasted goose and ham."

"No vegetables," said Simon, helping himself to more dal.

"Don't be ridiculous, Simon, of course there were vegetables. I'd do a very nice swede-and-sweet-potato bake, and we had jellied beets, of course. Brussels sprouts as well, but none of you except Archer liked those. Archer loved my Brussels sprouts, poor boy. We ate Christmas dinner together, our two families, but I did most of the cooking. Those were wonderful times—you children so sweet in your dress clothes. No one really dresses up anymore, do they? And hardly ever was food spilled on the napkins. Well, the meals were tasty, if I say so myself. But this meal is just lovely, dear."

"My father liked fiery curries."

The table turned to John.

"He started the day with eggs, but in the evenings, it was always a biryani or a curry."

"That was because of Rekha," said Nora, reaching for more wine.

"The actress?" asked Meterling.

"No. So, Archer didn't tell you?" asked Susan.

The table was quiet only for a moment, before the Forsters began speaking at once.

"She was more like a wife to him."

"She was seventeen when my father met her, and Mummy was still alive. It killed her."

"It didn't kill her. Aunt May never liked India or Pi, and that's why she stayed in Craywick."

"She caught pneumonia."

"Her constitution was very delicate, Susan. She might have died of anything. Malaria."

"How could she die of malaria in England?"

"Bronchitis then—Susan, this is ghoulish."

"Uncle John!"

"I'm being honest, Susie, not disrespectful."

"How can you discuss Daddy's bloody mistress and not see that as disrespectful?"

"Susan!" said Simon.

Susan rolled her eyes and looked away, while my aunt Meterling stared at John.

"I saw your mother once, after she died," offered Nora.

They turned to her.

"She was following Mrs. Vickers—oh, how is she working out, Meterling?"

"Fine, fine. Actually—"

"Anyway, she was following Mrs. Vickers—"

"You saw my mother?"

"I did. I was helping close up the big house after your father died, Susan, and Mrs. Vickers came up with another woman to clean. I was unpacking the dusters to place over the furniture, and I saw something out of the corner of my eye. I followed her following Mrs. Vickers as she scrubbed the entryway floor. The poor woman had her back to me, stooped over her pail and brush, and as she made her way to the stairs, there was May, following as well."

"What did you do?"

"Oh, I left and went back to what I was doing. I felt like I was intruding, really," said Nora.

"I would have spoken to Mummy! I wish—" said Susan, her eyes filling with tears she hurriedly blinked away. "Anyway, she's gone."

"Can you pass the wine, Mother?" asked Simon.

"Have some curry, girls," said John.

Lisa received the bowl of sweet potatoes, saying, "I love Indian food. Kavi likes Chinese, so we go a lot to the fusion places. The only thing I won't eat are some of the, ah—more demanding—dim sum, but Kavi loves it all."

"My parents used to cook Chinese food. They were in Penang for quite some time," said Kavita.

"Oh, my grandfather worked in Malaysia, but I think it was

Kuala Lumpur," said Meterling, thinking, *The Gin King had an island mistress! No wonder Susan dislikes me.*

"But you're from Pi, right? That's a really nice place," said Lisa.

Meterling smiled.

"It's like a little lost in time. Lisa and I went there, oh, three years ago? We stayed at a hotel on the beach south of Trippi and had a lovely time."

"Well, except our hotel room was robbed, but luckily we had our passports in the hotel safe."

"So the hotel safe was safe but the hotel itself wasn't?" asked John.

Lisa shrugged.

"Well, you might go to Meterling's town next time, although John and I like Tuscany. Simon edited a book on Tuscany once—didn't you, dear?—and we became hooked," said Nora.

The stories of Rekha and May's ghost were folded away.

Amid all the chatter, Meterling noted how quickly the meal was eaten. Simon kept refilling everyone's glasses with Riesling, which went well with the food. The champagne was long gone. Oscar was sound asleep. Funny how it had taken her so much time in the kitchen, but in two hours, everyone was done and waiting for dessert. She sliced the cake, added fruit, and arranged the sweets on small dishes to pass out, while Simon put on the coffee. Suddenly she felt a longing for him that surprised her with its ferocity. If they hadn't guests, she would go over and embrace him. As it was, she drank a small glass of water, and went to pass the plates.

Kavita was explaining Diwali.

"Some people see it as the time Rama returned after exile and the war to his rightful kingdom."

"And Rama is an avatar of Vishnu?" asked Nora.

"Yes."

"But your family connects it to the story of the demon king, completely unrelated to the *Ramayana*," said Lisa.

"Right. The story is that once there was a king, Narakasura, who kept praying to Shiva, and became more and more corrupt as his power, which actually stemmed from the amount of penance and prayer he had stored up as a young devotee of Shiva, grew. Anyway, Narakasura began to lead a fairly awful, debauched life, and started wreaking havoc on not only his subjects but on everyone and -thing around him. No one could stop him because of the boons he'd received."

"He stole earrings from the mother of the gods," said Meterling.

"Right, he stole from the gods, he pillaged other kingdoms, and he raped sixteen thousand daughters of the minor gods and goddesses."

"Sixteen thousand?"

"Yes. Finally, the gods went to Vishnu, who I think in the form of Krishna slew Narakasura."

"Another legend has it that Krishna could only defeat the demon as an incarnation of Lakshmi herself, who was churned out of the ocean a few days before, but I might be mixing up the stories," said Meterling.

"I've heard that as well."

"But tell the ending."

"So, as Narakasura lay dying, he came to his senses, and praised Vishnu for killing him and stopping the violence of the night. He asked that his death be marked with celebration, with lights, and feasting, and joy, so you have Diwali. As for the sixteen thousand women, they were deemed too sullied for marriage, so Krishna took them into his own harem, and apparently, they became sages."

A loud burst of firecrackers punctuated her words.

"So Diwali is a day of celebration, of washing away old wrongs, wearing new clothes and starting afresh," said Meterling.

"What an interesting story. I love fireworks, but John sometimes thinks they are too much like the bombing in the war," said Nora.

"That's right, but Nora, I don't dislike fireworks, especially tonight," said John.

"He loves to contradict me," she said.

That was when the air turned damp, the tea lights began to flicker, and my aunt Meterling's toes began to tingle.

Archer appeared as Simon's parents continued to eat, as Lisa and Kavita discussed acupuncture with Susan, and Simon rubbed his head.

"I'm sorry I'm late!"

My aunt's eyes widened.

"You didn't think I'd not show up to my wife's first dinner party."

"Ex-wife," she muttered under her breath. Could Simon see him?

"You will always be my wife, until—"

"Death us do part."

"What? Whose death?" asked John.

"John, you have a smudge of curry on your lip, dear," said Nora.

Meterling excused herself to bring more water to the table.

She refilled the jug in the kitchen, while Archer watched her.

"Archer, this is becoming impossible. I don't mean to be rude, but you can't just keep showing up whenever you like. It's—embarrassing."

He frowned.

"Embarrassing?"

"I start to speak to you, and people will begin to think I'm crazy. It's bad enough I'm tall."

"You never felt bad about your height."

"Don't change the subject. Anyway, you know I am no longer your wife. Why can't I have some life of my own?"

"What kind of life is this, Meti? Away from your family, your home."

"This is my home."

"London? London can't be your home. How will you stand the cold? You'll shiver in your sari. And what will you wear on your feet?"

"I'll wear a coat, Archer, and I'll wear boots."

"You can't be serious! Your beautiful skin will turn raw and red—"

"I had no idea you felt I couldn't take care of myself, as if I don't know how to protect myself from the elements."

"No, that's not what I mean. You don't belong here, that's all."

"You mean I *can't* belong here, that I'll never fit in because *you* never fit in."

"I wanted to give you everything, treat you like my queen, bathe your feet at night—"

"And where were you when my feet got tired and swollen during my pregnancy? Where were you when I had to tell my grandmother that I was pregnant? Were you there to witness her disappointment in me? Her heartbreak over you, the noble Gin King's son, the gentleman who promised to prove her trust? Her utter despondence at the fate that awaited me, a barely wed single parent?"

"I would give my life again to have spared you—"

"But you *did* give up your life, you did!"

"Meterling—"

Simon came to the doorway, hearing Meterling's voice from the kitchen. He saw Archer at the counter. He hesitated. He longed to go in and have a few words with him, if not throw a punch, but this was Meterling's conversation, not his, he told himself. They had to resolve things by themselves. Plus, he couldn't very well throw a punch at a ghost, could he? He returned to the table and made a remark about loud neighbors as he reseated himself.

"Which is why you should move," said Nora.

Meterling continued to address the ghost.

"How *can* you appear like this? It's one thing to haunt me, but Simon—how dare you! Don't you have any conscience? The man I married would never have pulled a childish stunt like this, coming to a party unannounced, intruding on our lives—"

"Meterling—"

"No, you must hear this! You can't disrupt our lives." She took a breath. "It took me months to get adjusted, to acknowledge you were gone. I nearly—I nearly went over the edge, and then, like a miracle, Oscar was born—ten little toes and ten little fingers. Yes, he's your child, but you died! Another miracle occurred; I opened my heart to Simon. My husband, Simon, your baby cousin."

"Simon—" began Archer.

"And who else do you think I'd have married? Only the kindest, gentlest man I know, the only one who loved you so deeply we could not even speak critically about you out of fear of hurting the other."

"Is this a marriage, Meterling? Where you walk on eggshells—"

"But we don't—we don't. Where did you get that idea? *We*—you and I—might have—we don't know," said my aunt. And though she could have burst into tears, she did not. She tried to look beyond Archer's ghost, see through him, as if he were a veil hiding a vista that she needed to witness clearly.

Then she turned around, marched out of the room, and rejoined her guests.

They did not seem in better shape than she did.

Susan was in tears.

Meterling was startled. She'd never seen Susan cry.

"Look here, now, Susan, pull yourself together. And you, Simon, look after your wife, she looks like she's seen a ghost!" said John.

"Was there any reason to bring up Rekha again, Aunt Nora?" continued Susan, ignoring Meterling.

"Susan—"

"Don't 'Susan' me, Simon. Archer's—" Susan stopped, biting her lip.

"It's all right, Susan, Archer's gone," said Meterling. Simon glanced at her.

"I was going to say, *Meterling*, that Archer is the only one who understood how I felt about Rekha."

"But I thought he liked her, darling."

"He tolerated her, Aunt Nora. We both tolerated her. And if he were alive, if he hadn't died so abruptly, so prematurely, he'd—he'd still be here."

"Susan—" began Simon.

"Don't 'Susan' me, Simon! If only Daddy had never set sight on bloody, bloody Muddy-pur!"

Simon started to laugh.

"I'm sorry, I can't help it," he told an alarmed Meterling, laughing some more, even as Susan excused herself from the table. Meterling followed her.

"He's so beautiful. It's so unfair," she said, looking at Oscar as he slept, oblivious.

Meterling nodded.

"It *is* unfair, Susan."

"Simon doesn't get it."

Shaking her head, my aunt led Susan to the bathroom and rummaged for a towel. Susan washed and dried her face. Meterling wondered what Kavita and Lisa must be thinking.

"I suppose you think I'm crazy," said Susan.

"Why would anyone think that?"

"It shouldn't still wound like that. So my father had a mistress."

"I don't think you can ever predict the emotional consequences of what our parents might or might not do," said Meterling carefully.

Susan bit her lip before speaking.

"Look, I know I've been pretty ghastly to you. It's just that I didn't want another heartbreak caused by some Indian woman . . ."

Meterling didn't say anything.

"God, I'm sorry—I didn't mean it that way," said Susan.

"You probably did," said Meterling.

Susan cracked a smile. "Yeah, I probably did."

"And we don't have to examine the inherent racism in your upbringing."

"Thank you, Meterling."

"Not today, anyway."

Susan dried her hands.

"I feel his presence sometimes, Meti," said Susan, using the diminutive for the first time.

Meterling hesitated, then said, "I sometimes think I see him. I don't think I'll see him again, though."

"It's probably natural, like the way when you are in a new city and you think you see old friends in the crowd," said Susan.

A burst of noise interrupted them. The Diwali fireworks from Neasden Temple had started.

"C'mon, let's make the most of it. Let's go outside and watch the display," said Meterling.

Going back to join the others, they saw the silvery remains of a burst of color at the window. It was a welcome distraction, and Kavita and Lisa looked less uncomfortable. After they trooped outside, Simon took a quick look back to see if Archer was around, but the room was empty. But why was his scalp itching? He heard a sigh.

"Why her, Simon?"

"Who else, Arch?"

"She was my wife."

"She was. I don't forget that."

"I would have—"

"No you wouldn't have. You wouldn't have kept away. You'd have swept her off her feet and absconded into the night."

"Unlike you."

"We didn't sneak away. Look, yes, Meti was your wife first. She will always be your wife first. And Oscar is your son. But he's my son, too. For godsake Archer, you're dead!"

"I know I'm dead!"

"Then bloody the hell leave us alone!"

"Simon."

Simon turned at Meterling's approach. She took his hand and led him outside.

In the garden, Simon lit the wicks in the pots lining the walls, and the effect was magical. Meterling squeezed Simon's hand.

"We used to set off firecrackers all day, my brothers and I," said Kavita. "Do you remember Diwali medicine?"

"What's that?" asked Nora.

"A digestive concoction—with, let's see, cumin and salt and honey—"

"Ginger and cardamom and camphor—" added Meterling. "Wretched tasting. But with all the sweets we'd eat, we needed something to counteract it all."

"Diwali medicine," said Kavita, breaking into laughter.

Meterling's guests stood on the steps to gaze at the pyrotechnical effects in the sky. Other corners of the city provided their own small bursts of garden fireworks—*pattasu* was the imitative word in Tamil for the *pat-pat-pat swoosh*—spiraling into plumes or confetti, unfurling into flowers. Like fairy lights, they sparkled into the sky, to disappear with noise. Light to usher in light after darkness.

Meterling loved fireworks as well and felt glad now, in a rush, to be away from Pi, where they might have had to travel to someone else's home to celebrate, following grief custom, and in the end, not feel like celebrating at all. On Pi, Nalani and Ajay, now asleep, would have already celebrated their first festival together. She leaned against Simon and he put his arm around her.

By the time goodbyes were being said, the talk was warmer than it had been all evening. Maybe because everyone was physically warmer, looked forward to their beds, and had survived an evening out with *company*, as well as an evening with memories, hearty promises to call and visit were made. Susan would meet Kavita and Lisa for tea; Susan would baby-sit Oscar; Susan would call on her aunt Nora more often.

"Bye," said Susan, surprising Meterling with a quick kiss on the lips. "It was, all in all, quite a party." One by one, they concurred.

"Happy Diwali!" shouted John as he helped Nora up the stairs. Sounds of firecrackers could still be heard in the dark; parties all over England were being held to celebrate the ushering-in of light after darkness.

Meterling went into the other room and scooped up Oscar, who stirred a bit, yawned, and went back to sleep. She should have done so the minute Archer appeared, she told herself, putting him back down.

"I will protect you with my life," she told Oscar.

42

In bed that night, Meterling let loose her desire ferociously, leaving Simon a little breathless and surprised. Later, he raised himself onto an elbow and gazed at his wife.

"What, my love?" he asked.

"Do you think he's gone?"

"I don't know. I hope so. I hope he's gone for good. I loved Archer, but—"

"I know."

"You can ask your ayurvedic doc when you go back to him."

"Hmm." She placed her hand on his chest. "Sometimes, I think we should take Oscar back to Pi."

"So you can eat mangoes?"

"Don't be absurd! But—I don't fit in, Simon! I wear the wrong clothes, I make the wrong foods—"

"What are you talking about? You looked gorgeous tonight—Susan especially envies your saris, and the food was bloody brilliant. She didn't mean what she said, you know."

"I don't know. She's protective, just like Archer. But Oscar—doesn't he deserve to grow up with his cousins?"

"They're all a decade older than him . . . Meti, I don't understand, aren't you happy here?"

"I'm happy with you. I'm happy with your family. I'm glad I'm getting to know Dr. Morgan—"

"Weren't you surprised when her partner turned out to be a woman?"

"Her receptionist. She's beautiful, isn't she? Simon, don't get me off track."

"I don't want to live in Madhupur."

"Why?"

"It's not my home. This is my place with you, with us. My job, everything."

"And how am I to cope, without my family? Your uncle had a mistress from Pi."

"What does that have to do with anything? I don't understand, you were so passionate just a while ago, and now you're so upset."

"Do you think that woman had a chance to say no? If she was working for him, and the boss wanted her, what power did she have to refuse? She might have even been married, with children."

"It's such an old story, Meti," said Simon, rolling onto his back.

"But it explains Susan's anger toward Pi."

"C'mon, don't worry about all that." He tried to put his arms around her, but she shrugged him off. "Didn't I promise you I would always hold you tight when you needed it, be your strength as you are mine?"

"It's just odd. I never thought of your family as having anything they'd be ashamed of, except, well—"

"Us? You mean the only strange thing is us." He paused. "My family has owned a gin distillery for over two hundred years, which I know to you is not a great deal of time, since you yourself are descended from one of thirteen original sages a millennium ago—"

"Shut up!"

He kissed her ear. "The thing is, our history is wretched. We've led masses of people to ruin their lives with alcoholism, we have twisted personal lives—there are stories!—and we continue on. Our lives are messy. Everything is messy, you know that. By the way, what was that poem about? Is Neela in love with you?"

"She's in love with everyone. She's protective, too. Simon, who's Mouxx?"

"What?"

"There was a postcard—look, it was stuck in this book."

"God, I thought I threw that out years ago." He frowned. "Archer—it was a long time ago," he replied, shutting his eyes again.

"Tell me."

"Archer wanted to marry her—decades ago. She was a banker's daughter, slumming in the East End. I was awestruck when I first met her—earrings down to her shoulders, very high heels; she looked just this side of a call girl. I thought she was fantastic."

"Yes?"

"Well, I was thirteen. I pretty much thought any girl over twenty fantastic."

"So Archer wanted to marry her."

"But his mother disapproved. She moved to Paris, and he never heard from her again."

"But the postcard?"

"I found it years later. After all that time. I guess she did get in touch, but my aunt must have hidden it. You know, she could have easily tossed it in the fire, but she stuck it in a book. Maybe it helped her conscience."

"To think—"

"—if Archer had wanted to read Conan Doyle instead of Miss Marple."

"Simon, it's not funny."

"I know. I was furious with my aunt at first, but when I found the postcard, Archer was happily ensconced on Pi, and seemed to have forgotten her. I don't know what happened to her. Probably went back to Bombay."

"Bombay . . . *Bombay?* Why?"

"Her family was there, and she was born there, too."

"So she was Indian."

"Oh yes, though she tried hard to shed her roots."

"So Archer was in love with an Indian girl before me."

Simon was silent.

"Your entire family is fixated on South Asian women."

"It was a good dinner, darling."

"Don't change the subject. Maybe we should move back to Pi."

"Tomorrow . . . let's talk about it later."

"Simon, do you think Susan will tell Oscar about Archer?"

"No. Susan might be crazy, but she'll always put Oscar's interests first."

"What if she decides it is in his best interest to know the truth?"

"That his mother once slept with her brother and then married him to cause him to die?"

"Well, no."

"Meti, let it go. I know it's easy for me to say, but you have to let the past rest, and stop blaming yourself."

"Susan?"

"Susan is mourning her brother, she's not mourning his marriage. And no, she will let us tell him the truth when he's old enough."

They were quiet after that, immersed in their own thoughts until exhaustion hit and they slept.

43

As they had planned, Meterling and Oscar met Susan at the park to eat lunch together about a week later. Meterling had not seen Archer's ghost since the day of the party, although once, at the grocery store, she thought she'd caught a glimpse of a white-suited man, but decided it was her imagination. Maybe he had gone away for good, as Simon hoped. Susan had brought Japanese takeaway complete with chopsticks, and taught her how to use them, but after a while, Metering just used her fingers.

"I found out about Mou," said Meterling.

"Moo? Oh, God, Moose. Or Mouse. That awful woman who never ate."

"I thought *you* never ate."

"Oh, I eat."

"Your family doesn't seem to have luck with islanders, or Indians, much—"

"I'm so sorry—"

"Forget it, Susan. There's so much in our lives to discover that is far better than raking up the past."

"Hmm. What will you do about the land, Meterling?"

"The fields? I thought I'd plant vegetables, and make a garden. I could lease some of it to farmers. Simon and I are going to keep the house. We'll redo it and make it lighter. I think it will be good to have a family home in the country for all of us."

"Archer . . . ?"

"He will always remain in my heart, Susan. He is half of Oscar, he's part of Simon."

"So many of my friends, well, they didn't understand . . ."

"Back home, hardly anyone understood or approved. Some stopped talking to my family."

"I didn't know."

"It was awful—neighbors we'd known for years, my distant relations. It was because I was a widow, and it was because I did not mourn enough. As if anyone knows what it is to mourn, as if you could assign a time period to grief."

"Aunt and Uncle wanted you both to wait a year, I remember."

"In the name of decency. But what was decent about Archer dying? What was indecent about falling in love with Simon? I didn't plan it, I didn't scheme—"

"It doesn't matter. None of it matters. They always say that in the end, those who stick by you—well, I'm one to talk."

"But at least you gave me a chance—you didn't close the door completely. You are trying to teach me to use chopsticks."

"Well—" here Susan smiled a little—"Oscar is my nephew."

"John was the first to accept me completely, without question. I will always remember that. In all those snide remarks, those little glances people threw at us, he just accepted us."

"Well, Meterling, if you want, now you've got me as well."

"Got you?"

Susan took a breath. "Got me as someone who can try to be a better sister-in-law."

Together, they sat bundled up in the park, in the weak sunlight of autumn, and looked out at the horizon.

PART THREE

Returning
(Nine Years After)

The great revelation never did come. Instead there
were little daily miracles, illuminations, matches
struck unexpectedly in the dark; here was one.

—*To the Lighthouse*

44

Oscar kept an eye out for the ferry. His mother had warned him it might be late. When *he* had taken the ferry, he had nearly gotten sick, the waters were so choppy. His father told him to look at the horizon, which helped, because he had not vomited. He liked the word "vomit" better than "throw up." He kept a list of words he liked, and next to each entry, he listed its synonym that he disliked. "Demolish" was better than "break," "tiffin" better than "tea," and "British" better than "Paki." He had been called "Paki" a lot walking home from school this past year, but he'd ignored the taunts. He had discovered if he looked at the name callers, they would beat him up (better word: "pulverize"), so he kept his head down.

What he did not want was for either his mother or father to find out, because if they caused a commotion, he was certain he'd be annihilated. Only villains in his comic books were annihilated by heroes—*poof!*, they were gone. In the real world the villains, it seemed, usually won. He had one friend, Asha from India, who knew karate. She rode the bus, and told Oscar he had to convince his mother to let him take lessons.

"I don't want to fight those goons."

"That's the thing. You just know karate and it gives you this, I don't know, aura of confidence."

"What's an aura?"

"Like a magic thing. My mum can read auras—mine is purplish, which means I'm a warrior."

"What color do you think mine would be?"

"I don't know—maybe pale blue, which is very good for an all-round best friend. But we'd have to ask my mum."

Asha's mother told him his aura's color was aquamarine, and said that he was braver than he himself knew.

"But he's a really good friend to people, too, isn't he, Mum?"

"That goes without saying."

"Only I already said it."

He missed Asha, and summer in England, and Pibs. Asha gave him a small pink quartz in a nylon pouch before he'd left, saying it was a stone to protect him in his travels. If they'd stayed put, they'd have gone to Craywick, which is what they did for three weeks in July ever since he could remember. He loved Craywick, their country house, where he had a room with twin beds and a secret panel. At least, he was certain it was a secret panel because it moved when he pressed on it. They used to leave Pibs home, with a neighbor to take care of him, but because he was now a *middle-aged* cat, as his father said, they took him with them. Pibs was usually the first one in the car. Pibs couldn't come to Pi, though, and Oscar tried to explain it to him.

"It's too far away, for one thing, and another thing—well, never mind the other thing,"

The other thing was that he'd noticed right off that cats slunk around on the streets in Madhupur, but he hardly ever saw one in anybody's house. Pibs was being taken care of by Oscar's London grandparents. Aside from missing Pibs, Pi was not bad—he got many points in school when he said he was going to an island for the summer holidays. He liked Great-Grandmother's big house, which had more secret-keeping rooms and parts than he'd remembered, plus the nice large swing on the veranda.

And there was even a funny cat that slept much of the time, curling onto itself. His mother said that was the cat that his cousins had adopted when they were his age. There were as well three small dogs, who also slept a great deal, in a tumble of long fur and floppy ears. No, Pi wasn't bad, but people kept pinching his cheeks, which sometimes hurt—old people did not know their strength—or kissing and cuddling him like he was a baby.

They would probably read *Treasure Island* and make maps in the next school year, Asha had told him, as her class had done. She had burned the edges of the map as their teachers instructed, even as her mother stood watch over her like a hawk. He thought he might read the book ahead of time, but then there were all the Famous Fives, plus *Swiss Family Robinson,* and the comic books. His father had remarked that he was swimming in reading matter, but Oscar didn't think so. He always worried he'd run out. Even to the doctor's office, he took two books, not one, as he explained to his mother, there was always the chance he'd like to begin the other before finishing the first.

Now he scanned the horizon. His father was looking at the schedule while his mother hovered nearby. It wasn't that it was scary in the terminal; just that it was very busy. There were people rushing about, but there were also people who slept soundly on bits of blanket or suitcase, some passengers, some homeless. One man cleaned his teeth absently with a stick. Oscar had spent some time staring at him until the man looked at him directly; embarrassed, Oscar had looked away. His mother gripped his shoulder. There! The ferry was coming in.

45

We jostled our way down the ramp, hand luggage in hand. Rasi gripped my wrist and I held on to Sanjay's shirt. We were like three little monkeys, I thought, inseparable, and now we were back on Pi. We had come specifically to see Aunt Meterling. We had meant to see Meterling years ago, but the years kept going by, despite our wishes. From America, Pi seemed distant and obscure, difficult to reach, as we fell into our American lives with a passion. We had returned once, but Aunt Meterling had been away in Kerala with her friend the poet, at an ashram, and only Simon and Oscar were at Grandmother's house. It was during a Christmas break, and high school called us back before we had seen a glimpse of our favorite aunt.

Now we were undergraduates, me in my sophomore year, Rasi, having skipped a grade, already a senior, and Sanjay a freshman. Our parents decided to let us go by ourselves this summer, thinking to join us later, or put off their trip until December. They thought it would be good for us, without them as interpreters and diplomats, as we navigated our way through family branches. "It is your country, after all, and you should get to know it, even as it changes," said Aunt Pa. I suppose she meant as *we* changed.

We had left the mainland in sunlight, but midway across, a thick fog descended, so that we could see only ten feet in front of us. I had hoped we could watch the approach of the island from the deck, but we stayed inside until the fog lifted. When it did, other passengers began to crowd on the deck, and we joined them. There in the distance, in the otherworldly beauty of late afternoon sun, in a clarity made pronounced because of the previous fog, was the island, green and lush. The balmy air blew against our faces in small breezes as the ferry made its way to the harbor, amid a murmur of voices that seemed continuous, rising in pitch and sometimes distinct. The waves sloshed against the boat, and I could see, behind a wire fence, the faces in the distance, waiting to receive the passengers

Getting visas at the Indian embassy back in New York, I thought we'd never make it, as a crowd surged and yelled at the slow officials. I made the mistake of glancing censoriously at someone pushing firmly to get ahead in line, saying, "No need to push!"—what gave me the right?—only to be yelled at by the man, who demanded, Could I tell him why his visa request had been denied for months and months? Could I, he asked, tell him why the embassy ignored him and treated him with disdain?, his voice pitching higher and higher as I froze, until Sanjay had the sense to pull me away. Now we *had* made it, our group of travelers—there, the mother with her baby, who kept up a monotone wail; the man dressed in khaki and expensive sunglasses, who looked like a journalist, but was more likely a banker; the trio of young women who were unbe-lievably lovely, blessed with similar long, honey-colored hair, ready to spend junior year abroad studying nonviolence—and we shared small smiles. What tales could we tell if we had lived in Chaucer's time? Now we waited while getting our passports checked and luggage inspected. This was always the nervous part of travel, when worry didn't just extend to us but to the luggage—had the Hershey's Kisses melted? Had the sneakers we brought for Oscar made it past luggage pirates? Already, we had been traveling for twenty-five hours. Finishing at last, we stepped toward the exit, past the security line, and I heard my name called out. Aunt Meterling!

We raced toward her and fell into her arms.

We rushed to speak at once.

Aunt Meterling, whom we hadn't seen in nine years, tall as ever, with gray now in her hair and full of smiles. She was only thirty-seven, but our family did always gray early. Aunt Meterling, who seemed full of the vital juice that seemed to belong to her alone.

"Is this Oscar?" Rasi exclaimed.

Oscar blushed as we hugged him.

"He's so big now!" I said. From five to nine years, a leap. He looked like Sanjay had looked as a little boy, all those years ago.

"And now you have turned into beauties," said our aunt.

Sanjay made a bow.

Uncle Simon joined us, bringing Aunt Meterling a bottle of water. More hugs, more exclamations. Our limbs relaxed. We had come home to our family.

The island smelled sweet, as it always did at twilight. We walked as the sun dipped and threw orange-pink clouds across the sky. I could never paint it, nor did I want to, but the sunset looked like a painting, more Turner than Maxfield Parrish. Billboards depicting new film stars in new movies vied with the colors, as did advertisements for laundry soap and vanishing cream. Men lounged on string stools in open shops displaying rows of plastic beads and glass bangles pushed onto newspaper rolls; it never changed, the glitter, the glitz of the market. A toy store caught Oscar's attention because a yipping metal monkey performed acrobatic tumbles, or maybe he was eyeing the wooden tops that could spin and flip over, still spinning. Vendors held open their palms, displaying small wonders, promising hours of entertainment. I gave Aunt Meterling another squeeze. It was glorious to be back with her, with us all.

When Aunt Meterling first left with Simon and Oscar for London, we felt like our favorite toy had been taken away. I remember we moped around until we were scolded. Uncle Darshan, hoping to distract us, brought home three puppies, one for each of us. It was startling how quickly we adjusted after that. Poor Scrap slinked away to Grandmother while our attention was caught by these yipping dogs. They were cocker spaniels, and won our hearts. Uncle Darshan got them from a fellow teacher who had retired to breed them. Grandmother called them One, Two, Three, but we named them Amitabh, Hemamalani, and Dimple. Aunt Pa said that when they'd had dogs in the past, they were given English names, so they could say "Come here, Tommie," or "Sit and stop barking, Reggie."

When we emigrated for America, all of us within the space of three years, we had to leave the animals behind. Nalani and Ajay promised to look after them, but they wound up in the big house. Grandmother, though she would not admit it, had taken a shine to Scrap, who was given dal and watery cream on the veranda, though one of the servant maid's children had to feed her nonveg food outside; mice supplemented Scrap's diet, and probably made her coat silky. The dogs, though, were given meat only once a week, also outside; the rest of the time, they were pampered vegetarians.

We didn't want to move to America; at least, I didn't. While I missed my parents, and knew it would be *very exciting* there, I wanted to remain with Grandmother. Who would take care of her? I worried. I knew she would miss us terribly, although she just scolded us if we told her that—before hugging us. My parents were firm, and a little embarrassed by my protests, and off I went on a Pan Am jet, to be joined by Rasi and Sanjay and my aunt and two uncles two years later. I don't remember the early years of getting adjusted to my new family life, but I remember school. I was leery of my new classes, finding American students loud, strange, and indecipherable at times. They kept thinking my accent was British, my clothes old-fashioned. The studies were dull as well, and it seemed there was more study hall than classes. Years later, people would still insist they heard a trace of England in my voice, or, sounding very surprised, tell me I had no discernible accent. When they said, *But I never think of you as island,* I knew they meant to flatter, bury my difference in a neutral pan-acceptance. My family was not without its own prejudices; "they" or "them" meant "American," and "American" meant something we weren't. "Not 'they,' 'us,' " I'd chant, to my mother's bewilderment. She kept Pi like a well-guarded shrine in our heart, built around us a seemingly impenetrable house of South Asian culture.

Rasi was the first to shake off island culture, listening to more rock and roll than Hindi film songs, getting a secret tattoo, and sneaking a boyfriend. Was this all there was, I wondered—music, tattoos, and boyfriends? I would be different, I told myself, immersing myself in Bharata Natyam. Unfortunately, I still wasn't very good at dance, and eventually gave it up.

Rasi already knew in high school she wanted to be a lawyer, but all I liked was art class. Sanjay was destined for something sensible, because as he himself admitted, even if he'd wanted to be a writer or an artist, as a boy, he couldn't; it would be beyond the scope of our family's imagination. Back in high school, he'd looked to science and math. As for me, I declared art history as a major my sophomore year in college, knowing my parents indulged me only because in their eyes, I would eventually get married, and if I wasn't going to become a professional in the sciences or the law, I could major in anything I wanted.

I thought I would be like my aunt Meterling. I would make radical choices, and live my life with honesty, not for the sake of society. By this time, I had thrown off my allegiance to Pi, and had given up my green card to become an American citizen. I did not necessarily want the citizenship, but it made sense. I lived in New Jersey, not in Madhupur. When the chance came, though, to visit Pi for the summer with Rasi and Sanjay, I leapt.

46

Freshly roasted, freshly ground, served in stainless-steel tumblers, coffee on Pi put all contenders to shame. Shanti-Mami was still cooking for Grandmother, and it was she who served us, with tears in her eyes. She also opened tins full of savories and sweets—Mysore pak and thatai. My grandmother's face seemed softer and more lined, her hands betraying tremors. We sat in the front room, which now had a bigger television set, the seven of us, on the floor, in chairs and on the charpoy, all talking at once, gesturing and laughing. It was a wonder Oscar didn't just clap his hands over his ears. Instead, he played with the hot rods Sanjay had brought him, while the dogs nosed him affectionately.

Meterling sat with Simon's arm around her. She was trying not to cry, I could tell. When you see someone after a long time, you wonder where the time had gone. What had really prevented you from keeping in touch, visiting? It is a terrible feeling, because the reasons are so selfish and petty. We hadn't tried hard enough, and at some point, we forgot. I had held on to her hand on seeing the old house, and exiting the car, barreled into Grandmother, who held us close. Grandmother did cry, and said it was a cold, but then said, well, why should she not cry; it was an occasion that called for emotion. She smelled as I remembered, only felt frailer.

Sanjay stretched out on a mat on the floor, Scrap happily curled next to him, telling Aunt Meterling of his plans to study yoga. This was news to all of us.

He told us he wanted to put school off for a year, and studying yoga the way he wanted required a full immersion in the subject. He would go to a shala in India, wake at four every morning, practice until nightfall, with breaks for meals and rest, and classes for chant, Sanskrit, and philosophy. It sounded like the ideal life for a South Asian, a prospect that should have made everyone proud—a real brahmachari role. Instead, everyone had objections.

"But why can't you just do yoga on your own?" asked our aunt.

"That sounds extreme, Sanju. Are you sure these yogis are reputable?"

"Are these places clean?"

"Mostly there are Westerners in these places, I hear."

I hadn't heard Sanjay called "Sanju" in ages. Grandmother reminded him of the guru with seven Rolls-Royces.

Patiently, Sanjay explained that yoga was not cultish, that it didn't involve Rolls-Royces and rampant sex. He was only going to India, he said, to study with someone in Mysore, which is hardly a foreign country, but that prompted another discussion entirely. I marveled at his patience. It was as if he had grown up in the space of the year. A well-aimed paper ball tossed at my head interrupted my musings. Well, nearly grown up.

After the second cup, before jet lag hit me like a strong wave, I toured the house. It was a ritual I did in New Jersey, and I did it here. My mother used to joke that it was my way of making sure everything was in its place. I went room by room, laying my hand on the mahogany bureaus and almirahs, tracing the dust on the wooden-framed mirrors. I looked out the windows, to see the views of coconut and mango trees, and beyond, the neighbor's walls and windows. I went up to the roof to stand by the clothes dried to stiffness on the line, noticing that the badminton racket that had been unstrung still lay the same way in the corner, near a broken umbrella. Plastic chairs were casually arranged to view the stars, breathe the night air. How could my grandmother climb the stairs to get up here? But it was her eyes that were going, not her legs. That is, she could still climb, resting heavily on each step, a smile like a sunrise on her face if anyone was there to greet her.

Nalani and Ajay joined us the third day. In the intervening years, Nalani had become a doctor, and she and Ajay had decided to remain in the city. After dinner, standing shyly before us, Nalani told us she was expecting. Ajay and she had tried for a baby many times before, miscarriage following miscarriage, and conception occurred when they were long past hoping.

"You know, we put in an application to adopt and it was accepted. We're getting a child from Trippi! Ajay says we might get them both at the same time. Imagine, two children at once!"

She was rosy with the news. We exclaimed our happiness. I

hadn't realized how much I missed her, my older sister-auntie. She was due in five months.

I looked up at the sky. The stars always seemed bigger in the tropical sky, and it seemed there were more of them.

"But that's only part of the good news," said Nalani.

We waited.

"Rasi, we have someone we want you to meet."

"Sure. A lawyer?"

"No," said Nalani. "In fact, it's a young man."

Our merriment vanished.

Sanjay spoke first.

"Nalani, Rasi hasn't even graduated yet," he said.

He turned to Rasi, waiting and cringing a bit for her reaction. It would be sharp and quick, and idiotically, I thought, *Don't let Rasi be brutal, because after all, Nalani is pregnant.*

Rasi shrugged her shoulders, and then nodded. "What's he like?" she asked.

I didn't realize I was holding my breath until I let it out. Sanjay and I glanced at one another. Maybe Rasi was humoring Nalani, but Rasi humored only Meterling, no one else. Only Meterling was spared her tongue, so I knew something was up. But Rasi didn't look upset or crafty, just calm. Nalani embraced her, and hugged us all.

As Americans, or more rightly, islanders living in the States, which is the way our family would see it, I wondered if Nalani expected resistance. But she was so open-hearted, it probably never occurred to her that Rasi might not agree, might argue against arranged and sanctioned meetings. For the boy in question would have been sanctioned, vetted thoroughly by our family.

Later Rasi said she was expecting it.

"I'm twenty. One can choose the battles."

"But this is a big battle."

"All I'm going to do is meet him. It's not as if I'm going to marry him and get pregnant tomorrow. Or vice versa."

"Rasi!"

"Oh, grow up, Mina. Life is also practical. I'll go to law school, and I've been in a lot of relationships."

"You've been in two."

"You forget how important some things are, like knowing the same food, the same customs. I want to be able to eat with my hands in front of the guy!"

"Are you kidding me? Food? Eating with your hands? Rasi, this is your life!"

"Like I said, I'm just going to marry—I mean, I'm just going to *meet* him."

I could only look at her.

"Maybe he can cook. You know, I get home from school, exhausted, and he's got nice hot bajis waiting for me—c'mon, I'm kidding!"

"So, you're not going to meet him?"

"Of course I'm going to meet him. Look, it will be just this once. If I go ahead now and meet this guy and say no, then the next time I'm asked to meet someone, I can say, 'Look, I tried once, and it didn't work out.' "

"That's terrible logic. People—the family—are a lot more persistent."

"C'mon, do you really think I'm going to marry some idiot just because Nalani thinks it's a good idea?"

I didn't answer.

"Forget it—and just deal with it, Mina."

Deal with it? It made no sense. How in the world did Rasi think her plan was going to work? Why did she even want to pretend she wanted to get married all of a sudden? Then I thought—oh, it couldn't be—but *could* she be pregnant?

"What are you talking about?" said Sanjay. In the background, we could hear the dogs barking. "First of all, if she were, she'd have told us. And second, to get married doesn't make sense—unless they got married within the month. And third—there is no third. That's it. She is just—ornery."

Ornery. I hoped Rasi would be able to tell us about pregnancy or an abortion, anything. But who was this new Rasi, this one who was fine with arranged marriages, of all things? It was as if the person I knew had transformed. I think I felt left out. She was being pushed out of the nest, which is one way to view marriage arrangements, but I always thought she would soar on her own, in a dramatic sudden sweep of wing. What I resented was the boy, whose name was Laksman, just as I had once resented Ajay. Who was he? Of course, I had time to adjust to Ajay as he courted us, because it was a package he got, not just Nalani, but all of us. At first, we had all resented Simon, too, but then I was ten, and now here we were, and—ha! This *was* Rasi's plunge, her sweep, her dramatic gesture: thinking of marrying Laksman! She really was agreeing to disagree, just like she was saying, and I knew that she would squash the idea of marriage like a bug. The nerve of Rasi, playing us like this!

47

It wasn't long after that I found Oscar sitting in the garden, in the bower toward the back. This had been Nalani's favorite hideout, and I needed to think. The monkeys only ventured in if there was food around, and since it was placed among the lemon trees, they pretty much left the area alone. Oscar was quietly reading, but looked up when he saw me.

"You look like you're in Pooh's forest," I said.

"I used to want to be Christopher Robin, when I was little," he told me.

"How come?"

"He had all his friends around him in the Wood, and he could go home and have his tea, too."

"I wanted to be Piglet."

"That's silly. Nobody *wants* to be Piglet."

"I did. First, he was a very pretty pink, and then he sometimes helped Pooh out when Pooh forgot all about him."

"He was so small."

I was still getting used to Oscar's British accent. At five, it had not been as pronounced, being mixed in with a child's high-pitched half-sentences.

"When I grow up, I want to be even taller than my mum, although it may not happen."

"I think it helps to stretch."

He looked at me with doubt, at someone who, after all, had openly declared her preference for Piglet.

"This is a nice place to read," I said, wondering why he wasn't on the veranda.

"I like to find places where I'm not bothered."

"Do people bother you?"

"Not so much here, but sometimes at school."

Instantly a funny look came over him, and he wouldn't say any more. I imagined he hadn't meant to tell.

"Do boys pick on you?"

Silence.

"I used to get picked on when I first moved to New Jersey."

He glanced sideways at me.

"Girls would call me names, and one boy would regularly steal my lunch."

"What did you do?"

"Nothing. I thought that's the way things were."

"Weren't you hungry?"

"I was really hungry, especially in the afternoon. One day, I fainted in class, and that's how it all came out."

"You told your teacher?"

"And my parents that evening."

"What happened then? Did the bullies stop?"

"They stopped taking my lunch, but they still teased me. Mum and Dad wanted to move me to a different school."

I hadn't thought about this in years. They did want me to change schools, but in a year, I'd be at the new high school, anyway, and things would be different. So, I stayed on.

Oscar seemed to be considering what I said.

"Really, you wanted to be Piglet?"

I sighed. "Really."

He looked at a lemon tree in front him.

"You won't tell, will you?"

When I said nothing, he went on. "It's just that I really like school, and I don't think the bullies will bother me too much anymore. And I'm going to learn karate to get confidence and an aura of protection."

"Is that like an invisible cloak?"

"Maybe," he said uncertainly. "Anyway, if you want to sit and read here, you can. I've got another book."

This is how I came to spend the afternoon reading about Matilda and the library.

48

I thought how easy it had been for Rasi, Sanjay, and me, on the island. In hindsight, we were rarely bored, and if we were, we had each other to complain to. I wondered if Meterling was right, what I had overheard the other night. She wanted to return to Pi, for Oscar's education. Nalani and Ajay were adamant: no one returns to the island for schooling; one only returns armed with degrees.

"All he will get here is learning by rote, and get involved in college-age politics. All these boys rioting and overturning buses, it's too much."

"There are all sorts of race riots in the UK, and anyway, you did well."

"Yes, but surely readying for Cambridge and Oxford—the seats of learning in England—"

"Seats of learning, Nalani? You once thought the English bastards and bullies."

"Oxford and Cambridge open doors. Oscar deserves better than schools here."

"I wonder how is it in America?" asked Ajay.

"Oh, Pa always says American education is a joke. Our children are by their nature brighter," said Meterling.

I had always thought my family's social views slightly outlandish but not dangerous, yet listening to them, I wondered if I had been too tolerant. They were middle-class, used to a very good life on Pi, and had gone without land or family to the States and become a different kind of middle-class. I still remembered one of my father's friends telling us the story of how people in a town north of ours had stared when his wife appeared at the A&P in a sari. Little children had made faces and pointed; but out in the Midwest, in St. Louis, because it was a university town, people were so enchanted with his older sister's sari, they invited her to model it at the local TV station. In the U.S., South Asian housewives carefully created their own upholstered American living rooms with fabric from Jo-Ann's and patterns from Butterick. My mother didn't, but that was because she was one of the rare women who worked. Aunt Pa had got to hand-stitched matching tea cozies and toaster covers before she said, *Enough,* and looked for a computer course to take.

As usual, my thoughts had wandered away from me. Hemamalani's chin rested lovingly on my knee. Absently, I petted her. I didn't want to evaluate my family, judge them without knowing everything, although of course I did. Who knew what was hidden in their past that they wouldn't talk about, ancient hurts and injustices that had shaped them? "Ancient" was the right word, because hadn't we been shaped from millennia of custom and decorum? All those laws to prevent the boat from being rocked. A woman's talents lay in how well she could roll a betel leaf, how many sons she produced.

Thinking I'd lay claim to my own talents, I thought I would go into Madhupur proper to get some sketch pads and pencils. I liked the Aspara-brand charcoals here, as well as the thick paper hand-sewn into notebooks. I wanted to sketch Grandmother watering the plants, as I had once done long ago, but this time, I wanted to catch her spirit in the arc of water splashing from her hand. I would never get married. I would break the chain of ordered life.

Still, I needed a guide for the practical things. Nalani took me on the bus, and we took Oscar along. I thought I'd get him a small set of watercolors, since I'd noticed the one in the house had all but vanished from frequent use. On the bus, I avoided eye contact with the men who leered in our direction; three years ago, I'd made the mistake of looking into a man's eyes, only to be "accidentally" brushed against, a hand snaking across my breasts minutes after my bottom had been pinched, hard.

Looking over Oscar's shoulder through the bus window, I saw the thatch-roofed stores giving way to brick and stone ones with Plexiglas windows advertising saris, electronics, and furniture. Stainless-steel ware was sold on the streets; tumblers and saucers and thalis lined up on rough blankets. Small and large chimes were sold on the street as well, and you could purchase songbird cages complete with songbirds. Small, colorful temples punctuated every few blocks, dedicated to both large and small deities, and vendors displayed coconuts, fruit, and flowers for purchase for special prayers. A priest was blessing a scooter with coconuts and lemons. Three years ago, if we were on foot, I'd insist we stop in at all the temples, pray and receive prasad. Now, outside one temple, I saw a holy man, with dark, long, curly hair and mustache, ash stripes covering his arms and chest, taking a break with a cigarette.

A thin, unsmiling proprietor looked up as we entered the art-supply shop, and a thinner and saried woman followed us as we browsed the aisles. I can always rely on art-supply stores and stationers to get my senses engaged and, weirdly, my senses calm. This store was tightly organized, with pyramids of candy-scented rubber erasers and boxes of unsharpened pencils. Paintbrushes were neatly arranged in open cups, one reason the woman in the sari was probably following us. Pads of foolscap, tracing paper, and heavier drawing paper enticed, as I ran my finger dreamily along their spines. Oscar was much intrigued by a paper tiger mask, but in the end, decided he really didn't want it. The proprietor still didn't smile as Nalani insisted on paying for my purchases. Well, there was no need for him to smile. He wrapped up the sketch pads, brushes, pencils, and watercolor set individually in brown paper and twine. Because it was so hot, after getting coconut water, we headed for home. I wanted to ask Nalani more about this Laksman, but instead we chatted about her pregnancy and the adoption while Oscar stared out the window.

I told Rasi about the holy man smoking in front of the temple.

"Do you think he just goes up to the counter and says, 'A pack of Camels, Hari Om'?"

"With a special discount, *yaar*, and I'll pray for you?"

Somehow this struck us as hilarious.

"I'm sorry I was angry before," said Rasi.

"That's okay." I hesitated. "I just don't understand why you agreed to an arranged marriage after your whole life has been about, you know, nonmarriage."

" 'Nonmarriage.' I like that. Anyway, I agreed only to an introduction. Look, the whole charade will be over. Nalani will be happy, my parents will be happy. I'll have seen one boy, that's all, and I can say no to all the rest. I told you, I can say, 'I've tried it your way, but now please leave me alone.' "

"But won't everyone think if you agreed to one meeting, you'll agree to more?"

"I don't think so. It will get everyone off my back."

"Or you could wind up with someone on yours."

"Ha-ha."

49

O scar didn't remember if the top half was white and the bottom painted green, or the other way around. Try as he might, the image wouldn't come to him. He really wanted to make a picture of the ferry for Great-Grandmother. He wanted it to be a surprise, and frankly, he wasn't confident if any of his cousins could keep a secret. They seemed to like talking a lot. His father had given him some coins for ice cream the other day, but they hadn't gone because of the rain. The change was still in his pocket, so he wondered if he could just get to the dock and look at the ferry. He could even make a quick sketch.

Quietly, he slipped out the gate and headed for the bus stand down the road. He had to remember the name of the street, so he wouldn't get lost on the way back. He hoped he had enough change. He was the only one waiting as it creaked to a stop. The sign said 50p, so he took out the coins and put them in a small iron box. The bus driver didn't even look at him. He took a seat behind him, but an old man yelled at him. He didn't understand, but then he noticed a cartoon demonstrating that the first seats were for the elderly, so with face red, he took another seat farther back, beside a woman holding a baby. The bus lumbered toward the stop they took to the art store, but the dock was nowhere in sight. He tried to ask the woman next to him.

"Boat? Ferry? Water?"

She stared at him, but a man turned around and told him the dock was only a few more stops away. The man kept looking at him, and was about to ask him something, but Oscar hunkered down and studied the No Smoking or Spitting sign imprinted on the back of the seat, looking up every time the bus groaned to a stop. Many stops later, he arrived at the ferry terminal. He exited the bus, and headed determinedly for the water, ignoring the Kampa Kola sellers and peanut vendors. Finding an empty bench, he opened his notebook. The quay was busy, with sellers shouting out their wares, or arguing over traffic maneuvers. Passengers waited for the ferry to arrive in the terminal. Children ran about, some glancing at him curiously. He waited for a ferry, and when it finally did arrive, he took notes. The bottom was green. There were flags and decks and stairs. For two hours, Oscar was occupied. Finally, getting up and stretching, he realized he needed to use the bathroom. He looked around uneasily. He wondered if he could use the terminal's bathrooms even though he wasn't a passenger or waiting for one. His need proved greater than fairness, and he walked slowly into the building. He remembered where one was from last time, and entered. When he was washing up, a funny man with a mustache sidled up to him, making his hair prickle. Asha had told him that people sometimes stole children just like that. His father always told him, look for a policeman if you feel scared or get lost, but there wasn't any he could see. Clutching his sketch pad, Oscar ran out, hoping he wasn't being followed. The late-afternoon sun was comforting as he made his way to the stand and got on a bus.

The problem was that he forgot where to get off.

50

I assumed he was in the garden, reading. Aunt Meterling might have thought the same, but it was nearly tiffin, and Oscar was always hungry for Bournvita and Amal biscuits. Uncle Simon casually said he'd just go have a look, and Ajay accompanied him, "to buy a paper and betel leaf." Aunt Meterling was inside; otherwise, she would have started to panic. The benefit of having a large family was that if anyone got lost, a search party could easily be assembled and dispatched. Rasi, Sanjay, and I set off as well.

"Should we call the police?"

"No, that will just cause more chaos."

"It's not chaos yet."

We thought he might have headed to the beach, so we went there. This is where our fear kicked in, because the bay was large, deep, and the water choppy.

"He's a sensible kid," said Sanjay.

"But what about the undertow?" Ever since I read *Garp*, I worried about undertows.

Rasi began to ask people if they'd seen a little boy, but she had no luck.

"I wonder if Meterling has told him about Archer," said Sanjay.

I wondered as well. It seemed we had all agreed, almost implicitly, that no one would say anything. In England, it would be easy to keep it a secret, but on Pi, anyone might talk, let loose a comment.

"She'll tell him when the time's right," said Rasi.

"But when is the right time? If I were in his place, I'd want to know," said Sanjay.

"But why does it matter?"

"Seriously? It's not so much that Simon isn't his biological father, but that he wasn't told."

I didn't reply.

"It's not like Archer was a criminal. Oscar has the right to know," said Rasi.

"Even if he were a criminal, Oscar still has the right to know," said Sanjay.

"But what about the psychological damage, then? Imagine how haunted you might be if you knew your father was violent."

"That's nonsense. It's still part of where you come from. It doesn't determine anything, but—"

"Why are you two arguing? Archer wasn't a criminal, Oscar can be proud of him, and it's up to Simon and Meterling to decide."

It looked like it was going to rain, and I hoped the uncles had found him by now. There were only a few people about, because of the darkening skies. Some were already taking shelter under thatched baskets overturned on their heads. Others raised umbrellas as the first drops hit, the skies opening to let out a steady downpour. Thunder rumbled, and the sky lit with a sudden flash of lightning.

51

e had sat on the driver's side, to the port, but on the return trip, he forgot to switch sides. Still, if he could just recall his way, he should be in time for tiffin. If he got off the bus too soon, he could walk, but it would be harder if the bus overshot his street. It occurred to him that this was an Adventure, and aside from not knowing Tamil, he felt excited. He could Explore, Remember, Record, as they always said in school. He had counted six stops—oh! that's what he might have done, counted stops, but it didn't matter now, he was going to have an Adventure. And to do that, he needed to get off the bus.

He took a breath, and jumped off at the next stop. He thought he remembered those palm trees, but soon realized there were the same trees everywhere lining the road. A plump woman in a sari with a net bag in her hand hurried by him, glancing at him curiously. Adults never bothered with him in England. Here, how did people immediately sense he was a foreigner? The street was crowded, and he had to be alert to escape being pushed about too much. He felt in his pants pocket and discovered the few coins he had left were gone. There wasn't a hole, so he must have been pickpocketed. Maybe when he had been jostled getting off the bus. The thief must be very cunning, he thought, but also disappointed with his spoils. Luckily, he had Asha's pink quartz in his shirt pocket, which, considering the situation was probably a good thing.

What with keeping from bumping into people, and the noise

of the traffic whizzing by, there was hardly much to Explore or Remember. He was getting tired of walking and craning his head to see if he'd reached home yet. He wondered now if anyone was getting worried. He hoped his absence was still unnoticed. It had been a silly thing to do after all, venture out without telling anyone, and taking a bus. Raindrops hit the pavement before he noticed that he was also getting wet, and then the thunderstorm burst. He took shelter under a shop awning, but there were many people there. Lucky souls who remembered their umbrellas took no notice of the rain and continued on their business. A cache of children jumped into the muddy puddles, their legs now striped with dust and water. He looked at his rubber sandals, and without further thought, joined in. The water was not at all cold, and his feet created droplets as he lifted them up. His companions didn't say anything—one girl smiled at him shyly. It was strange that while he was on holiday, island children had school. Their clothes looked very clean—children most likely from an orphanage, because schoolchildren would probably have stayed inside. He was fascinated with orphanages. But how had they got out—did they have day passes? He wasn't sure how orphanages worked, but was sure it didn't involve heedlessly and joyously jumping into puddles.

The rain stopped just as quickly as it started.

Very soon, too soon, there came a teacher rounding the children up, hitting their legs with a cane. He just shook his cane at Oscar, snapping at him to get in line. Oscar stood in a puddle, and then noticed a woman with an enormous toothless grin staring at him. Made uncomfortable with her attention, he ran after the group of children. Maybe they could direct him to his house. Just as he was reconsidering, thinking maybe that wasn't really a good plan and he ought to find a policeman, the teacher surprised him by pulling him roughly by the collar and giving him a push to walk faster.

They entered a courtyard, which was so different from the bustle of the street. Here, two low, whitewashed buildings abutted one another. Two women were doing the laundry by the side of an old palm, while scents of cooking came from a small shed farther away from the women. Oscar realized he was hungry, and wondered if it would be all right just to stay for lunch before he told the teacher about his mistake. He was certain he was not missed at Great-Grandmother's house.

The students were made to queue up in two lines. Oscar hoped they weren't going to do a head count, but it seemed they were just waiting to be addressed by the headmaster. He spoke rapidly in Tamil, and then more haltingly in English, announcing the sports schedule for the afternoon. Oscar was surprised how much there was planned. The headmaster then asked everyone to assemble quietly and orderly for lunch, at which point the lines erupted into pandemonium. The children noisily entered the building on the left, and sat down at long tables. Oscar was surprised at first, imagining everyone would sit on the floor. Quickly, stainless-steel plates were passed around, and several men and women went up and down the tables, efficiently serving rice, dal, a tangle of green vegetables, and yogurt. Gingerly, Oscar tasted the food, and discovered he was not just hungry but ravenous.

Finishing his plate, he put down his spoon, wondering if they would have seconds, when he saw the schoolmaster coming toward him. The other children stared at him. Would the police come for him now? Rising up quickly, he ran out of the building and into the street. It didn't look as if the headmaster was pursuing, so, panting, Oscar caught his breath. Maybe the headmaster realized he could be in more trouble if it came out that he'd mistakenly ushered a foreign child into the orphanage. Oscar walked on.

This side of the street started to seem a little more familiar, because wasn't that mango stand the same his aunts and uncle took him to? He wasn't allowed to drink any juices, but fruit was okay, as long as it was cut in front of him. The owner of the stand knew how to cut the mangoes into frog and turtle shapes, and served them with a toothpick. He realized he was still hungry. He wondered if they were already eating at Great-Grandmother's house. For the first time, he thought about his mother. His clothes were still wet. He had been gone over four hours, he estimated, and she was certain to be furious. If he kept on this side and went farther, he should reach his street quickly, unless he had overshot it.

More and more buildings appeared familiar, but with slow-growing alarm, he recognized that he had gone the wrong way. The terminal was ahead. Could he have really walked all that way? He could not make out the ferry, so he must still be some distance away, he reasoned. He felt embarrassed just turning around, walking the other way again, and seeing everything and everyone all over again, so he thought he would first go down a side street. Cities were laid out in grids, he knew, so a side street should take him to a street that ran parallel to the main road. Bougainvillea and jasmine bloomed from the thick vines that dropped from gardens hugging the street, which inclined steeply. One side of the street burst with heat while the side he walked on was cool. Voices and laughter drifted from restaurants perched high on the third storeys of buildings that lined the street, and looking up, he could see waiters carrying plates of two-foot dosas, and skillfully streaming coffee from individual saucers to tumblers. The joke was,

Sanjay said, the waiters could pour a vertical length of liquid as wide as their arms, so you asked for a yard of coffee.

In the distance lay the sea.

If one street would take him to the parallel street, then three would take him to the beach. If he turned left at the beach, he would be walking in the right direction to Great-Grandmother's house. He reminded himself he would need to climb up steeply at some point to rejoin the main road, but surely the water at the sea's edge would refresh him. And he certainly needed more shells for his collection.

Splashing into the water, he discovered the waves were rougher than he expected. They were fast as well, as he darted in and out to grab the tiny shells that were uncovered on the wet sand. The bigger ones eluded him, though. There were only a few people about, and no one paid him any attention. Soon he was absorbed in filling his pockets, which grew damp and heavy. Beach fleas nipped his toes. Left, he told himself, he needed to turn left, and then left again, but by now his legs were tired. In fact, his whole body ached.

"Oscar!"

He turned.

It must have been the wind. There was no one there. He flopped down on the sand and fell asleep.

The fleas woke him up. He batted them away, wondering how long he had been asleep. Had the sun been as low as it was now when he first reached the beach?

He was supposed to turn right. No, it was left. A small panic rose in his stomach. By now, he knew his parents would be worrying, and if he was truthful, he too was just a little scared. He could hear men shouting to each other in the distance, and a woman's voice rising to scold someone. What if he were never to find his way back? Would he wind up homeless, sleeping on the beach? He saw a pack of dogs come in his direction. Island dogs tended to be short-haired, pointer-like, and sometimes painfully thin. Mina had told him they were wild, scavenging for food and sleeping on the beach. He wished she were here. He must have been daft to come by himself—that's what his father would say. They might be really mad by now. It must be close to dinnertime. He knew that night fell quickly on the island, but the sun was not yet ready to make its descent into the water.

"Oscar!"

Scrambling to his feet, he turned around. No one.

"Look here."

A few feet away, sitting against a small sand bank away from the water, was a man with a walking stick. He was white, a tourist most likely.

"Are you lost?" the man asked.

Oscar wasn't sure whether to reply. The man looked kinder than the headmaster had, but his mother had long ago warned him not to talk to strangers. Asha told him that kids were kidnapped often, and tortured and drugged, although she admitted she didn't know anyone *personally* to whom that had happened. It was, however, another reason to learn karate. Oscar wondered how karate would help if the kidnapper had a gun. Well, Asha had said, if he has a gun, you are out of luck. Oscar clutched the stone she had given him for protection.

Oscar noticed the man had bare feet, and somehow that was reassuring. It also seemed that the man was slightly transparent. Oscar wondered if he was an angel. Asha told him that when her cousin's neighbor from Yorkshire was involved in a car accident, he had seen an angel, who kept telling him that it would be all right.

"I just came from the ferry," the man said, indicating the right with his hand. "I'm going to the town center, if you're going that way."

Oscar considered. It would be nice to walk with someone, nice to go home somehow—he didn't even know his address!—or at least go to the police station. Already he felt glad to get his bearings a bit.

The man smiled, and slowly made his way across the beach, and Oscar, following, was relieved to see some wooden steps leading to the street. Two men selling shell necklaces and straw pinwheels called out to Oscar, but he paid them no mind. He felt safe with this man, although he had already decided to refuse if the man offered him candy, but Oscar didn't think he would. The man just walked in front of him, leading the way.

"How did you know my name?" he asked the man after they crossed two streets.

"A lucky guess. You look like an Oscar."

The main road was upon them. His legs hurt and he wished he could take a bus.

The man seemed to understand, for he slowed his pace.

"I'm glad you trusted me. You must always listen to your stomach, Oscar. It will tell you everything."

"You mean my gut?"

"Yes. If it gives you a queasy feeling about someone, listen to it. But of course, always use your intelligence. Assess any situation carefully."

"Are you a spy?"

"A spy? No. Why do you ask?"

"I don't know. A spy would have to be careful about people, I guess."

"People are pretty good for the most part."

By now they were walking at a steady pace and the streets were more crowded than earlier, as people streamed out from work and the restaurants.

The mango stand he'd noticed earlier was a chain, he now realized, but a tailor shop he remembered looking at from the bus when they went to buy art supplies was a landmark. In front of the tailor shop was a family selling young coconuts, which he also now committed to memory, just in case he needed further landmarks. Right next to them was a stand advertising Sanctuary Chai. Of course, people weren't landmarks, but their businesses could be. Then again, he might never get the chance to go anywhere by himself again.

"So, young man, what would you do if you got lost again?"

"I'd ask a policeman. I'd might not stray off the path again, but how can you have adventures if you don't take chances?"

"True enough. Still, a good explorer takes precautions. You want a good map, protective gear, a compass, a flashlight, insect spray—"

"But that's a planned journey, not an adventure!"

"Well, you can always be prepared for an adventure by carrying a compass."

"But how will that help if you are lost?"

"Well, it's always good to ask a policeman. But if you had a compass, and you knew the ferry was west—"

"Which it has to be, because we are east of India," said Oscar, feeling utterly foolish for not figuring that out.

"—you would know you are heading east. You could also look up at the sun."

"But we aren't supposed to look at the sun," said Oscar.

"True enough."

Oscar wondered if he should tell the man he didn't know

Great-grandmother's address. Still, if he was an angel, maybe he would just take him home.

They walked a while in silence.

"Have you had many adventures?" asked the man.

"No. This is probably my first one." Oscar frowned, and continued, "My mother and father have a lot of rules about where I go."

"Are they strict?"

"No, not really. I don't know, they're all right." He paused, and then asked,

"Have *you* had lots of adventures?"

"Oh, yes, I've traveled a great deal."

"Have you been to Everest?"

"Well, no."

"My dad says one day we might trek there together, but it's a hard trip, and there's plenty of preparations to make—years and years worth, but we might go on a balloon ride sooner."

"See the mountains from above, you mean?"

"Well, not Everest, but maybe the Alps—they have climbing classes."

"I hiked in the Pyrenees one summer. I was nineteen."

Oscar waited for him to launch into a story. Adults always got a funny look in their eyes when reminiscing, their faces going soft, if not slack.

"It's a good idea to carry water, even if it seems heavy at first."

Oscar nodded. His father had told him the same thing last summer.

"And you can always ask for directions. People are usually glad to help, and if they set you off in the wrong direction, well, it's just another adventure. Good shoes are important."

Oscar wondered if a story would follow now. On the whole, it seemed grown-ups offered up lots of advice.

"I came to Pi not much older than you. My father brought me and my sister, and the very first day, a monkey stole my cap. Susan shrieked, and I never laughed so hard."

"They are a bit scary. My aunt's name is Susan, too."

"Well, my sister didn't much care for walks after that. The monkey didn't snatch it off my head, mind, just grabbed it from the grass and ran off."

"Did you chase it?"

"No, sometimes you just lose a hat. Life is full of peculiarities."

"My parents are probably looking for me by now."

"Not much farther, now."

"Where are we going?"

"Oscar!"

It was his uncle Ajay, with his father close by. He ran up to them, and his father swung him up off the ground. Nearly breathless, he began to tell his story, and turned to introduce the barefoot man, but the man was gone.

"But he was right behind me—he helped me find the way back!" said Oscar, as his uncle raised his eyebrows and his father frowned.

"I'll go get us some juice," said Uncle Ajay, heading toward another of those mango stands.

"What did your friend look like, Oscar?" asked his father.

"He was barefoot, Daddy, but he had on a funny white suit—and a pink tie! I suppose you're thinking I'm fibbing, but I'm not."

"Oscar, let's not tell your mum about your friend."

"Why not?"

"Well, first of all, she doesn't know you were lost, and second, she'll be upset you tagged along with a stranger."

Uncle Ajay gave him a cup with a straw.

Listening to Oscar's adventure, they began to walk home.

"Not a word of this to your mother, or she'll be livid."

Oscar noted the street name once again.

As it was, his mother was livid anyway, having found out the truth.

52

I had let the cat out of bag, so to speak. Coming home from the beach, I'd asked Nalani if Oscar had returned, not realizing my aunt was steps away.

"Why would you think I would not want to know?" shouted Aunt Meterling.

"You'd worry needlessly—and look, he's home, safe and sound."

"Simon, what if you hadn't found him? Was I just supposed to be twiddling my thumbs while you act the hero?"

"I was hardly acting the hero. We went out to search for him, that's all, and we found him."

"And I was headed in the right direction," muttered Oscar, who looked as if he knew he should probably slip away, since the attention was no longer on his having left home without permission.

"You! I expected more of you, Oscar! You know better than to go anywhere by yourself!" she said.

"But Mum, I had help from this man—"

"What man?"

"He was so nice—he was even wearing this clean white suit

and—" Oscar frowned—"and a pink tie, like he was dressed up for something special."

Meterling seemed to weave on her feet.

"Mum! He showed me the way to get home! He *helped* me!"

"He helped you? He spoke to you?"

"Did you know about this?" she asked Simon.

"I didn't want to worry you."

"Why do you keep repeating this? I worry. I'm a mother. For godsakes, Simon!"

"C'mon, Meterling, he's just a boy, that's what boys do, they explore," said Simon.

"But he saw Archer!"

We all stared at her.

Now Meterling did sit down in a chair, and Ajay went to get her some water.

"Mum, who's Archer?"

"Oscar, sit down a minute," said Simon.

We should have all left the room, I suppose, but it didn't occur to us. We remained rooted.

"Oscar, your mother was once married to my cousin, a wonderful man named Archer. Archer Forster," said Simon.

Meterling drank the water gratefully.

"The Craywick house actually belonged to Archer, and he left it to your mum. Archer was your—biological dad, but he died before you were even born. I met your mother just before you arrived, and we got married."

Oscar thought a minute.

"Am I a bastard, then?" he asked.

"No!" we all said in unison.

"And how do you know such a word anyway?"

"That's what Asha's dad calls her puppy because they don't know who his father was."

"Well, Archer was your father."

"Okay." Oscar sighed. "But why are you mad about the man on the beach? Because I'm not supposed to talk to strangers? But I had to, or I would have stayed lost."

"When your father died, he was wearing a suit and tie just like you described. I think it was him."

"Cool!"

"Well, be that as it may, it still gives me a start. He shouldn't be here—he should have long gone! He wasn't supposed to ever return."

"You've seen him, too, Mum? You've seen the ghost of—Archer?"

Meterling looked miserable. She seemed to recollect herself in a moment.

"You are too little to go wandering off on your own. Anything could have happened!"

"Not so little," Oscar muttered, almost involuntarily.

At which Sanjay ushered Oscar out of the room, out of harm's way, since Meterling began to look as if she were going to say more on the subject.

We were all silent now. The secret had been let out, and Oscar seemed to take it well. But this news about Archer's ghost was exciting. What did it mean? What did the ghost want? And would we see it too?

The wind blew warm air, ruffling the palm fronds. The moon was in first quarter, a thick crescent in the sky.

"It looks farther away tonight," said Rasi.

"We could go up on the roof."

"Do you get the feeling Meterling thinks this ghost is going to snatch Oscar away?"

"I don't know. I don't really believe in it, anyway," said Rasi.

"I do. There are always spooky things going on, Rasi, a lot more than we know."

"Science fiction. C'mon, let's go to the roof."

To cool down, Meterling went to pick lemons. There was a tree located at the far end of the garden. She still felt shaken at the idea Oscar had so casually sneaked out of the compound. And Archer—what was he doing back, after all those years? Why did he pick this time to return? A ghost who desired what he couldn't have: his boy. Would he dare try to take him away from her? Taking him would only mean that Oscar had to—no, she wouldn't think such thoughts. She plucked some fruit; she would slice it open, grate some ginger, and make some tea. She'd eaten some hot bajis at lunchtime with small cut green chilies, and her stomach felt a little queasy. The lemon felt good in her hand.

And there he was, up in the branches in his white suit and pink tie.

"I came back to Pi," he said, though it was redundant to say so.

Meterling said nothing.

"I'd forgotten how cold England could be," he continued.

"You can feel the temperature?"

"I can smell it." He shivered.

"Why did you come back? Why are you here now?"

"You mean since that Diwali party?"

"Yes. Why on earth have you returned?"

"This is my home, Meterling, or at least it was. I'm better off on the whole where I began, and now that I've gratified some of my longing, I can finally reincarnate."

"Gratified? Reincarnate?"

"I can't hope for union with Ishvara just yet."

"Archer—"

"Don't be annoyed. I just wanted to see you one more time, make sure you were being looked after, make sure that idiot Simon loved you enough."

"I don't think you have to worry about that."

"I hoped he wouldn't be enough for you, but that would just prolong my existence."

"I am making all of this up in my own head, aren't I? To compensate for my guilt—which frankly, doesn't even exist—in marrying your cousin, for remarrying at all. Archer, too much time has passed for us to even have this conversation."

"But I need the conversation. I'll always be with you, rooted in a corner of your heart."

"But Oscar? Oscar needs the chance to live. You can't take him."

"Take him? Meterling, you're mad. And anyway, even if I could, you should know that the longing of a Bhuta remains unfulfilled. That's the tragedy of our lot. And that's why some living people are like ghosts—deep in unfulfilled longing. But I met him, Meti. I met my son. He spoke to me. He's smart, and sweet, and trusting."

Meterling looked away.

"Will you find a priest or someone to help you reincarnate?" she asked.

"I think there's one on Biswan Road, but I might go further. I need to ask you something. When he's ready, when he asks, tell him more about me. I don't think he will mind much, really, my—your—boy."

"*Our* boy, Archer." Meterling's eyes filled with tears.

"Don't cry, Meti. We can't change what's already happened.

You could never have prevented my dying—no one could have, not even me."

"I wish you could have known Oscar—know him. I wish we could live simultaneous lives."

"But we can't."

"I was so angry at you."

"It's fine, it's all perfectly fine. I guess I was angry, too. Death must do that."

"I'm in love with Simon, you know."

"I know you are. Of course I was jealous."

"We didn't plan any of this."

"None of it, my dear. Well—" Archer brushed himself off a bit, and straightened his tie. "Well, it must be time."

"Time?"

"I've seen Oscar, I've seen you—it's time to go for good. Maybe I am reconciled enough to go peacefully into the next life."

"Archer—thank you."

"Goodbye, my dear, dear Meterling. And don't ever wilt."

Ever so slowly, as my aunt Meterling watched, he turned on his heel, and walked away until he disappeared. Only the garden was before her, only the lemon tree.

Somewhere inside, a door closed, and a window opened. Meterling turned to go back in.

53

Two Rovers were hired and two drivers. Shanti-Mami packed us pooris, potato subji, curd rice, idlis smeared with chili-dal powder, and mango pickle neatly in stainless-steel containers, as well as thalis and a couple of blankets. Jugs of water, plus a tin of her special rava ladoos and Scottish shortbread, also came with us.

Nalani thought we could do with some diversion and planned a picnic for all of us in Akkase Park. She used to go camping with the girl guides up into the mountains, and loved eating outside with a fire. It would be a change for Oscar, too, we thought. At first, Grandmother said she was too old, that picnics were for young people, but Ajay convinced her.

"Paati, you'll be driven there to sit down. No exertion," he said.

Grandmother, Ajay, Sanjay, Oscar, and I rode in one car with Raman, our driver, and Aunt Meterling, Uncle Simon, Nalani, and Rasi rode in the other with Mr. Joseph. Food and blankets packed, we set off in the early morning when there was mist coming off the ground. The sun, when it emerged, was a giant orange in the sky, almost too beautiful to look at. We had our windows down, and soon got absorbed in the unknowns of Pi traffic. Gaily painted trucks, auto rickshaws, motorcycles, cars, and buses honked to make sure everyone was aware of them, and then honked again to pass, turn, or check the volume of their horns. Raman told us that this was the best time to be going to Akkase, because the city would reach very high temperatures, and we should not worry if we got lost, because he had GPS, which was news to all of us except Sanjay. The amount of stuff that was coming from computer technology, the driver said, was going to revolutionize the island.

The radio played film music as we navigated the last rotary to head to the mountains. In thirty minutes, the car in front stopped on the side of the road.

Raman went to investigate, as we got out to stretch a bit. It was the first rest stop of a total of four. Nalani, of course, needed the facilities often, but so did Meterling. The country-side started to get prettier as we left the city at last. We left the highway for Old Commissioner's Road, where there was more foliage and thatched and mud houses, not brick. It was not long before Western-style toilets disappeared at the rest stops. Grandmother had fallen asleep, and Oscar nestled in the place where her blouse ended, before her sari tuck began, a roll of soft brown flesh that had comforted us all at one time or another. In half an hour, Sanjay and Ajay were asleep as well, while I looked out the window, as the landscape sped by, until my eyelids too became heavy. In the other car, Rasi later reported, they sang songs. First Aunt Meterling began a tune from an old film, so familiar that even Rasi knew the words. Song by song, they sang a repertoire of film hits from the fifties and sixties.

Adding to the beauty of the island was the variety of terrain. Mountains, forest, and shore, all in a space that was not too difficult to explore. No wonder Captain Geert Pieter thought he had stumbled onto an enchanted island in 1726, thinking it might indeed be peopled with "elves of hills, brooks, standing lakes and groves." The greater magic was that the Dutch did not find it until the eighteenth century. Life here was so leisurely, in spirit at least, if not in actuality. Of course, we were on vacation, away from the all-nighters cramming for exams and papers, the days regulated by the buzz of the alarm clock, and weekends at home in front of the drone of the television, where all the studying could be nullified only by endless repeats of old shows.

We stirred as the car began to climb up into the hill country. We passed a coffee estate, and I saw a sign advertising Banac's Best, Ltd. I could smell the roasting beans, a fragrance that was said to increase one's intelligence. Skinny trees jutted out as coffee plants thickly enveloped the hillsides. We drove up a dirt road, with a background of almost violet-colored mountains. There was mist in the air still, and the freshness that comes from altitude. As we rounded a turn, a field of lilac primula caught me by surprise. I heard Grandmother's intake of breath. The driver said these were the royal carpets Akkase was known for as he brought the jeep to a stop.

We got out, stretched, and waited for the rest of the family to climb out of the other car. From where we stood, we could see a vast view that was largely preserved in its natural state. Some sixty miles further was a bird sanctuary near a lake. Birds, coffee, mountain, and flower jostled for space. Oscar declared he was hungry, which made sense to all of us, as we had driven so long. Uncle Simon and Ajay set up the blankets under a tree, until Grandmother pointed out that the monkeys would not hesitate to steal the food and scamper up the leaves. So, we settled on a grassy open space, and set about opening the contents of our picnic. That must be why eating outdoors is so captivating: unpacking food from containers, stretching out on mats and blankets, not minding if an ant comes by for a crumb. The drivers went off for a smoke and their lunch.

After eating, we split up to explore. There were many other travelers about, and Grandmother happened upon an elderly woman who, it turned out, knew Grandmother's sister's doctor. They might even find shared family, I thought, smiling to myself. That's how it was on Pi. The woman's son and his wife had brought her out for a visit, but when Grandmother stopped to chat, the couple wandered away for a walk, as we did as well. Akkase was a paradise for young lovers and hikers. Soon, even in our party, the couples went off on their own, Ajay helping Nalani up a steep path, Simon drawing in Meterling for an embrace. So, Sanjay, Rasi, Oscar, and I walked by ourselves, Oscar carrying a stick in case of tigers.

We didn't see any tigers, but what I was thinking of was snakes. We didn't see any of those, either, except for a slender fellow that darted away. I wondered about Dickinson's "tighter breathing," how she got it just right in that poem. I shuddered in the way one does in the aftermath of seeing something alarming, shivering in its memory. Rasi and Sanjay had walked ahead with Oscar leading, and I hurried to catch up.

When we came back, after investigating a pond, a view, and a splendid old tree full of monkeys, we found Grandmother deep in conversation with her new friends. This was Mrs. Shukla, we learned, a retired professor of astronomy—who had, we were astonished to learn, a side interest in astrology—and her son, Rajendra, and his wife, Asmati.

"There is so much we don't know, with the universe constantly in motion, and so much mystery," she laughed, as our faces betrayed our surprise. She had learned to read charts, making her a South Asian woman who excelled in two things a woman of her time did not ordinarily do.

"Mrs. Shukla is as revolutionary as Rukmini Arundale," said Grandmother.

"No, no, I just would not listen to those oldies who said only men can be versed in certain arts. We both have the same brains inside, don't we—nice gray matter that is waiting to be filled with knowledge."

Nalani and Ajay arrived, receiving a good deal of teasing because their clothes showed signs of leaves and dirt.

"We were merely sitting on the ground, you fools," Nalani protested, waving away our sounds of cooing.

Introductions were made, and made again, when Simon and

Meterling arrived. They too looked like young lovers, smiling quietly and accepting hot cups of tea. We drew forth the biscuits, and shared Asmati's homemade fruitcake. Asmati and Rajendra were visiting from Kerala. We listened to Mrs. Shukla's story of studies, her marriage, and moving to Kerala from her original home in Kanyakumari.

"Do you know the story of Kanyakumari Devi?" Grandmother asked us. "She was jilted at the altar by Shiva, and all the food for their wedding was left to turn to stone. That's why the sand there resembles rice grains."

"Why would he jilt her?"

Grandmother laughed. "He was supposed to arrive exactly at midnight, the time Narada selected as auspicious for the wedding, but on the way, an insomniac rooster crowed, and Shiva, thinking it was morning, and therefore too late to marry correctly, went home."

"That makes no sense."

"The point is that he had to leave her unwed so the demon she was destined to kill would try to marry her and initiate the battle that would leave him dead by an unmarried girl. That was why the gods created her."

"Yes," said Mrs. Shukla, "I heard that the rakshasa in fact was the one who tricked Shiva, so that he could take his place, but of course, our Kanyakumari could see right through that deception."

"But wasn't it Narada who tricked Shiva, because on no account could the wedding take place? Oh, there's another story too about Kanyakumari. They say the diamonds adorning her statue's nose are so bright that they could light the seas for the catamarans," said Nalani.

"A holy lighthouse."

"But instead of safely guiding boats home, the light made the boats crash onto the rocks. That doesn't happen anymore, because they keep the door to her shrine shut."

"They open it five specific times a year, though. You know, the sand at Kanyakumari is also tricolored: red, pearl, and black. As a child, I once visited, and we collected the sand," said Grandmother. "We used it to decorate our Navratri golus."

"What's a golu?"

"It's when we arrange dolls on the steps of a tiny stage, for the nine-day festival, when we honor Saraswati, Lakshmi, and Durga with special poojas."

"Oh, a doll festival," said Oscar, disappointed.

"Yes, a doll festival," I said, tickling him.

"Durga-Kali too was created to kill a demon," said Rasi.

"But she kept on killing after the demon's death, so she became anger uncontained."

"And had finally to be subdued by Shiva."

Meterling hid a smile.

"Do you think we could go there, Mummy?" asked Oscar.

"Not on this trip, darling, but on the next one, perhaps."

Mrs. Shukla patted his head.

"My home is also famous for being a place where our rajah and his son ousted the Dutch East India Company by capturing their commander. I named Rajendra after him. But this was before the Geert fellow found Pi. Holland was already in decline," she said.

So we discussed history and mythology, and inevitably, the talk came round, as it always does, to partition. By the time we were ready to leave, Grandmother and Mrs. Shukla, who had by now discovered they had at least two common acquaintances, were still discussing Gandhi, and how they wore kadhi.

Mrs. Shukla and her family said goodbye to us warmly. She looked at Rasi a moment longer and smiled.

"Remember, be sure to look at the moon the third day after it is new," she said.

I wasn't sure she was really addressing Rasi, but it seemed that way. Overall, a mysterious encounter. The moon would be full that night, which was all I knew.

54

It would be nice to come here each summer, Mum."

Oscar played with a loose thread on his shirt as he said this. Swiftly, Meterling snapped it off, and then tousled his hair.

"Why do people do that? To my hair?"

"They're just showing affection. Do you really want to come back each year?"

"Yeah. Great-Grandmum is getting old, and I think it's important to see her. Plus, I like it."

"How about moving here? See her all the time?"

"Mum."

Meterling sighed. "You really want to learn karate?"

"Yes."

Arrangements were being made to invite Nalani's friends the Krishnaswamis and their son Laksman over to the house. Grandmother got a new sari for the occasion, and as in the old days, all of us were told to behave properly and dress nicely. Sanjay and I still couldn't understand Rasi's reasoning, and

went to seek Aunt Meterling's thoughts. We found her looking at Oscar's painting of the ferry, which Grandmother had
framed and hung near drawing models of Grandfather's buildings and photographs of our ancestors. A large portrait of Lakshmi, shimmering and seated on her lotus, faced a portrait of
Saraswati playing her sitar. Oscar's watercolor looked good; for
all his trouble, he got all the details.

Aunt Meterling continued to surprise me. When we asked
her if Rasi was being foolish for agreeing to meet this boy, she
smiled.

"Why foolish?" she asked.

I never could keep a secret from Meterling.

"So that's her plan?" she said when I told her. "Well, I
wouldn't worry, you two. I hear he's a very good boy, has lots
of prospects."

"Auntie?"

"Ah, you think because I married Simon, I'd be against
arranged marriage. Not at all. I think we have a selection process that's been in place for thousands of years, and it has held
its own."

"But so many things can go wrong."

"Of course. But that's true of all marriages. When Archer's
sister, Susan, first got married, she had a terrible time adjusting. She used to spend nights at our house, weeping in my
arms. But after the initial shock of sharing space—things like
finding dirty socks carelessly strewn about, or even other more
irritating habits—you get over it. Susan did."

"So her marriage worked out, then."

"Well, her second marriage has. The first husband turned
out to be a philanderer. She's doing very well now, I think."

Sanjay and I glanced at each other.

"Look," she said, "nobody knowingly wants his or her child

to marry badly. That's why backgrounds are checked and horo-scopes consulted. Of course, I'm not talking about dowry."

Or sati, which is all anyone wanted to talk about at my uni-versity, even as our parents insisted that the ancient texts never required it.

I thought of the story of Kanyakumari. She was a good role model, a warrior who helped her people. I always thought of Rasi as a warrior, keeping Sanjay and me from harm. Maybe I would have to become a warrior as well. I don't know why that thought occurred to me, but it had a nice ring to it. It was funny, though, that Rasi was going about her ordinary life, and somewhere, perhaps a mixed-up rooster had crowed. Bad tim-ing and a preplanned life crept back like a wave returning to the shore, while a new suitor and a new life appeared.

55

Laksman arrived at the house on an auspicious Wednes-day. In two days, we would have a new moon. Aunt Pa told me long ago that women were powerful three days before and after every full and new moon. I had argued that women must be entitled to more than just twelve days a month, but she said it made up for the monthlies, and men, as far as she knew, had no powerful days they could specifically claim. Because every day is a man's day, teased Sanjay. Aunt Pa had been kept up to date on the Krishnaswamis. She may have even spoken to Rasi on the phone, but Rasi didn't tell me.

Oscar and I were out on the veranda, while Sanjay sat on the swing and played us what he knew so far on the guitar.

Raman, the driver, had found him one. All Sanjay knew so far was "Blowing in the Wind," which he must have repeated a dozen times already.

"I'll get better when I get calluses," he said.

"I seriously doubt it. It only has three chords."

"How do you know?"

"I've been watching you all afternoon."

Oscar was on his stomach, drawing.

We were expecting Laksman to come with his family, but he sauntered in alone. Introducing himself, he apologized for coming early, but said that he had been at a cricket match nearby and wasn't sure when it would end.

"It was a terrible match, it ended very fast," he said with some disgust.

I was struck by how affable he seemed, his hands stuck in his pockets, a broad smile on his face. Poor sap, I thought. I hesitated at taking him inside immediately, because he might throw the house in a tizzy. There was a word. What was its etymology? I put the question to the boys.

"It rhymes with 'dizzy,' like 'You make me dizzy, Miss Lizzy,' " said Sanjay, aiming the lyrics at Oscar, who giggled.

"And 'tipsy,' it might have to do with things ajar," I said.

"I think it's German," said Laksman. He frowned, adding, "It sounds German, anyway."

"Do you know German?"

"I was born there, actually, in Leipzig. I'm here visiting my parents."

"Are you studying there?"

"In Warwick, actually. Civil engineering."

"I've been to Warwick. It's on the way to Scotland," said Oscar.

"Well, that's one way of describing it," said Laksman, nodding.

In a few minutes, his parents arrived at the gate, along with his sister. They looked more cosmopolitan than I expected, dressed in subtle, expensive clothes. His sister sported a large red bag that looked like it could hold three others. She looked a little bored as we introduced ourselves and took everyone inside.

Grandmother had just finished pooja, and offered prasad, beaming. A very auspicious arrival. Nalani led them to the charpoys and chairs, and went to get drinks. Ajay and Simon had gone off for a walk and would return later, so it was just us seven and their four.

"Thank you, darling," said Laksman's mother, taking the chilled nimbu pani from Nalani. How easily she said that, without sounding snobbish.

His father told us how they had lived abroad until a few years back, when he and his wife returned home. "At heart," he said, "we are Madhupurians, but Laksman is—"

"European, darling, as is Sita. She is starting her studies in Warwick, too."

Sita smiled. Clearly, she wanted to be back there. Unlike Laksman's, her accent was not a curious blend of German and English, but completely British, an urban manner of speaking that sounded hip and cool and trendy.

Nalani told us how she had met Seema, Laksman's mother, at an art gallery. "I heard a voice say, 'But where is the rabbit in that picture?' So I told her where to look."

From that, they had started a conversation that led to tea at the Royale Tea House on Ningumbakum Road. Soon, Nalani and Ajay were invited home for dinner, which was where Nalani spotted Laksman's photograph. For a minute, I wondered why they thought of Rasi and not me, but obviously, that was because Rasi was a year older.

"Ordinarily, we don't believe in long engagements, but we want Rasi to finish university first," said Seema.

Grandmother beamed even more.

Meterling and Rasi came in, and after introductions, an uncomfortable silence descended. Even Sanjay had no jokes for the occasion. We sat on our seats, not wanting to offend, not wanting to look foolish or needy. Some of my grandmother's rarely glimpsed hauteur returned, but only briefly. She knew who she was, and Rasi was her granddaughter. Rasi, meanwhile, just held herself with an elegance that surprised me. She answered questions that were asked about her studies and her parents efficiently. I wondered if she had practiced for graduate-school interviews.

"Maybe," suggested Laksman's father, Prem, "the young people should go for a walk together," indicating Laksman and Rasi. They agreed.

When they returned in three quarters of an hour, they were engaged.

56

He's Mr. Darcy without the pride."

"Then he can't be Mr. Darcy. And since when did you want a Mr. Darcy?"

"We all want a Mr. Darcy, Mina."

"Bend it like Beckham and don't marry Wickham."

"What?"

"Something Nalani said."

"Who's Beckham?"

"Soccer player."

I had had to wait until night to talk to Rasi by herself. We were in our large bed, with the mosquito blaster plugged in. It had begun raining outside, and I could hear the patter of water on the roof. The summer monsoon would be upon the island soon, but we'd be back in the States before then. The window let in the night breeze.

Rasi raised herself on an elbow. "Anyway, the thing is, I like him. I didn't think I would, and I really wanted not to, but I don't know, he's kind of nice, don't you think?"

I opened my mouth to reply, but Rasi kept talking.

"He only agreed to see me to please his parents. He's leaving for England in a week, anyway. So he hadn't planned it, either."

"Wait a minute," said Sanjay, coming in and dropping onto the bed. "Isn't his sister supposed to be married before him?"

"Of course, but get this. She's already engaged to this French guy who Laksman's parents aren't that crazy about—a total soap opera—so we'll get married after them."

"That's why they want you to finish your degree."

"Well, no way am I getting married without my degree, plus there's law school."

"You don't even know him!"

"I know he's kind, responsible, likes sports, likes animals . . ."

"That's like a personals ad. You only spoke to him for twenty minutes."

"An hour. How long does it take to know a person? I read

that in one second you know if you are or are not attracted to someone."

"Yes, and that women over thirty who aren't married will never get married."

"Attraction is a lot different than knowing someone, Rasi. I mean, what if you get in an accident? Will he just go off and watch cricket? What about money? Will you have a joint checking account or separate?"

"And," I said, "he could be a philanderer!"

They both stared at me.

"Well, you don't know!"

"*I* could be a philanderer. Are women called philanderers?"

"I think they're just called brazen." Sanjay yawned. "I can't believe you're getting married. It's so—" He searched for a word.

"Terrific?"

"Peculiar."

"Shut up."

"It's all we seem to do in this house. Get married, have babies, get married, have babies."

Rasi sighed.

"The thing is, I trust him," she said. "I know it sounds crazy, but I don't know, I think he makes sense. I like him."

"Like finding the perfect puppy at a shelter, and knowing that one before all others is yours."

I began to laugh, but Rasi seemed hurt.

"You can't understand, and you won't until it happens to you. It's not anything you prepare for. You go for a walk with someone and there's a vibration in the air, a shift of some sort—"

"A moon wave."

"—and your heart cracks open."

. . .

We were quiet after that, in our own heads. Sanjay lay across the foot of the bed. If men could be called odalisques, then Sanjay would be one, always at ease stretched out. I would always have a lot to learn about love. I never thought Rasi would accept an arranged marriage, but then perhaps she too, like our aunt Meterling, was merely following her heart. Who could predict what the heart will dictate, and who among us has the courage to listen? My trailblazing aunt and cousin, daring the rules, Eastern or Western, defying the customs of what was accepted or expected, and choosing freely. Would I be brave and honestly answer my heart when it called? Would I face the truth if it met me eye-to-eye, and accept it, or would I turn away, be ruled by convention?

Nalani came in wearing one of her Juliet gowns, and quietly slipped into bed with us. She too had defied convention, by choosing adoption, something our ancestors would have not allowed.

"I heard you talking," she said, sighing as she freed a pillow for herself. In five months, she would have a baby *and* a five-year-old, but for now, she cuddled, our dreamy cousin who wished on paper fortunes and made matches for other people. She stroked my hair.

"You could be next on the list," said Sanjay.

"Don't get any ideas. I'm Kanyakumari," I said automatically.

"What?"

"Is this a private party?"

We turned our heads to see Aunt Meterling at the door.

"Come in, come in, there's plenty of room," called Rasi.

There was. No matter where we were in our lives, married or not, with babies or not, we would always have room. We only imagined we were adrift like Wynken, Blynken, and Nod, fish-ing for stars, but our shoes always led us home, into a reality that seemed more touched with enchantment than most. Aunt Meterling laughed when she saw us, a giant belly laugh that lifted our spirits, and must have woken the house. That was fine, for waking by laughter was always good.

ACKNOWLEDGMENTS

This novel began in a green-tinted notebook presented to me by three kind graduate students from Southampton College in 2001. It is a pleasure to thank them and to thank the Paden Institute for Writers of Color and the Fine Arts Work Center's Long Term Residency Program for support during the writing of this book.

Thank you to Rosemary Marangoly George, who read, scolded, and encouraged; Rachel Harding, who cheered on; and Lillias Bever, who kept up the conversation.

Thank you to Caitriona Barclay, who gave me permission to fabricate a love story.

Thank you to Diane Cooper, Ani Kalfayan, Florence Ladd, Maureen Clyne, Scott Hamashige, Naomi Horii, Bhanu Kapil, Willow King, Emily Wilson and Joy Wallin, Karen Tei Yamashita, Brian Kiteley, Carole Maso, Vicky Tomayko, Harini Subramanian, Agnes Chouchan, Megan Smith, Chris and Michelle Hogas, Jeffrey Green, Michelle Ryan and Dean Chapla, Quincy Troupe, Henry and Arlene Geller, and the Ashtanga Project for support, advice, inspiration, and good cheer.

Johnny Jenkins and Chris, Danielle, and Nina of the Laughing Goat provided sweet welcomes and fine cappuccinos no matter my mood; and Marcia Douglas always offered wise guidance and deep support of my work.

ACKNOWLEDGMENTS

Richard Freeman and Mary Taylor, and all of the teachers at the Yoga Workshop, gave me solace and strength, and I would not have made it through a dark year without them, nor the light ones before and after.

I owe much to Southampton and Sag Harbor, Long Island, where friends, students, and colleagues supplied coffee, Sunday dinners, and over-the-counter wisdom, especially Lisa Bonsal; Kathryn and MaryAnn; Jeanelle and Terry; and Doug and Bessim.

I owe much to my colleagues and students at Naropa University.

I owe much to Boulder, where I found great neighbors, a wonderful farmers' market, and made lasting friends.

Thank you to my Nineteenth Street neighbors, Amanda Rankins-Stark, Ben Holland, Ben Oliver, Niko Wojczuk, Brigitte and Tom, David and Pamela, and Jack and Jenny.

Thomas Crown, Katie Heath, Luke Iwabuchi, Megan O'Brien, and Sue Zemka gave hugs and words sorely needed.

At the eleventh hour, both Andrew Wille and Dennis Mathis provided comments and notes for which I will always be grateful.

Thank you to Emi Ikkanda, who asked good questions.

Thank you, Andrea Cavallaro.

Thank you to Elise Capron who enthusiastically and consistently sent e-mails and e-vitamins.

I am always deeply grateful for the presence of Ann Close and Sandy Dijkstra in my life.

Thank you to everyone at Knopf, including my exceptional copyeditor, Patrick Dillon; Caroline Zancan; and Chris Silas Neal.

My parents, Subashree and Shankar, Shreyas and Meena, and my extended family as always provide love.

Finally, I would not have finished this book without the generosity and love of Anashua Sinha and Shridar Ganesan. They believed in the work and gave me time, space, and compassion.

A NOTE ABOUT THE AUTHOR

Indira Ganesan is the author of two previous novels, *The Journey* and *Inheritance*. She has held fellowships from the Paden Institute for Writers of Color, the Mary Ingraham Bunting Institute at Radcliffe College, the W. K. Rose Fellowship, and the Fine Arts Work Center in Provincetown. For her first novel, she was selected as one of 52 Best Young American Novelists Under Forty in Granta's 1995 campaign; her second novel was a Barnes & Noble Discover New Writers Book. Her essays and short fiction have appeared in *Antaeus, Black Renaissance, Bombay Gin, Half and Half: Writers on Biracialism and Biculturalism, Glamour, Mississippi Review,* and *Newsday.*

A NOTE ON THE TYPE

The text of this book was set in a typeface called Méridien, a classic roman designed by Adrian Frutiger for the French type foundry Deberny et Peignot in 1957. Méridien, as well as his other typeface of world renown, Univers, was created for the Lumitype photo-set machine.

Composed by
North Market Street Graphics,
Lancaster, Pennsylvania

Printed and bound by
RR Donnelley,
Harrisonburg, Virginia

Designed by
Iris Weinstein